# SURRECTION

# SURRECTION

A NOVEL

BY

## Will Martin

THE NEARING SKY PRESS

ISBN: 979-8-9853258-0-5
e-book ISBN: 979-8-9853258-1-2

*For Jeanie*

# ACKNOWLEDGEMENTS

For countless readings and for helping me shape the story, I give special acknowledgement and appreciation to Paul Sloan, Geoff Macdonald, and Eve Porinchak.

As a first-time novelist, I am grateful for the support and advice of many other friends and professionals, including (in alphabetical order) Malika Anderson, Charles Annis, Clark Akers, Lisa Bubert, Shakura Conoly, Doyle Duke, Morgan Entrekin, Skila Harris, Joe and Sally Huston, Kris Kemp, Dwight Lewis, Paul McNabb, Porter Meadors, my wonderful wife Jeanie Nelson, Gordon Peerman, Nat Schmookler, Elaine Weiss, and Adena Williams.

# MAPS OF EASTERN KANSAS AND

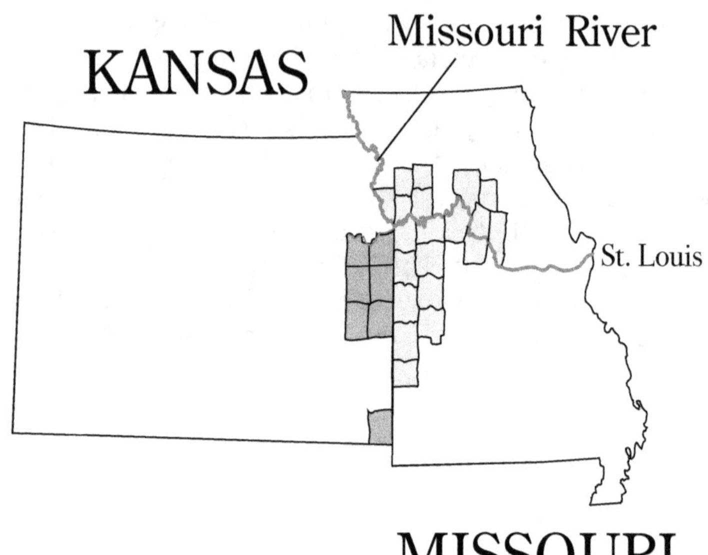

# WESTERN AND CENTRAL MISSOURI

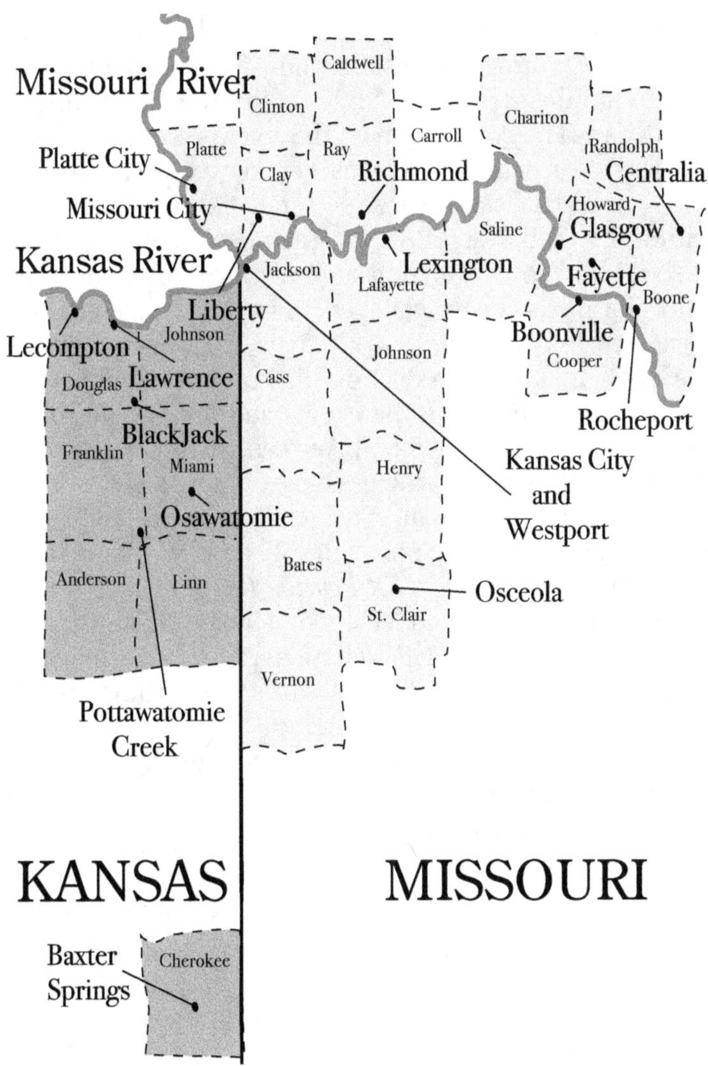


Graphics by Brite Ideas, Houston, TX

# AUTHOR'S NOTE

*Surrection* is a work of fiction based on historical events in the border area of Missouri and Kansas during a period of nine desperate years before and during America's Civil War. The novel follows the events from the "border war" over whether Kansas Territory would enter the Union as a slave state or free-soil state to the guerrilla war within the Civil War. However, my novel is not a history. It should be read as fiction on a platform of history. My selection of the historical events is an arbitrary one, designed for storytelling, but I believe the selected events are key to an understanding of a little-appreciated piece of history. I learned about the events and their background from a number of non-fiction sources, including personal accounts, newspaper articles, biographies, and works of historical non-fiction, all of which I gratefully acknowledge. In particular, I acknowledge T. J. Stiles' magnificent biography, *Jesse James, Last Rebel of the Civil War*, which inspired my interest and led eventually to this novel.

A number of real-life characters who participated in these historical events make up a supporting cast. In some cases, I have imagined their personalities, their motivations, their conversations, and occasionally certain of their actions. Other characters, notably the protagonist and his father, are fictional.

So foul a sky clears not without a storm.
William Shakespeare, *The Life and Death of King John*

# PROLOGUE: THE STORM COMES



Eastern Kansas Territory

In the afternoon, thunderheads piled high, at first gray with white tops, then darkening to a dusky charcoal with patches of pure black. At the edge of the western horizon, where the prairie meets the sky, a break in the clouds formed an opening like an aerial canyon, and the sun poked its rays through the space, backlighting the gathered bulk of the thunderheads and spraying a beam of pale yellow on the distant land. As the dark mass advanced, the sky looked like a bruise. Lightning forked the clouds. In the forefront, the clouds tossed into a malign froth. Small gray clouds whipped away from the mass and drifted toward the land like upside-down smoke.

The man was plowing with a mule, pressing the animal to finish before the storm. He had come from Massachusetts when Kansas Territory opened for settlement in 1854, and he was still learning about the storms in this part of the country. From the field, he had a good view of the farmhouse and shed of his neighbor, beyond the tall grass, roughly a quarter-mile away. The neighbor was Dutch—what folks in these parts called someone from Germany—who had come to America in December 1850.

Earlier that morning, the man had seen three riders on the road, trotting from the neighbor's land, purposeful but not hasty. He was busy with the plowing, and he gave them no further thought. Riders on the road were not uncommon, and both he and his neighbor had visitors in these days—fellow settlers from Northern states who came to discuss the troubles with settlers from those Southern and border states that were intent on making Kansas a slave state when its time came to enter the Union.

The man gave no thought to political matters now, and he concentrated on beating the storm. The wind picked up and hissed through the new green leaves of the stand of trees nearby. The big limbs waved and moaned. The rain came, trickling at first, then in sheets, and the man unhitched the mule and ran with it toward his house.

From the center of the black cloud mass a gray-white protrusion emerged, stretching in a long, skinny shape, wavering down through the liquid cloud sea, searching for contact with the earth. The funnel lengthened in a matter of seconds, extending thousands of feet, reaching all the way to the ground, scraping it now like a great claw. The day's dim light turned to a smoky gray-green gloom. The rain came harder, and the loud, deep howl of the tornado came closer, like a train grinding across the Missouri River countryside. "No, no, no, no, no, no," he huffed as he ran, punching out each "no" with every stride and tugging the mule's halter.

He saw the storm hit the farm of his neighbor like a bomb. The funnel's snout spewed earth from a plowed field, sucked up a wagon, and shattered the shed into splinters, spinning the debris in its funnel cloud as it tore across the land. The man yelled to his wife and son who were at his house, but the distance was great and the storm's roar swallowed his words.

There was no chance the man could make it to the house before the tornado. He left the mule and ran to a swale nearby in hope it could provide shelter. He ran hard and dropped into the marshy depression, slid beside the creek that traced its gulley and pressed his body to the ground, trying to melt between two large rocks. With his fingers, he dug into the ground in the bottom of the ravine, as if he could grip and hold to the land as the big wind came.

The funnel lifted as abruptly as it had appeared before it reached the man's land. The pelting rain quit. The storm passed. The man closed his eyes and exhaled deeply. The soft purling of the creek was now the only sound. He could still taste his fear. His legs quivered as he gathered himself, staggered to get his footing, and stood upright. The mule moved toward him. He looked at his farmhouse—it was untouched. He saw his wife and son waving and running to him. His family was safe. He waved back and lifted his arms to the sky.

Then the man thought about the neighbor whose farm had taken the direct hit from the violence of the storm. The man ran toward his neighbor's house, calling his name. When he neared the cabin, he saw a body lying in a wet heap in the nearby field, flattening the grass. He walked slowly to the lifeless form lying on its side, its right arm crooked behind and left leg twisted over the right, angling the left hip into a contorted position. The face looked blankly upward, both eyes open toward the clearing sky, the mouth agog from a scream—or from gravity's pull on the jawbone.

Yes, the body was that of his neighbor. The man slowly, reverently, minced closer, closer, and then saw the right ear had been ripped off. There was an ugly black bullet hole in the forehead a few inches above the left eye. He dropped to his knees and touched the body, poking it as if to stir life in the still flesh. "My God," he whispered. He fingered the hole where the bullet entered, and he couldn't keep his eyes off the raw smear where the ear had been sliced from the skull.

# PART ONE
# WAR BEFORE WAR

# 1

## JABEZ

Jabez Cooper: *For me, the war began in Kansas before it even became a state, not in South Carolina. Started in 1856, when I was just fourteen, not 1861. My life as a guerrilla fighter in the war started then, for all intents and purposes. I would not join a guerrilla band for seven more years, but my fate was sealed in 1856 in Lawrence, Kansas. I was there, a Missouri boy, with my pa and hundreds of proslavers from Missouri and Kansas called Border Ruffians. We had come to arrest abolitionist leaders, destroy abolitionist newspapers, and scare hell out of abolitionist residents of the town.*

*"Run 'em outta Kansas," said pa. "The big-money abolitionists have paid the way of low-life Eastern settlers to come to Kansas and vote against slavery. They're just like a plague of locusts descending on our part of the country, and we have to clear out the infestation."*

*Pa helped form a posse to take care of Lawrence, and he wanted me to go along. "No" was not going to be an acceptable answer. I knew I had no choice. Or so I believed. The slavery issue was not a thing I cared much about, but I did have some curiosity about what Kansas looked like, as I had only been across the river to Leavenworth, which looked no different than Missouri. Hadn't ever seen an abolitionist either, since there weren't any in my hometown of Liberty, Missouri. I was curious to see what abolitionists looked like. Traveling with a group of hundreds sounded like an adventure, to boot.*

# WAR BEFORE WAR

*As we traveled to Lawrence in May of 1856, I admired the beauty of the tall prairie grass fields and the hardwood forests showing their fresh green leaves. Nature in the territory looked so peaceful. I laughed when I thought about what pa had called the residents of Lawrence and imagined a town full of locusts who hated slavery. These were thoughts of a boy who had no idea of what was to come.*

*We arrived and set up camp outside Lawrence and waited as the members of the posse sifted in. Pa was a blacksmith and farrier, and I was his apprentice. He had put together a traveling forge we brought in our wagon, and we did our best to help the assembled men who had needs or problems with their horses' hooves or with their knives.*

*On May 21, 1856, our posse rolled into Lawrence. I mark that as the day when the war began. My life was to be changed in ways I could never imagine.*

# 2

## SOWING THE WIND

May 21, 1856, Lawrence, Douglas County, Kansas Territory

Jabez Cooper stood in the middle of the camp outside Lawrence, Kansas, staggering from the force of the mass of men moving in every direction on ground made muddy by horses letting their water. He'd never seen so many armed men. In fact, he'd never seen so many people in one place. They were from all over, from Kansas, Missouri, Alabama, Georgia, and South Carolina. Every man was carrying a hunting rifle or shotgun. Many had pistols jammed into their belts or into sashes tied around their waists.

"Listen up!" yelled Sam Jones, the county sheriff. Then, as the men slowed and turned their heads in his direction, the sheriff swiveled in his saddle. He removed the last of a soggy cud of chewing tobacco tucked into his lower lip, tossed it into the dirt, and spat a well-aimed stream of tobacco juice to the ground. "Today, the goddamn abolitionists will bow and kiss their free-soil dirt beneath my feet."

One of the deputies passed by and handed Jabez what looked like a printed circular. Scared he'd miss what Sheriff Jones was going to say, he barely looked at it, but when Jones struggled to get the crowd's attention and began muttering to no one in particular, Jabez took time to puzzle over the handbill. It was titled "The Law" and the first paragraph read:

> If any free person, by speaking or writing, shall assert
> or maintain that persons have not the right to hold
> slaves in this Territory, or shall  print, publish, write,
> circulate, or cause to be introduced into this Territory,
> any book, paper, magazine, pamphlet or circular con-
> taining any denial of the right of persons to hold slaves
> in this Territory, such person shall be deemed guilty of
> felony and punished by imprisonment at hard labor for
> a term of not less than two years.

Jabez waved to his father and held the paper out to
him. "Pa, what does this mean?"

Ashford "Ash" Cooper sauntered over, grinning. "Jay-
bezz," he drawled, "that's one of the reasons we're here.
The folks who run the damn Lawrence newspapers are
violating Kansas territorial law by writing their abolitionist screeds."

Jabez was wide-eyed. "They're going to jail?"

Ash Cooper winked. "Damn right. After we eliminate
their presses. And that's not all, we're gonna deal with a
hotel that also violates Kansas law. Look down that page
and you'll see."

Jabez read on. It was a quote from the federal grand
jury of the First District Court of Kansas Territory:

> The newspaper known as the *Herald of Freedom* in
> Lawrence has from time to time issued publications of
> the most inflammatory and seditious character. Also,
> the paper known as the Kansas Free State has engaged
> in similar publication. We respectfully recommend
> their abatement as a nuisance. Also, we are satisfied
> that the building known as the Free-State Hotel in Law-
> rence has been constructed with a view to military oc-
> cupation and defense, and is regularly parapetted and
> port-holed for the use of cannon and small arms, and
> could only be designed as a stronghold for resistance
> to law, thereby endangering the public safety and en-

couraging rebellion and sedition to the country; and we respectfully recommend that steps be taken whereby this nuisance may be removed.

Jabez squinted and turned his head to show he couldn't fully take it in. "What does it mean, pa?"

Before his father could explain, Sheriff Jones waved his hat and yahooed again for attention. The men of his posse pressed close, some on their horses, some on foot, all—except Jabez—with guns and Bowie knives. The air filled with the smell of leather, sweat, whiskey, and tobacco spittle.

"All right, all right, all right, hear me," Sheriff Jones said. "By order of the federal court for this territory, we gonna disarm and arrest a hotel." He punched out the last words slowly, and the crowd laughed and cheered. Jones smiled and winked. "We gonna disarm and arrest a hotel," he repeated as he turned in the saddle. "It's built like a damn fort—they're gittin ready for the worst kind of treasonous war, and that hotel cannot stand. We gonna take down that hotel because the court has declared it a nuisance."

Cheers erupted again. Jabez chuckled.

The sheriff continued, "Nother thing, the newspapers in this town been violating the law of this Territory. We're gonna put a stop to their crimes." Sheriff Jones lifted his arms to the sky as the crowd roared louder.

"Gentlemen, that ain't all. Our federal Marshal, Mr. Israel Donaldson here, has his own federal posse, about a hundred Kansans, and he has some criminal writs. First thing today, he is gonna arrest the leaders of these abolitionists for treason in tryin' to set up an illegal abolitionist government for our territory. You can't have two governments for a territory or state. These people are claiming our duly elected legislature is bogus because so many of you Missourians voted over here, and they say they gonna resist the laws our legislature has passed. They's trying to set up a separate government—abolitionist. That's treason."

Ash stepped forward and took the sheriff by the arm. Jabez flushed with pride. He knew his father was going to speak.

He and his father lived in Liberty, Missouri, not far from the Kansas border, and they had come with a contingent of about four hundred fellow Missourians. His father, as a blacksmith, farrier, and knifesmith, had arms and shoulders well-muscled and hands strong and laced with prominent blood vessels. His thick black mustache was beginning to show flecks of gray, but Jabez thought of his father as a young man who could do any task.

Jabez was an apprentice at the forge in Liberty. To serve the camp that the posse had set up outside Lawrence, he and his father had come by a mule-drawn wagon that carried a grindstone for knives and a portable forge—a firebox set on metal legs, a bellows behind the box, a small but sturdy anvil, bags of charcoal, and basic blacksmith tools including hammer, tongs, and clenching iron. For farrier work, the kit contained bags of horseshoes and nails, a shoeing knife, and hammer.

Both father and son wore the Ruffian garb of maroon flannel shirts, and theirs were embroidered with the symbol of a heart over the pocket. Like many in the camp they had streaked the shirts, and their faces too, with campfire ashes and wet, black gunpowder to underscore their roughness. A feather of a blue jay—his mark, he claimed—adorned Jabez' wide-brimmed hat.

Sheriff Jones waved again to the crowd. "I want you all to listen to my Missouri friend, Ash Cooper. We been friends since when I lived in Liberty. Many of you know him, he's an important man in dealing with these abolitionists. He helped organize the Missouri wing of this posse. He's got opinions, by God, and he ain't afraid of speaking out. I want you to hear him."

The crowd pressed close to hear Ash's words. Some men pulled out their revolvers as a demonstration of their fierce intentions. A few popped aimless shots toward the empty horizon. Jabez scowled, clenched his fists and pulled his arms close to his body. Ash put his arm around his son's shoulders. He whispered, "Don't worry, boy. Everything will be fine. They's just getting a bit excited." Jabez forced a smile and swallowed hard, his eyes flicking around the crowd.

Ash hopped on the bed of a wagon, put his hands on his hips, and turned his body slowly in a full circle, making eye contact with as many in the crowd as he could. "Thank ye, sheriff. I believe I can speak for every man here when I say Kansas and Missouri are common soil. Kansas is an extension of Missouri, and the border is only an artificial line in this common soil, about as meaningful as a shadow. By logic, Kansas must become a slave state. It's only natural. But there are criminals who are out to foil us. They's called abolitionists. We all know this damn town is crawling with the scum. They ain't a proslavery man in Lawrence, only Yankee abolitionists from…" He raised his hands and paused, making the crowd wait for the revelation. "…New England—the hellhole of abolition."

The crowd roared again. Jabez felt the thrill of seeing his father move the posse like a tent evangelist.

Ash continued, "Sheriff, they's all nuisances. Can we send them back to New England?"

The crowd laughed and hooted. Jabez was laughing and full of pride.

Someone shouted, "Or can we shoot the vermin!"

The crowd roared louder.

The sheriff's brow scrunched into a knot of concern, and he held his right arm aloft. "Whoa! Hold up there. I'm responsible for carrying out the command of the grand jury and the court. Let me tell everyone, there is to be no bloodshed—unless there is armed resistance. There will be no blood if the Yankee residents of this town lay down their arms and don't fire on us. Now, if they shoot, that's 'nother thing."

Sheriff Jones pressed a palm against the saddle horn, leaned forward and looked at the other side of the crowd. "We gonna arrest that hotel, and we gonna arrest and shut down the seditious newspapers been printin' antislavery crap." Jones leaned toward the ground and spat for emphasis. "Matter of fact, I personally will have vengeance against the miserable som'bitch abolitionists who tried to assassinate me last time I was in this town to carry out court orders. Shot me in the goddamn back. Doctor said I missed the Grim Reaper by a matter of inches. And I tell you, it's right painful to sit on a horse now."

The sheriff called for David Rice Atchison, former United States Senator from Missouri. Atchison's hometown was Liberty, Missouri, and he and Ash Cooper were close. Atchison was cut from Southern Senatorial cloth, proslavery and a friend and follower of Senator John C. Calhoun. Observers in Washington called his speaking style both stentorian and sententious. Atchison had led six thousand Missouri men into Kansas to vote last year, and he had worked with Ash Cooper to organize the Missouri men in the sheriff's posse.

The senator lifted his arms above his head, palms turned to the heavens, and said in a voice honed by years in the halls of power, "You all know the eastern press is calling us Border Ruffians. Well, I accept that sobriquet and consider it honorific. Yes, today I am a Border Ruffian and proud of it. I am also a Kickapoo Ranger, a Doniphan Tiger, and a Palmetto Guardsman. I am one of you. I'm also a Kansan, and I'm proud to say there's a lovely town named Atchison in this territory. Now, I want everybody to know that, whether you are from Kansas or Missouri or Alabama or South Carolina or anywhere else in the South, you are working today for the administration of President Pierce, and you will be well paid. Tear down their boasted Free State Hotel. Yes, riddle it till it shall fall to the ground. Throw into the river their printing presses, and let's see if any more free-nigger screeds will be issued from them. These people are scum immigrants from New England Yankee land, they are an infestation. I would rather see Kansas sink into hell than be free-soil. If there is armed resistance, will every one of you swear to bathe your steel in the blood of those sons of bitches?"

Cheers rose, and the men lifted high their rifles and knives.

The sheriff cut in, "Gentlemen, I am the law here." He paused.

The crowd stirred.

"I am the law here," he said more loudly. "Murder is a crime, and my posse and the marshal's posse are gonna execute court orders, and that's all they gon' do. Now, if the citizens of Lawrence be stupid enough to resist or to shoot one of us like they did me last month, then that's a different story. 'Nother thing, you boys can't take no plunder, that's a crime too. Now, do y'all hear me?"

There was an awkward silence. Then, a group of South Carolinians who called themselves the Palmetto Guard raised their banner, a flag of vivid red with a single white star in the center and *Southern Rights* written across the top in white letters. Some Missourians thrust up their flag with the words *Slavery for Kansas*. A makeshift banner read, *Removal of Nuisances*.

The crowd roared in a rage.

Jabez felt his pulse race, and he leaned against his father. "Pa, is there gonna be a battle here? Will people get shot? Killed?"

"Hush, son. We got this under control. Abolitionists

would be beyond stupid if they try to put up a fight. Don't be scared."

"I ain't afraid," Jabez lied.

The posse was primed and ready to enter the town, but they had to wait for the federal marshal to make his arrests first. Jabez saw that his father could barely contain his energy. He followed as Ash darted through the waiting crowd. Ash found a group of men from Alabama that a Colonel Buford had brought only a few weeks ago to settle in Kansas, and Ash began to tell them about Lawrence. "Last December, after the Free-State'ers interfered with an arrest by Sheriff Jones, almost two thousand men camped on the banks of the Wakarusa, a short piece from this camp, ready to take over the town. But the territory's governor, Shannon, came to Lawrence to talk with the abolitionists. They fed him whiskey and wine and got him drunk, and he signed a peace treaty he was too soused to read. We had no choice but to honor it. This time, we gonna get the job done.

"I tell you one more thing," Ash said, "the Free-State people are hypocrites of the first order. In their bleeding hearts they don't believe the black man is equal to the white. People tell me the illegal constitution of the illegal Free-State government not only bans slavery but also bans black people from settling in Kansas. Now ain't that a purty thing? The Free-State people don't want to have nothin' to do with a man whose skin is black. That's a goddamn fact."

*

Shortly before noon, United States Marshal Donaldson sent his deputy, W.P. Fain, into the town to make the arrests of the leaders of the antislavery government. Fain took a small troop of eight men, and they proceeded to the Free State Hotel. Sheriff Jones and one of his deputies tagged along. The proprietor, Colonel Shalor Eldridge, received Fain and Jones with restrained courtesy. "Welcome to my hotel. What can I do for you?"

Fain said, "I'm here to arrest your leaders of the Free-State government. Robinson, Reeder, Lane, Smith, and Deltzler have been charged with high treason for setting up an illegal second government in this territory. Sheriff Jones has orders from the court to remove the two newspapers for printing antislavery filth and to remove your hotel as a fortified nuisance and threat to public safety. He'll deal with that assignment later. "Understand, together we got some eight hundred deputized men. If one of your abolitionists pulls out a gun, like the man who shot Jones last month, all hell will blow, and a lot of your people could die, and there will be nothing left of Lawrence." Fain placed his hand on his hip, palm open over the butt of his revolver and turned just enough to accentuate the threat.

Eldridge received the threat without changing his expression or replying. But he was burning with anxiety inside his calm exterior. He planned to use a combination of friendly compliance and hospitality to stave off the threat to his hotel, but he knew his gambit was a long shot. Slowly he read the writs and looked at Fain. "Lane and Reeder are not in this town, not even in the territory. Governor Robinson was arrested in Missouri on his way to Washington about a week ago, for what crime we can't imagine, and we heard they'll send him to jail in Kansas. There are only two men on your list who are in town now, Smith and Deltzler."

Fain looked irritated, and he responded to Eldridge through clenched teeth, "Find Smith and Deltzler and bring them to me for arrest."

Eldridge launched his campaign to save his hotel. "We will cooperate. We don't want bloodshed. I'll send some men to find the accused, but before you and Sheriff Jones do anything to my property, I'd like to discuss the matter over midday dinner at my hotel."

Fain sneered and declined the invitation, but Jones accepted and said he'd like to bring Atchison too. Eldridge said the Senator was more than welcome, and Jones sent his deputy to fetch Atchison. While the sheriff awaited Atchison, the accused Smith and Deltzler arrived. "My job here is done," said Fain. "I'm taking these men to jail."

Jones and Atchison followed Eldridge into the hotel dining room. Eldridge appeared relaxed, but his pulse was racing, and anxiety made his voice shaky. Though he was almost crippled by fear, Eldridge had a plan. Liquor and wines from the hotel's cellar had served to lubricate a truce that averted bloodshed during an earlier standoff with Border Ruffians, and Eldridge knew of Atchison's affinity for drink and hoped to capitalize on it. Missourians didn't call the Senator "Old Bourbon" without cause. Eldridge would offer Jones and Atchison his best, starting with a shot of Kentucky bourbon. The Senator knocked down the first shot, and served himself another, holding the bottle up to the light to determine how much remained.

"Lord, this is good," said Atchison, grinning and sighing. "We make some fine whiskey in Missouri, but there ain't nothing like Kentucky bourbon." When wine was served, Atchison stuck with the whiskey. "Bourbon is my wine."

After Eldridge saw that Atchison was buzzed from drink, he moved to make his case that the destruction of the newspapers and the hotel was not necessary. He knew he had an uphill climb, so he was prepared to stretch the truth. "Most folks in Lawrence don't care one way or th'other about abolishing slavery. Let it continue back in the South, just don't bring it to Kansas. Folks in this part of Kansas got their minds on making a living out here on the frontier, working their claims, or building a business. We have residents from many states other than the New England ones—Pennsylvania, Missouri, Ohio, Illinois,

Kentucky, Tennessee. There is not a radical in this town or even this Territory, except for John Brown and his sons who live down around Osawatomie. As to my hotel, you can see that it is built for hospitality, not for warfare. Ridiculous to call it a fort."

After a long silence, Atchison reached a smooth hand across the table, laid it on Eldridge's arm, and spoke in a voice soft and patronizing. "Colonel, we know you want to save your hotel, but even if we believed what you just said, there is nothing we can do. The law has spoken, and we are but its agents."

*

Jabez ran to his father when he saw the sheriff and Atchison returning to the camp after their meal with Eldridge, and he yelled, "Pa, they're coming back!" Ash spread the word, and soon hundreds surrounded the two men on horseback.

"What happened?" Ash quizzed the sheriff and Senator. "We going on with this work or we going home?"

Sheriff Jones laughed and shook his head. "Not to worry. He tried to hornswoggle us, said this town had nothing against slavery, but we didn't fall for his lies. Let's get rolling. Bring the cannons down from the hill, get everyone together, and we're gonna march down to the hotel."

A mix of excitement and anxiety jolted through Jabez. He and his father rushed to their wagon to load up their camping gear and secure the traveling forge. Ash said, "Jabez, you drive the wagon. I'm gonna ride with the sheriff on our extra mount." Jabez took the reins of the two wagon mules and slid off the brake. He had never felt a thrill of importance quite like this moment.

The posse swept into Lawrence. At the rear, horses brought five cannons. A choking dust cloud kicked up by hundreds of horses and mules followed the entourage to the center of town.

Sheriff Jones led them to the front of the Free State

Hotel. In a voice loud enough for everyone within a block to hear, Jones said to Eldridge, "Colonel, as you know we are here by order of the district court to remove three nuisances, the newspapers known as the *Kansas Free State* and the *Herald of Freedom*, and your Free State Hotel. We ain't here to harm your people, but for the safety of those you represent, I demand you deliver to me all the firearms in Lawrence. It better be one hundred percent, or we're gonna have a bloody mess on our hands. I may not be able to restrain my men if your people don't disarm. I'm giving you five minutes." One side of the sheriff's mouth crinkled into a smirk.

Eldridge read the court orders. "Sheriff, we want to comply with the law, but I do not see anything in the orders about taking guns. And, look a-here, I am not Caesar. I can't make the men give up their private property. But I can give up the guns the town owns, and that includes a few Sharps rifles and our brass cannon. And I will assure you, we have notified the residents not to resist the posse."

The sheriff grumbled, "Fine," and walked away to address his men again.

"Fellows, I'm putting Ash Cooper in charge of demolition. His boy Jabez, who's his apprentice, is gonna help him. Ash will choose a group of y'all to go down to the newspapers to start things off. Ash, y'all come back to this spot when you finish."

Jabez felt another surge of pride. His father had been given an important duty, and the boy knew his father would do it well. *This'll be known all over the country. Probably a day for the history books too. And I'm in the middle of it.*

Ash yelled, "Missouri men, South Carolina men, come with me!" Jabez followed his father and the posse mob to the *Herald of Freedom* office. It was vacant, and Jabez could see Lawrence residents rushing to the outskirts of the town.

Ash said, "Well, they ain't nobody here to open the door and welcome us, so we need to do it ourselves," and with that the Ruffians swept into the newspaper office and smashed the printing press and type. Ash pointed to the paper's library and files. "Get this too. Throw all this crap into the river." While roughly half of the men followed this command, Ash led the remaining half to the Kansas Free State offices, where the men duplicated their destruction of press and type and their seizure of the library and files. Jabez pitched in with transporting the seized property to the Kansas River, but soon the men tired of lugging the papers to the river, and they scattered them along the street or piled them into Ash's wagon.

The newspapers were finished. Jabez ran to his father, and Ash shook his hand. "Good work, boy." The two led their group of ransackers back to the sheriff 's command post in front of the Free State Hotel.

In a loud voice now growing husky, Jones read the grand jury's indictment of the hotel as a disguised fortress for future warfare against slavery.

Colonel Eldridge protested and begged for mercy. "Please, sheriff. For God's sake, please do not destroy my innocent property."

Jones flung out an arm as if sweeping away Eldridge's plea. "Take all personal possessions from the hotel immediately. I'm giving you an hour."

While waiting for the deadline, the members of the posse who had not participated in destroying the newspaper offices, began taunting Eldridge and the town residents who were helping him. These Ruffians had missed all the fun of smashing the printing equipment, and they were becoming increasingly impatient as they waited to take down the hotel. Finally, the hour grace period expired, and the men raced into the building to remove the remaining contents, pushing the items through the windows on each of the three floors. Shortly, a moat of broken beds, chests, chairs, and scattered bedding surrounded the building. The men discovered the wine and liquor cellar in the process and passed the bottles around.

As the posse emptied the hotel, the sheriff called up the five cannons. Jabez ran to follow the horses as they pulled the cannons in a slow and ponderous effort to array the artillery facing the hotel. Jabez had never seen, nor even imagined, what was about to happen, and his heart was pounding.

After the stripping of the building finished, Jones gave Senator Atchison the honor of ordering the first shots. Ash took Jabez by the arm and crowded close to Atchison. Jabez could smell the whiskey on Atchison's breath.

"Start at the top. Let 'er rip," cried Atchison.

Five cannons fired at this signal, but by miscalculation the balls cleared the roof of the hotel, rolling down the nearby street.

The small crowd of town residents who remained to watch laughed and cheered at the artillery failure. Jabez looked at his father in disbelief. "What happened, pa?"

Atchison muttered an oath and then bellowed a second command, but the result was the same as the first volley. "Aim at the second floor." This time, five cannonballs hit their mark, but with negligible impact on the stone exterior. The structure stood. "Again," cried Atchison, until the hotel had been hit by twenty balls. The edifice still stood.

Sweating from the heat and the frustration, the sheriff cried, "You men with the keg of gunpowder, bring it here and blow the damn thing down." There was a roar and a cloud of smoke from the explosion, and glass shattered on the first and second floors. But the building still stood.

"Cooper, torch the goddam nuisance," Jones commanded.

Ash and Jabez collected a group of men, and they brought stacks of papers and books from the destroyed newspaper offices and lit fires. Jabez basked in the flames, his chest pounding with pride. Soon, only part of one stone wall of the Free State Hotel stood, like an ancient ruin ringed by smoking ashes.

The sheriff ran to the wall, lifting his hands in triumph. "Gentlemen, this is the happiest day of my life. You are now dismissed." He swung his body to the saddle and trotted his horse out of Lawrence. A small group of men joined him.

Ash and Jabez returned to camp to make preparations for their return to Missouri. Jabez's face was all smiles. He was waving his arms like windmills and whooping, "We did it, we did it. I 'spect we made history today. What a show. Pa, thanks for bringing me along. Thank you. Thank you."

Ash put an arm around his son's shoulders. "Damn glad you agreed to come and be part of this. You did good work. If your ma was still alive, I know she'd be proud of you. I sure am."

Back in the town, most of the Ruffians weren't about to leave. The torching of the hotel had added to the fury of the posse. They finished the wine and liquor liberated from the hotel and blazed through the town, smashing into houses and seizing money, jewelry, and clothes and wrecking furniture. For good measure, they burned the house of the governor of the Free State government, Charles Robinson.

In the late afternoon, the last of the posse filed out of Lawrence, their horses and wagons draped with dresses, coats, pants, and shirts. A white wedding dress hung off the shoulders of one rider.

# 3

## ON THE RIVER

May 23, 1856, Westport, Jackson County, western Missouri
Jabez knew he was too young to be in a saloon, but he—
and his father—wanted to be part of the celebration in
the hotel saloon in Westport. The Missourians who had
sacked Lawrence streamed into this port town at the edge
of Kansas City, looking for whiskey and beer and an opportunity to brag to the locals about their exploits. Jabez
was not about to miss this scene, so he pulled the front of
his hat down to his eyes. He was tall, so that helped, and
his face was dirty from the events of the last few days,
masking the youthfulness of his face.

The saloon was packed, noisy and smelling of bodies
unwashed for many days. The smell of alcohol provided
a deodorant of sorts. Jabez saw two bearded men yank
pistols from their belts and hold them overhead. One of
the men shouted, "See this gun? By God, if a abolition
crosses my path, I'm gonna give him a black-powder how-
do-ye. We didn't git to use our guns this time, but if them
abolitions don't git to gittin outta Lawrence, we'll go back
and git it done."

The crowd roared, raising knives or guns in agreement. Everyone was laughing and clicking glasses. Jabez
laughed too, but he and his father were not drinking.

A clean, well-groomed man approached the father and
son. Jabez could see the man was clearly not one of the
Ruffians and probably not a local. He noted that the man
had a refined air.

"Good evening, my name is Edwin Fielding." The man spoke in an accent unfamiliar to Jabez. "I am a newspaper correspondent for *The Times* of London, England, and I have come to report on the troubles in Kansas Territory."

Ash introduced himself and Jabez. Fielding handed each of the Coopers his card. "Here's my card. I expect some of my articles for *The Times* will be re-published in American papers. I hope you will read them."

The father and son stared at the cards before stuffing them in their pockets. This was not a custom they knew. An awkward period of silence followed, which Fielding broke by asking, "Have you come from Lawrence?"

Jabez figured the man spoke to them because they weren't drinking or waving weapons around. Jabez let his father do the talking.

Ash eyed the man in a sideways glance and said, "We just arrived from that hellhole. Are you an abolitionist reporter?"

The man smiled. "I am not from the States. I am an Englishman, and I am here to report on facts, not to take sides. I arrived in Westport this afternoon on the steamboat, *Arabia*, coming up the Missouri River from St. Louis, and I was planning to continue tomorrow to Lawrence. However, it seems I've missed the big event in that town. Wish I could have witnessed it. Bad timing, I should say."

Before Ash could speak, Jabez blurted, "You sure missed some history being made, mister. We whipped their tails."

Ash took over, "I'll tell you what you can say to your people back in England. These abolitionists are traitors. They set up an illegal government. They's not obeying the laws of the territory's legal government. They's trying to prevent slaves from even being brought on Kansas soil. It was high time we took down that den of vipers. If you ask me, we let 'em off too easy. Shoulda wrecked the whole damn town—not just a hotel and couple of newspapers.

We shoulda burned everything and shipped 'em all back to New England. Sheriff oughta let us. They don't call us Border Ruffians for nothing."

Fielding smiled. "I like that term Border Ruffian. Sounds very British. But tell me what happened in Lawrence. Could you take it from the beginning and give me the details, please?"

Yelling over the din of the celebration, Ash recounted the events of May 21 in a storm of words and dramatic gesticulations. When Ash finished his account, Fielding turned to Jabez. "Young man, are you a Border Ruffian too?"

"You bet. I'm not so keen on slavery like my pa is, but I believe in law and order. Both of us were deputized. I helped my pa carry out the demolitions ordered by the court."

Fielding seemed puzzled. He asked, "You are not trying to make Kansas a slave state?"

"That's what pa wants, and to me it doesn't matter. We have no slaves, never have, and don't want them. I'm keen on law and order, though, and we laid down the law."

Fielding turned to Ash. "Is that right, you don't have slaves and don't intend to?"

Ash made no direct reply to the question. "It's a matter of what abolitionists are tryin' to do to the South, to Missouri, and to our way of life. When my son gets a little older, he'll see."

Jabez could sense Ash's irritation at his remarks. Then Ash abrubtly said, "C'mon son, we have to find a place to sleep tonight." Father and son said good night to the Englishman.

*

Fielding found other Ruffians to interview, but he could see that many of the drinkers were past the point of self-control, so for safety he returned to his hotel. Back in his room, Fielding tapped shreds of Missouri tobacco into his pipe. He struck a match, and the lusty smell of pipe smoke filled the room. From foregoing whiskey at the saloons, his mind was clear, and he spent the evening writing notes of his encounters that day in Westport.

Fielding also had time to review notes he had made during the earlier parts of his journey. He recalled his first day on the river, on the riverboat *Arabia*, when he had a conversation with a physician from South Carolina, a Dr. Sempronius Mayfield. The doctor was a dignified man in his early forties who had volunteered to come to Kansas for the spring and summer to support the proslavery forces there. Fielding recognized he was speaking with an educated individual who was dedicated to the institution of slavery and who believed that slavery was a natural condition for Negroes, a conviction informed by medical science—so the doctor said—about what he called the natural inferiority of the Negro. For his articles in *The Times*, Fielding was eager to learn the basis of Mayfield's prejudice. Fielding was acquainted with the peckerwood logic of white supremacists, but he had never met an educated man who supported racist views on supposed medical grounds. *Medical grounds for slavery?! What a story for my readers!*

"I haven't personally performed the medical research on the ethnology of the Negro race," said Dr. Sempronius Mayfield in a Carolina accent as soft and rich as warm butter, "but I am a friend of an eminent New Orleans physician who has done the research in great depth and who has written extensively about the subject in medical journals and Southern publications. That man is Dr. Samuel Adolphus Cartwright." Mayfield raised his chin, a signal that he believed he was about to recite the utter truth.

"Dr. Cartwright was asked to investigate the scientific case for the inequality of the races and the appropriateness of slavery. Here in America, we can see with our own eyes that Negroes are limited in intelligence and motivation and are suited for a protected servile status. But it was Dr. Cartwright who provided the *scientific* proof.

"Cartwright examined the history of the Negro race, noting that Negroes have always been enslaved when encountered by other races, whether Caucasian or Arab. He studied the biblical foundation for their slave condition. We know from the scriptures that Noah cursed the Negro descendants of his grandson Canaan to a servile status for all time, so there is biblical truth supporting slavery."

Fielding interrupted, "Doctor, you mentioned medical, scientific proof. Was that in addition to Cartwright's study of history and the Bible?"

"Oh, yes, he studied the mental inferiority of black Africans, and the special physical qualities the Lord has given them for servile labor. These factors he outlined in his paper. There's much more. Cartwright even discovered two diseases that are particular to the Negro. The first is what he calls *drapetomania*, a mental disease that stimulates the desire to flee from servitude. If the *drapetomania* persists, the white master should take strong measures—whipping for example—to discourage them from running away.

"The second disease affects both mind and body, *dysaesthesia aethiopica*. This disease results in a weakness of intellectual faculties and a torpid physical state, like a person half asleep. *Dysaesthesia aethiopica* is more prevalent among free Negroes. Slaves under the guidance and supervision of white masters are far less inclined towards this disease."

Dr. Mayfield paused and drew a deep breath, letting his audience of one digest the scientific disclosures. He took his coat lapels in either hand, lifted his chin another inch, cleared his throat, and continued.

"We therefore can see that slavery is the African's proper state, so that they can deal with these diseases and with their limited intelligence and make more progress than in a free state. In truth, slavery is the only state in which the race can be refined and elevated, and for this reason God has given to the white man a sacred trust and guardianship for the good of both races."

Fielding shook his head and thought, *My God, can anyone believe the scientific "proof" Cartwright offered? Insane. And those alleged diseases?*

In his hotel room, Fielding put away his pipe and recalled another conversation on the *Arabia*—this one with Dr. Mayfield and another of the passengers. This conversation was about the sources of conflict over the slavery question in Kansas Territory. The morning after their discussion about the so-called scientific underpinnings of slavery, Fielding joined Dr. Mayfield at breakfast. As they ate a breakfast of greasy meat and chicory coffee, Fielding fired off a series of questions about why and how a state of near civil war had developed along the Missouri-Kansas border. Mayfield was at a loss to explain the intricacies of the political history, other than to say that the issue was about whether Kansas Territory would enter the Union permitting or banning slavery.

Mayfield said, "I have come to help assure that slavery is permitted in the future state of Kansas. I believe I am acting as a patriot trying to hold this Union together, because if Kansas is abolitionized, such a state of affairs cannot stand, and these United States will become the Divided States of America. My state, South Carolina, will be the first to secede, I can assure you. Beyond that simple truth, I can't give you the details of political history, but I can introduce you to a history professor named Bird, whom I met yesterday. Come, and let me do so."

Franklin Bird was a history professor at St. Louis University. Bird was traveling to Kansas City, where he would be giving a series of lectures about, of all things, nineteenth century American history. Fielding could not believe his good fortune.

Bird said he was honored to have the opportunity to talk about history and to educate a writer for a famous English newspaper about the background of what had become an undeclared border war. The three men sat at a table in the dining room, drinking chicory coffee and enjoying sweet pastries.

Bird brushed away the crumbs that had gathered on his ample stomach and began, "It's all about the connection between slavery and power. Slavery is the issue that bonds the states of the South together. Slavery is the economic engine of those states. Their economy is agrarian. Aside from land, Negroes are the most important asset of southerners. The Northern states have a diverse economy, with manufacturing a much more important element than in the South. There is a clear difference between the culture of the South, which Northerners say is dominated by an indolent, pleasure-seeking planter class enslaving humans as chattel property, and the culture of the North, which Southerners say is dominated by money-grubbing racial hypocrites and foreign immigrants."

Mayfield abruptly stood to interrupt, almost knocking over his chair. He stretched to his full height, lifted his chin, held his coat lapels tightly and snapped them for emphasis. "By God, the Yankees have no idea about our Southern culture, because they are only interested in piling up as much money as humanly possible. And they keep their workers in a state of subservience too, exploiting their labor for starvation wages. They don't treat them with humanity or provide food and housing like we do the slaves."

Fielding was writing notes furiously. "Thank you, Sempronius, let's hear more from the professor."

Professor Bird chuckled. "The clash of cultures and economies has resulted in very short tempers, as you see."

Mayfield snapped, "Damn right."

The professor continued, "The division and sectionalization of our country is played out in a competition for power. You may have heard the term, "slave power." Well, it has nothing to do with the power of the slaves. It's about the power of slave owners. It's about the power of the slave states. One of the key factors of power is control of Congress. The number of seats a state has in the House of Representatives depends on population, which has been accreting each year in favor of the antislavery Northern states. But the advantage in the Senate, where each state possesses equal voting power, has been balanced between North and South, and any change in this balance could depend on whether new states enter the Union as 'slave' or 'free.' If Congress allowed slavery in the new state, it would align with the power position of the Southern states, and of course *vice versa*."

Fielding looked up from his notebook and asked, "Where do things stand now in Congress. Is there a balance?"

Professor Bird replied, "At the present time, there are fourteen slave states and seventeen free states, and there are two territories poised to become states in the near future, Minnesota and Oregon, and they will be free states. Needless to say, the South is nervous about Kansas Territory and also Nebraska Territory. Under the old rules by which Congress determined the slavery issue in a new state, each would have been a free state upon admission because its geographic location is above a line Congress drew across the Louisiana Purchase lands west of the Mississippi. But, two years ago Congress changed the rules and erased the geographic line. The new rules, called the Kansas-Nebraska Act, specify that the residents of each new territory will decide prior to admission to the Union whether it will be a free or slave state."

Mayfield stood again to interrupt. "Congress did the right thing. Each state should decide its destiny, not be forced one way or the other by Congress."

The professor paused and arched his eyebrows. "In my opinion, gentlemen, the Kansas-Nebraska Act was a monumental policy blunder and a failure of leadership at the national level. The mechanism for deciding the slavery issue—votes of the residents—created incentives for antislavery and proslavery forces to send thousands of like-minded settlers to Kansas to vote. In the Eastern states, especially the New England states, antislavery advocates arranged for financial support of settlers moving to Kansas who would vote against slavery. Southerners likewise organized and supported settlers to move to Kansas and vote for slavery. Why would Congress want to settle such an important question by inciting a competition to supply the greatest number of settlers who would vote for one side or the other? Conflict in Kansas was inevitable as a result of this Act, especially on the frontier, where everyone is armed, and gun justice prevails."

"What do you think will be the outcome in Kansas?"

"It will be a close call in Kansas. I predicted at the time the Act was passed that the conflict between the two groups of settlers in Kansas would lead to violence, possibly even civil war. And sure enough, conflict in Kansas erupted right away. When the first elections were held to create a territorial government, the proslavery leaders in western Missouri led thousands of residents across the border to vote illegally, and these votes made the difference. And then it happened again last year—at least six thousand Missourians voted in Kansas. They elected a legislature that passed a set of laws legalizing slavery in the Territory and criminalizing attempts to ban slavery. Now you would think the Kansas officials would not allow the Missourians to vote in the Kansas elections. But here is where the border war began. The Missourians were heavily armed, and they threatened the lives of election officials who opposed their voting. Some of the Missourians intimidated antislavery Kansans from voting. Antislavery Kansans cried 'stolen elections' and said they would not follow bogus laws passed by a bogus legislature. They created their own legislature and elected their own governor. So, today, there are two governments and two sets of laws in Kansas Territory. Kansas is a tinderbox."

Dr. Mayfield was not smiling. He told the professor that there was more to the story and suggested that the account was drily academic and slanted toward an abolitionist view. Professor Bird assured Mayfield that he was trying to give an objective account, and yes, he realized there are many parts of the complex history of slavery and of Kansas Territory's struggle. This is simply a summary, he said, and if the doctor wished to add anything or correct any errors, he would be pleased to hear.

Dr. Mayfield grumbled. "The only thing I'd say is, what's the difference between a Missourian coming twenty or thirty miles to vote in Kansas and an abolitionist coming from New England to vote?"

Edwin Fielding turned from his recollections to his preparations for sleep. He smiled as he reflected on his good fortune to be assigned to cover this momentous development in American history. He could not wait to be in Lawrence.

# 4

## OLD MAN BROWN

Jabez Cooper: *We soon learned that the abolitionists were not going to run out of Kansas just because we came down on Lawrence. They had suspected what was coming, and they had organized militias. And there were some who had been itching for a chance to war against Missourians. What we did in Lawrence gave them the spark to light their flame.*

May 22–25, 1856, Miami County, eastern Kansas Territory
"Vengeance! God must have His vengeance! There must be blood," wailed old John Brown. His son had told him of the May 21 sack of Lawrence. Old Brown's scream was high-pitched, a squeal so high that the tone made mockery of his imperative. Then he clenched his massive jaws and thrust his gaunt and weathered face forward, craning to right and left as if looking for a recipient for his rage. His luminous eyes glowed in anger. His son John Jr. repeated what he had heard and added there was no resistance, no shots fired by Lawrence residents. "Cowards!" old Brown screamed. "They're so weak they didn't even put up a fight."

Old John Brown was a fifty-six-year-old white New Englander, solemn as a graveyard—a man who never laughed—and religious to the extreme, a strict Calvinist in the mold of the throwback Puritans. His God was judgmental and vengeful. Brown believed with all his faith that he was a divine agent chosen by God to lead

Negroes from slavery, an institution that he considered the work of Satan. Going beyond a mere embrace of abolition, he believed that Black and White were brothers, equal brothers. In recent years he had dedicated his life to helping Negroes, and he had contemplated the adoption of a black child. In upstate New York he had created a utopian community composed of his family and the Negro families that had been granted land by the abolitionist Gerrit Smith.

Brown knew prominent abolitionists in the East, and he became active in raising funds for Sharps rifles and ammunition to be sent to antislavery New Englanders emigrating to Kansas. He served as a conductor on the Underground Railroad. Believing slavery could be ended in America only through the shedding of blood, he contemplated various options for provoking an uprising by slaves that would ignite the war he believed was necessary. As early as 1851 he was sketching plans for a raid on the federal arsenal at Harper's Ferry, Virginia.

Five of old Brown's sons—John Jr., Jason, Owen, Frederick, and Salmon—and their families had migrated to Kansas in early 1855 to stake land claims as the territory opened, bringing eleven head of cattle, three horses, a plow and various farm tools, two small tents, some seed corn, two squirrel rifles, and a revolver. The group established a family compound some fifty miles south of Lawrence, called Brown's Station, near the town of Osawatomie, and began a farming life. All were ardent antis. John Jr. and Jason joined an antislavery militia called the Pottawatomie Rifles, and John Jr. became its captain.

Old Brown pondered whether he should postpone his idea to seize the arsenal at Harpers Ferry and move to Kansas to assist his sons in resisting the attempts by Southerners to make Kansas a slave State. He put the question up for a vote by his family and the Negro residents of North Elba, one vote each. After the vote was made for Kansas, old Brown, his sixteen-year-old son Oliver, and his son-in-law Henry Thompson traveled by wagon to Kansas in October 1855 to join the other sons. In addition to his personal possessions, old Brown brought a stash of weaponry including Sharps rifles and short double-edged broadswords.

On May 22, Brown's son, John Brown Jr., was in his Kansas field planting corn when a messenger brought him the news of the preceding day's events at Lawrence, and he spread the word to the antislavery militias nearby. Thirty-four men of the Pottawatomie Rifles, including John Jr. and Jason, gathered and headed to Lawrence to provide aid to the antis. John Jr. ordered one of the men of the Rifles to round up reinforcements who would join the force later.

Traveling with the Rifles, but not as members, were old Brown and his sons Owen, Frederick, Salmon, and Oliver, his son-in-law Henry Thompson, and neighbors, James Townsley and Henry Weiner. Townsley provided a wagon with a team of dappled grays. The wagon was tightly packed with the men, their guns, and the broadswords.

Along the way to Lawrence, the combined group decided to camp and wait for reinforcements.

During the night, the men held a council around a campfire. Old Brown stood, tall as he was, his wide shoulders loomed over the men seated on the ground. The glow of the fire in the dark night made his figure look like a medieval painting, etching the prominent bones of his gaunt face, his weathered and leathery skin, and the wiry muscles roping his trim body. He prayed at length, beseeching an Old Testament, angry God to help him smite his enemies. After the prayers, Brown addressed a plan he had held in his mind for some time.

"It's time to fight fire with fire, time to strike terror in the hearts of the proslavery people. Terror! We must make an example to show the Ruffians they can't run us out of Kansas."

Old Brown scratched out a list of pros who lived in the general vicinity of Pottawatomie Creek and who had been active in what Brown perceived as persecuting the antis under the provisions of the slave laws. Brown listed two men, Doyle and Wilkinson, who were involved in a grand jury attempt to indict the Browns for defiance of a territorial law enacted by the proslavery legislature. On his list, Brown included a man named Sherman, who had a tavern that was a center of proslavery activity and the seat of the local court. Old Brown completed his list. "These pukes are ignorant and Godless vermin who are servants of Satan. We must remove them from Kansas. From this Earth! We are the Lord's agents. Let His will be done."

After Brown finished, the group rose and broke into private conversations. Many in the Rifles were skeptical of Brown's plan. The next morning, May 23, Old Brown announced that he and his group would split from the Rifles and head back home. He spoke in a loud and theatrical voice. "We will complete my plan. Our mission is God's mission—to prevent the utter destruction of the antislavery families in our community."

Old Brown and his men sharpened their swords on a grindstone at the campsite, then broke camp. They proceeded in the direction of Pottawatomie Creek and bivouacked beside a small stream in a grassy ravine, fringed by a stand of sycamore and cottonwood trees. Here the horses could feed on the spring grass, and John Brown could lay out the details of his plan.

The next day, Saturday May 24, Brown was in a lively mood, despite the news of the past two days. He led morning prayer, and while making breakfast, he sang to himself the refrain from his favorite hymn, "Blow Ye The Trumpet." *The year of jubilee is come! The year of jubilee is come!*

Shortly after the waning gibbous moon rose on the night of May 24, the group of eight men left the ravine and walked in the moon's light toward the Pottawatomie Creek area, where the proslavery families lived. They carried the swords and two revolvers. At around ten o'clock they reached the first house, the home of a settler named Mentzig, and knocked.

"Wha' duh ya want?" growled Mentzig.

"Can you show us the way to the James Doyle cabin?" said Old Brown.

No word was returned. Mentzig poked a rifle barrel through a chink between logs.

The group scattered away and moved on to the next cabin, which turned out to be that of Doyle. As the group neared the Doyle cabin, two guard dogs charged from the darkness, snapping their fangs and barking. Townsley slashed the neck of one of the dogs with his broadsword, killing it instantly. He chopped a gash in the croup of the other dog, and it limped into the woods.

Old Brown knocked on the door, and he heard a voice within ask who was there. Brown said, "We're looking for Allen Wilkinson's cabin."

Doyle opened the door to accommodate the visitors, and his wife and five children crowded around the entrance. The Brown group rushed into the cabin, pushing Doyle to the floor.

Doyle scuttled to his feet. Old Brown asked, "Are you all members of the Law and Order Party?"

"Yayus" said Doyle in his Tennessee drawl. "Y'all leave me and my family be."

The others in the Brown group herded Doyle's wife and children to the back of the one-room cabin.

Old Brown pushed his face into Doyle's and said, "We're from the Northern Army, and we are here to take you prisoner. If you come peaceably with us, you will not be harmed."

Doyle's wife burst into tears.

Doyle said "Hush, Mother, hush."

"Where are your horses?" said Brown.

"They's out on the prairie," said Doyle.

Old Brown pointed to Doyle's children. "You have some grown boys here, and we must take them too."

Mrs. Doyle's eyes were as big as biscuits, and she had a stricken look on her face. She put her hands together as if in prayer to Brown. "Please don't take these boys, they ain't done nothin'." She began to weep and moaned, "John is just fifteen years old, please don't take him."

The woman's pitiful pleas stopped old Brown. He stood motionless for a full minute, and everyone was silent. Brown finally spoke, "All right, woman," and the men took only the father and the two older sons out of the cabin.

Outside, the three were walked a couple hundred yards or so from the cabin. Old Brown held a revolver in front of James Doyle's face. "You have committed unspeakable sins in supporting slavery." With this judgment, Brown fired point-blank into Doyle's forehead. When Doyle fell from the fatal shot, old Brown turned to his son Owen. "Stab him in the heart. That's where Satan has put his evil."

Owen obeyed, thrusting the sword into Doyle's chest.

The frantic Doyle boys struggled to escape. Owen and Salmon wrestled one to the ground and hacked his head. They stabbed him in the side for good measure. The other son broke free and ran about fifty yards towards the cabin. The Browns chased him, knocked him to the ground, and sliced his body with their swords, cutting off some of his fingers as he fought to defend himself. Then they cut off his arms, hacked his skull, and stabbed his chest.

The men silently washed the swords and their hands in the creek. The group moved toward the cabin of Allen Wilkinson, who had served as a court officer in the attempt to serve warrants on old Brown and his sons a month prior. Like James Doyle, Wilkinson was a well-known hater of abolitionists.

At the door, old Brown rapped and cried out, "Show us the way to Dutch Henry's place."

Wilkinson began to answer, "Well it's yonder down the creek . . ."

Brown took a breath and tried to speak in a honeyed tone. "Come out and show us the way, we're not from here."

Wilkinson stepped outside.

Old Brown's stern demeanor returned. He seized the man by the arm and demanded, "Are you a Northern armist?"

"What the hell does 'armist' mean?" said Wilkinson, "I ain't never heard of a armist."

"Are you a member of the Law and Order Party?"

"I reckon I am," Wilkinson said, throwing back his shoulders.

"Do you oppose the Free State Party and the abolition of slavery?

Wilkinson clenched his jaw and shot back, "You damn right I do."

"Then you are our prisoner. We're from the Northern Army. Do you surrender?"

Wilkinson grunted a "Wha?" but he was swept inside the cabin by the Browns.

The Brown party spread through the cabin, looking for what they could use, and they picked up two saddles and a gun.

Owen said "We're taking these saddles and we're taking this prisoner to the camp. We'll take your horses too." Owen had Wilkinson by the arm and led him out of the cabin.

Old Brown watched his men take the prisoner into the brush a short distance from the house. He looked on with pride as they hacked his head with their swords and cut his throat twice.

Old Brown turned to his sixteen-year-old son, Oliver, who was trembling. "I know this is hard on you, son, but you know this is God's war, and you have been a brave soldier. Be calm in knowing our Lord approves this."

The Brown party was now frantic, moving back and forth and in circles, electric with the adrenaline and energy the slaughters had released. Old Brown called them to attention, and the group moved up the creek toward Henry Sherman's cabin. Dutch Henry, as he was called, and his brothers known as Dutch Bill and Dutch Pete were immigrants from Germany, and all three had a long history of threatening Free-State settlers. Dutch Henry's tavern was the scene of frequent meetings of pros and the site of the local court. Finding no one at Dutch Henry's place, the company diverted to the nearby cabin of Dutch Henry's friend, James Harris. It was now around two in the morning on Sunday, May 25.

The cabin door and windows of the Harris cabin were made of cotton cloth framed in wood. With his sword Brown split the cloth door down the middle, and he and the other men slipped through and crept to the bed where Harris and his wife and young child lay.

"Get up, we're the Northern Army."

The cabin had only one big room, and three other men were asleep on the floor. Brown kicked at the men on the floor and demanded they stand. He pulled Harris from the bed. "Where is Dutch Henry? No one is at his place."

Harris stumbled and tried to gain his balance. "He and his brother Pete left during the day to go out on the prairie to find some lost cattle."

Brown looked at one of the men who had risen from the floor. "We know you. You are Dutch Henry's brother Bill and a member of the Law and Order Party. All you

Shermans have threatened Free-State settlers. You're under arrest. You are a prisoner of the Northern Army. Your brothers will be prisoners as soon as they return. Where do you all keep your horses?"

Bill Sherman rubbed his face to wake up fully. He looked at the floor. "In the field behind Henry's place."

Brown directed Frederick to round up the horses. Meantime, his men scattered through the house, searching for plunder, and they grabbed a saddle, two rifles, and a Bowie knife.

Old Brown positioned himself in the threshold of the door. "Bill Sherman, we'll deal with you shortly, but first we have some questions of these others."

Brown and Frederick took Harris and the two strangers outside. One by one, old Brown pushed his face so close to their faces that noses almost touched, as he asked each of them a series of questions about their support of the Law and Order Party. Each smelled the hot and stinking breath of the old man. None of them panicked, and each answered "no" to the questions. Being satisfied, the Browns brought the three back indoors.

Old Brown turned to Frederick, "I know you didn't like my plan. But you can see I am acting as a fair agent of the Lord. If they ain't guilty, I let 'em go."

Then, returning to the cabin, Brown gave instructions to his sons Owen and Salmon, who took Bill Sherman a distance from the cabin. Brown followed behind and watched. There was no interrogation, and they came down on him with the swords, cutting off his left hand as he raised it in defense and splitting his skull in two places. Owen said, "Now your black heart," and pushed the blade into his chest.

John Brown had moved his personal war against slavery to a new level. "Glory to God," crowed old Brown. "His will has been done. We have drawn our first blood and lit the fuse of a holy war.

# OLD MAN BROWN

June 2, 1856, Black Jack, eastern Kansas Territory
Henry Clay Pate ran a proslavery newspaper in Westport, Missouri. He had organized a vigilante militia known as the Westport Sharpshooters, and he had brought some of them to serve as deputies of Sheriff Jones in the destruction of the newspapers and hotel in Lawrence on May 21. Following the killings in the Pottawatomie Creek area, the federal marshal in Kansas deputized Pate and the Sharpshooters as a posse to arrest John Brown and his accomplices. Right away, Pate's posse captured Brown's sons John Jr. and Jason in Osawatomie and put them in irons. The posse burned the homes of the Browns and scattered their livestock.

"Why are you arresting us?" asked John Jr. "We are completely innocent. We were in Lawrence when these killings took place, and we have many witnesses."

Clay Pate waved some papers. "We have writs for your arrest. We have no choice but to carry them out. If you have an alibi, tell it to the court, not to me. Meantime, where's your father and your brothers? They're going with you to jail."

"My family is not here in this settlement, as you can see. I have no idea where they are. Jason and I just returned from Lawrence."

Pate sent the brothers to be jailed, and his posse then moved north and camped near a small settlement known as Black Jack, between Osawatomie and Lawrence, on the edge of the Santa Fe trail. Pate and his men camped in a thicket coursed by a small creek, a spot in a stand of prairie grass surrounded by maple, cedar, black walnut, black willow, sycamore, blackjack oak, and osage orange trees, interspersed with young saplings, bristly greenbrier, buckbrush, black raspberry and multiflora rose.

Shortly before dawn, guns fired into the camp, and Pate scattered his men into the wood. There was a pause in the firing. Pate heard a booming voice. "I am John

Brown, agent of Our Father in Heaven, who has commanded me to wipe slavery from the future of Kansas. We will not allow Missourians to invade our land. We have many men on our side. We outnumber you, and we are heavily armed. Reinforcements will be here in minutes. Do you surrender?"

"Hell no," shouted Pate, and guns fired from both sides.

After two hours of battle, some of the Missourians had enough and began draining away. In a fit of paranoia, Pate conjured up the fantasy that his reduced force was then outnumbered four to one.

A young man in the Brown force leapt on his horse and rode between the two opposing forces yelling, "Father, we have them surrounded." The rider was Frederick Brown, and unbeknownst to Pate, Frederick suffered delusions from time to time, this being one such case.

The coincidental misfiring of the minds of Frederick Brown and Clay Pate led Pate to wave a flag of truce. He requested a meeting with old Brown, and with a lieutenant he went to Brown under the flag. "Captain Brown, we are prepared to leave this battle under flag of truce. Can you assure us safe passage?"

Brown waved a revolver at Pate and spoke in a yell, "I will have nothing but unconditional surrender."

Pate snapped, "Sir, I refuse to surrender."

"Then you are a prisoner of the Northern Army." Brown and a half-dozen of his men surrounded Pate.

Pate stiffened. "Sir, this is a violation of the rules of combat. I am here under a truce flag. You cannot take me prisoner. Release me."

"I spit on the rules of combat. We answer to a higher authority, God Almighty, who despises slavery and those who support it."

Brown seized both of Pate's arms and pushed Pate as a shield ahead of Brown and his men in a march toward the Missourians. The old man pressed the barrel of his revolver against Pate's skull.

As they walked along, Old Brown spoke in a low and harsh voice. "I can kill a man as easily as I can kill a dog. If a man stands between me and what is right, I would take his life as cooly as I eat my breakfast."

When the group neared the posse, Brown again spoke in a loud voice, loud enough for the posse to hear. "We demand an unconditional surrender."

Pate again refused, but Brown's grim face showed his men that Brown would kill Pate if the posse did not surrender. The battle had worn out the Missourians, and they had been told, albeit falsely, that they were surrounded. So, they laid down their arms. Brown and his men kept the prisoners for a few days, until a U.S. cavalry unit happened to find the camp and forced Brown to release the men.

Pate told one of the cavalry officers, "I refused to surrender, but my men could see Brown would shoot me in the head if they didn't. I owe my life to their peaceful surrender, and thanks to them I live to fight again. That old abolitionist took me with a devilish trick—a dishonorable violation of the code of armed combat. I came to take old Brown, but old Brown took me."

# 5

## INVASION

Jabez Cooper: *When old John Brown captured Clay Pate at Black Jack and forced Pate to surrender, Pa was fit to be tied. He and Pate had been friends but weren't any longer.*

*Sometime after the Black Jack disaster, Pa came running into our forge, gripping a newspaper in his fist, holding it high and shaking it, and said, "Jabez, ever one of our newspapers is making a call to arms against the abolitionists in Kansas. Look at these headlines in our Sovereign Squatter, 'War to the knife and knife to the hilt—Let the watchword be extermination of abolitionists total and complete.' We gotta do something. Kansas is in civil war, Son. The abolitionists are tearing Kansas Territory apart with murder, arson, and robbery against innocent pro-slavery settlers. John Brown and his boys are bloodthirsty murderers. We must take blood for blood. That fanatic Jim Lane has come back from the North bringing over a thousand Yankee pukes and forty wagons of arms, and he and Brown are everywhere on the attack. They're trying to run every resident who's for slavery out of Kansas. Meantime, there's a flood of new abolitionists coming in from the east to vote our people out. Something's gotta be done."*

*My pa raved on for the rest of the morning, his face getting redder by the hour. I tried to calm him, because he had heart problems and I worried he was heading for a heart attack. But I couldn't even slow him down. He said, "I'm more concerned about my health if I don't raise hell. Did you know it has gotten so bad the territorial governor*

*Shannon—who they say is on our side—resigned and fled for his life to St. Louis? Here it says in the Squatter that he claimed governing Kansas is like trying to govern Hades."*

*The next day, Pa came to our forge, and he said our friends Senator Atchison and Sheriff Jones were raising a posse in Missouri to go back over to Kansas. Said the plan was to sweep through John Brown's town and up to Lawrence and on to the abolitionist capital at Topeka. Wipe 'em all out. If they catch Brown they'll kill him, Pa said, for attacking Pate's posse. Pa said he was joining that posse, but that I should stay and run our shop while he went to Kansas. I wanted to go, and I said it was no different from Lawrence, but he said, "no" because it was going to be a lot different from Lawrence. People probably were going to die. I still wanted to go, but as always, he was the boss.*

*A few days later he was gone by wagon to Kansas, along with almost fifteen hundred Missourians. Can you imagine that number? Pa took his traveling forge, with blacksmith tools, fuel, and a lot of horseshoes, so he could work his magic and take care of the horses. But Pa wouldn't be in the background working metal and dealing with hooves and horseshoes. He was ready for fighting, too. I worried whether he would be shot, but truth to tell, I was very proud of him—at that time.*

*A posse of fifteen hundred is a mighty thing to behold. More like an army than a posse. When it rolled into Kansas a small group of about two hundred fifty, including pa, split off from the main group and set upon Osawatomie, near where the Browns live. Old Man Brown was there, and Brown and his little army put up a fight, but soon retreated. Our Missouri men burned the town to the ground and killed one of Brown's sons, but the old man escaped. Even though Brown retreated, the abolitionists worshipped him for fighting—like he was a hero for shooting at Missourians but getting whipped.*

# 6

## RETURN TO LAWRENCE

Jabez Cooper: *The posse turned its sights to Lawrence and Topeka. What began as about fifteen hundred men had almost doubled in size, as it added more men coming from Missouri and picked up proslavery recruits in Kansas. They had more than just John Brown and his little band to fight, because the abolitionist militias led by Jim Lane were on the move, attacking proslavery Kansans and looking for a chance to stop the big posse.*

September 14–15, 1856, Lawrence, Douglas County, eastern Kansas

John Brown and his group moved about the eastern Kansas countryside, evading arrest and battling proslavery settlers. An information network among abolitionists assured his elusiveness, and through spies he tracked the movement of the growing posse headed by ex-Senator Atchison and Sheriff Jones.

Brown arrived in Lawrence, where he received word that the posse was only a few hours away. The old man was on fire. He passed the warning out to the community, and men and women, and boys gathered on Massachusetts Street in the space between two earthen forts built after the attack in May. The problem was that so many of the men who could provide a defense had joined Jim Lane in action against proslavery settlers in other parts of the state, and Lawrence now was outmanned by the Missourians. The townspeople sorely needed the absent residents and the thousand-member volunteer army Lane had brought to Kansas.

Brown took a dry-goods box from a store and placed it near the middle of a group of around three hundred. He waved his arms and whistled for attention. He looked like a scarecrow with his bony body and tattered clothes and his hair splaying in all directions. His appearance was comical, but he spoke calmly and in a voice of authority. "Gentlemen, there are almost three thousand Missourians down at Franklin. They will be here in two hours. We must organize the defense of this town."

The news about the size of the posse had a deadening effect on the gathered crowd. They hopelessly gripped their various weapons—Sharps rifles, shotguns, pistols, Bowie knives, and pitchforks. "Good Lord, save us," cried one. "There ain't no way we can stop them."

"That may be true," said Brown, "and now is probably the last opportunity you will have of fighting the slavers, so you had better do your best. I'm not afraid to die, and I know my time on this earth is almost up. If I die, I will have given my best for a cause that God has called for us to follow."

A boy was helping a woman load a shotgun left behind by her husband who was away with Jim Lane and telling her how to shoot it. The woman said to Brown, "How do we do our best, if we have never fought before?"

The crowd was waiting and listening for the mad warrior to tell them how to make war. Brown was still standing on the box and he raised his voice for all around.

"When they attack us, don't yell and make a great noise, but remain perfectly silent and still. Wait until they get within twenty-five yards of you, get a good look at your object, be sure you see the hind sight of your gun, then fire. A great deal of powder and lead and very precious time is wasted by shooting too high. You had better aim at their legs rather than at their heads. In either case, be sure of the hind sights of your guns. By God's grace and men shooting too high I have so many times escaped. If they had shot lower, I'd be as full of holes as a riddle."

Captain Sam Walker, one of the leaders of the Free State militia bands that had attacked proslavery strongholds, gathered a group of eighty horsemen to serve as a cavalry. Captain Joe Cracklin organized a makeshift infantry. Some men pulled out the town's cannon that had been reclaimed in the recent raids and a stash of cannon balls fashioned from the salvaged type of the newspaper *Herald of Freedom*, which had been tossed in the river during the first raid on the town in May.

Walker called to a wiry young man who had a fast horse. "I want you to go to the territorial governor's office in Lecompton. There's a new governor, name is John Geary. Tell him his Territory has been invaded by Ruffians, and our town is about to be wiped off the map of this Territory." The governor's office was only fifteen miles from Lawrence, but no one expected the governor would be able to arrive before the Ruffians attacked. All they could do was hope.

*

Within a few hours, the Ruffians approached the outskirts of the town. Sheriff Sam Jones and David Atchison rode together at the sharp point of the posse. Jones mumbled to Atchison for the third, maybe fourth, time, "Wish I hadn't held our men back in May. We shoulda burned Lawrence to the ground then. We woughtn't be here today. This time, total demolition."

Around four in the afternoon, Sheriff Jones took a hundred men forward as an advance guard, followed by the main body. Sam Walker and his eighty riders emerged from Lawrence, rode and met the advance guard, and wheeled around, as if in a panic. Then, as Jones' men chased, the eighty spread out and turned to fire at the sheriff's men. The Missourians retreated to a ravine, and after regrouping charged toward the town. By this time, the foot soldiers had established a line, and they pushed the Missourians back to their camp outside the town of Franklin for the night.

Sam Walker and John Brown spread the word to the people of Lawrence to expect the Missourians back at the gates of the town the next day. To the surprise of the townspeople, a large force of U.S. cavalry troops arrived in Lawrence during the night, as a peace-keeping force, and Governor Geary arrived the next morning.

John Brown avoided contact with the governor and the troops, as he was a wanted man. Walker informed the governor of the details of the attack and retreat by the posse. "There's about three thousand of them. Thank God, they only sent a small scouting party, and we turned them back. When they return, they'll bring all three thousand. Is there anything you can do, governor?"

Governor Geary went with a small entourage straightaway by carriage toward the camp of the Ruffians. Along the way, the governor met a new advance guard of three hundred Missourians, dressed in red shirts, led by Sheriff Jones and Ash Cooper and heading toward Lawrence.

The governor spoke a curt demand, "Who are you?"

"We're the territorial militia. Appointed by the governor of this territory," said Ash Cooper. "Who in the hell are you?

"Well, I'm the new territorial governor, John Geary, and I'm ordering you to turn back. Take me to the leaders of this illegal army."

"We're here to finish a job we started in May, when we should have wiped these traitorous abolitionists off the face of Kansas," said Cooper. "We ain't gonna take orders from a stranger claiming to be a new governor."

Geary had no papers with him to prove his authority. He turned to his entourage and asked if any of them knew these men, so that they could attest to his position.

One spoke up and said, "Yeh, I know Sheriff Jones. Everybody else must be from Missouri. I'll talk to the sheriff."

After a few minutes of parley, the sheriff returned to his men. He leaned forward in his saddle and spat tobacco juice on the ground. "This here is a new governor, all right. And he has federal troops with him back in Lawrence. He wants to talk with Atchison and me back at our camp. Let's head back there."

The advance guard turned around and escorted Geary's carriage through Franklin and to the bivouac camp on the banks of the Wakarusa River. Geary met with Sheriff Jones, David Atchison, and Ash Cooper in Atchison's tent and told the Ruffians he had U.S. Cavalry troops, which they would have to fight if they did not disband. "This is an illegal militia or posse or whatever you want to call it. I'm the new governor of this territory, and I order you to disband. If you attack Lawrence and engage U.S. Army troops, you will start a civil war, not only in Kansas and Missouri but throughout this entire country. I know of you, Senator Atchison, and I know that as a former member of the Senate you would not want to be responsible for throwing the country into a war that would take many thousands of lives."

Jones, Cooper, and Atchison walked a distance sufficient to provide privacy for their parley. Geary and his party could not hear the words of the three Ruffians, but they could see them gesturing with their hands and arms and sometimes by spitting to the ground.

One of the governor's aides said, "Looks like it is Senator Atchison versus the sheriff and the other fellow."

The three men returned to the tent where Governor Geary was waiting. Atchison did the talking.

"We sure as hell don't agree with your order, Governor, but we will not defy it. We would not take arms against the Federal army. Most settlers in Kansas will be exceedingly critical of your order, Governor. The legislature of this Territory was elected fairly, and it is proslavery. As I am sure you know, the abolitionists have acted treasonously in defiance of the legislature and the laws of Kansas Territory. Our posse came here to break up this nest of vipers and send them packing."

Geary was stone-faced. He said, "Wise decision" and turned and walked to his carriage.

Jones, who was working his jaws over a slug of chew tobacco, spat a stream of juice on the ground, grunted a "gah—damn …" and walked to his tent.

The Ruffians left Kansas, winding their way back to hometowns in Missouri. John Brown departed too, heading toward eastern states.

# 7

## LOSSES

Jabez Cooper: *The years between 1856 and the summer of 1859 were hard and bitter. The worst thing was, I lost my father. Pa passed away January 14, 1859. Heart finally played out on him. I was crushed, my heart broken.*

*He was blue, very sad, during his last three years. When he returned with Senator Atchison and the big posse in '56 from their failed mission to eliminate the abolitionist strongholds in Kansas, Pa was more torn up than I had ever seen.*

*He said he knew when Governor Geary turned them back, it was the beginning of the end for the slavery cause in Kansas. "They'll flood Kansas with eastern abolitionists. Then they'll outnumber the proslavery settlers. Then they'll take control of the legislature. Then they'll write a constitution banning slavery and present it to Congress to become a state, a state where a man can't own a Negro.'*

*Pa was red-hot mad at his friend Senator Atchison for making the posse comply with the governor's order to disband. They had been so close—not only in politics—but true friendship. Even though the Senator was a high and powerful man, he was a friend to a blacksmith, a good friend. After that failure in Lawrence, Pa could barely speak to Atchison.*

*Pa told me, "We had old John Brown and the abolitionists in the palms of our hands. If we had taken down Lawrence and Topeka, we'd a-scared every New Englander back to Massachusetts.'*

*I tried my best to calm him. Said going against the governor woulda brought on a war with the federal army. Said the United States government was not going to allow Border Ruffians to fight its army. Pa couldn't hear that logic.*

*Pa even believed Sheriff Jones should have wiped out Lawrence the first time. "If we had burned down Lawrence back when we only just wrecked the newspapers and hotel, it woulda sent a chill wind through abolition land. We shoulda run out all the Free Staters in the territory at that time. We woughtn't a-seen abolitionists flowin' into Kansas, they woulda been scared to come. Then there would be no doubt that Kansas would enter the Union as a slave state. Now, it is looking like the Free-Staters are in the majority, and there's more comin' every day."*

*Pa worried all the time about the slavery issue. Soon, he let himself go physically too. He started drinking whiskey. Had never drunk a drop before. Liquor gave him release to rage against the abolitionists. Not that he needed any additional help to speak against them. After about six months of watching him drown in whiskey, I tried to get him to stop drinking. But he said he couldn't—said it would be like losing a dear friend.*

*He ruined his body too—put on an awful weight—he had a hung belly that made him look foolish. He was a proud man, but he was destroying his pride as he destroyed his body.*

*Whiskey and the ruin of his body were one thing, but it was politics that killed him. All that anger poisoned his heart.*

*Railing about slavery was the mysterious part of him. He was such a kind and gentle man with people of all sorts, rich, poor, black, white. Why was he so sore about slavery?*

*I tried to calm him down, get his mind on something*

*useful. "Pa, will it really be so bad if Kansas is a free state?"*

*Well, that was a mistake, because rather than calm him, it made him boil over.*

*"Jabez, if I told you once'st, if I told you twice'st, I told you a hunderd times. If Kansas is free-soil, slaves will stampede from Missouri, cross the border to Kansas and go up the underground railroad. Worst, abolitionists will come out of Kansas into Missouri and steal slaves."*

*"Pa, why are you so bothered about keeping slavery alive? Why are you willing to kill over it?"*

*Well, that was like putting a match to a fireworks rocket. He blew up. Maybe it was the first time he ever yelled at me.*

*"Dammit son, are you that stupid? Don't matter if we own slaves or not. It's the way of life in the South. People here in these parts of Missouri need slaves for farming. We ain't gonna let a bunch of radical abolitionists tell us how to live. I tell you, if Kansas enters the Union as a free state, this Union will come apart at the seams. Lot of people talking about secession."*

*I was worried back then whether his heart could stand it. So I stopped talking politics with him. And I told him for his health I'd do the heavy work at our forge. He could just continue to teach me the trade. He could file horse hooves and that sort of thing, but lay off using the hammer doing metal work. That suited him fine. The bad thing was it gave him more time to spend at the courthouse and the saloon. At both places folks talked—all the damn time— about the Kansas problem.*

*As time went on, what really got my pa's goat was not so much the growth of the number and power of Free-State settlers in Kansas, but the problems we had with a group of Kansans called Jayhawkers. Nobody knows where that name came from, but we sure knew what a Jayhawker was—marauders in the name of abolition who used that cause as an excuse for robbery.*

*Two Jayhawker chiefs got under Pa's skin the most, James Montgomery and Charles Jennison. Each led a pack of low-lifes who said outright their mission was to rid Kansas of proslavery settlers. Montgomery was the original Jayhawker. He was a former preacher, and he was called a praying fighter. His example made me start questioning religion. I'd already had some doubts—guess I just wasn't built for faith—but hearing about this man of the Bible who became a villain just about finished me with religion. Montgomery and his men tried to convince everybody that his fighters needed to live off their victims. He called it "self-sustaining." So, horses and livestock were stolen on every raid, along with money, jewelry, and anything of else value that could be carted off. The rest was burned. Western Missouri was flooded with proslavery settlers he had run out of Kansas. Montgomery even stole the house of a Kansas settler he ran off, to use as his own. Jennison was one of Montgomery's Jayhawkers in 1857, and later he set up his own Jayhawking gang. Both of these men led raids into Missouri, and folks in western Missouri had to set up defense militias to fight Jayhawkers.*

*Then old John Brown came back to Kansas in the summer of '58, making trouble again. He was a wanted man in Kansas from his previous episodes. Disguising himself with a long white beard, he took an alias, Shubel Morgan. This past December he led a raid into western Missouri and stole about a dozen slaves. His men killed one of the slaveowners. Brown was chased by the law, but he managed to take those slaves through the snows of Kansas and Iowa and on to Canada. They say it was over a thousand miles.*

*When pa heard about the raid Brown made, he flew into another of his furies. He told me, "See, what'd I tell you about how the abolitionists will be stealin' slaves here in Missouri. You need to listen to me. We shoulda killed that sonofabitch at Black Jack or Osawattomie or Law-rence."*

*I told Pa that politics and fightin' for slavery was not something I wanted to spend my time on. I had had enough political adventure, and I wanted to be with my pals and ride horses and hunt. And I had a girlfriend too, Cait O'Kelly, a beautiful Irish girl. He seemed to understand, but he made me swear to something. He made me promise to join the Self Defensive Association. That was a group of proslavery men trying to defend against Jayhawkers. It was a group of people I knew. Friends of Pa, friends I had grown up with. I kept that promise. I considered it my duty.*

*On the second day of the new year, 1859, Pa and I were working in the shop, and he toppled like a big tree uprooted and blown down by the wind, falling stand-up-straight, without his feet even moving, and he was dead before he hit the floor.*

*Pa and I were very close. All my life he had been my hero. Even after he fell apart. I miss him so much. With Ma dead too, and having no brothers or sisters, I was alone. I suppose you'd say I was an orphan.*

*One thing I'll never know is what Pa would be like today, after the war, after slaves were emancipated. Would Pa have come to accept it if he was still alive? This mystery part of Pa, the slavery part, where did it come from? Why was he so keen to fight for the right to own Negroes? It had to be something beyond property rights, because he never owned a slave and had no intention to. I never will be able to understand why he would be willing to kill someone over the right to own people.*

*Losing Pa was not the only sadness visited upon me in 1859. My girlfriend, Cait O'Kelly, moved from Liberty across the state to Columbia. I still have in my mind a picture of her from those days, her long red hair and bright eyes and a dash of freckles on her cheeks. Her arms and legs were like willow branches, and she moved with the smooth gracefulness of a dancer. She was smart and had never-ending energy, a tomboy who loved the outdoors. She cut a dramatic figure in Clay County, and I sometimes wondered why she chose me. She could have had her choice of more likely men than a blacksmith. But she laughed at my jokes, and she loved to ride horseback and walk in the woods with me. Most of all, we were friends who could talk and share feelings.*

*Pa had been buried for only a matter of weeks when I heard the news from Cait that her parents were moving and she would go with them. The revelation was a terrible blow on top of Pa's death. Cait and I swore to stay connected, to write letters and to meet occasionally. Soon the time between letters stretched out and drizzled down, and there was no visiting because of the distance. Then, the letters from Cait stopped. My heart broke again.*

# 8

## AT THE JAMES FARM

Late October 1859, James Family Farm, Clay County, Missouri

The afternoon sun warmed the clear, bright fall day and highlighted the autumn trees, whose leaves had reached their peak of color. Jabez rode his horse under canopies of maple, oak, hickory, sassafras, sycamore, and walnut. He loved this time of year. The colors, the light, the chill of morning then warming during the day, the end of harvest, the smell of curing tobacco in the barns—all gave him an emotional uplift and a heightened sense of energy in this season.

It was hunting time too, and Jabez was arriving at the farm of his friend, Frank James. It was a long way from Liberty to the James farm, so he would spend the night at the family's house, and tomorrow, Jabez, Frank and the James' slave Briggins would rise early to go on a hunt for antlered bucks. Frank might even take his bow in addition to his rifle. This was Jabez's first visit to Frank's family farm, which was somewhat distant from Liberty, and he was taking in the beauty of the rolling countryside. He passed through the gate and saw a young Negro woman waving a greeting.

Jabez introduced himself. The woman said, "My name is Queenie. You here for the hunt?"

Jabez swung down from the saddle. "Yep. Frank and Briggins and I are going for big antlers tomorrow."

Queenie put her hand on her hip and cocked her

head. "This must be your first time here. Ain't never seen you before."

Jabez led his horse through the gate. "Right. Ain't never been here before. I'm pleased to meet you. Where'd you get the name Queenie? I like it."

Queenie smiled. "Maria is my given name. I came up with the name Queenie, because I'm smart and strong too. Frank liked it, and started calling me by that name. He says I'm the queen of all the slaves in Clay County. Missus still calls me Maria."

Jabez nodded. "That's interesting. Are you a sister of Briggins? I've met him before at my blacksmith forge in Liberty."

"Naw, we're not kin. But I'll tell you—he's smart and strong too."

Jabez and Queenie walked down the road to the house. Jabez pointed at four horses in a pasture. "You probably know Frank has the reputation of being the best horseman in the county. I think that's because he has the best horses."

"I know he is the best. He was trained by his kinsman—an uncle or cousin named Wild Bill Thomason. His family has a farm a couple miles down the pike. Wild Bill is a mountain man, hard as a rock with his hair all the way down below his waist and sticking through his Indian belt. He has lived with Indians, and he would spend a season living alone in the mountains trapping beaver for the fur company, hunting deer and buffalo too. He taught Frank how to ride horses and shoot like a Comanche Indian. Pistol, rifle, and bow. Wild Bill and Frank would go out into the woods and live for days on end. Frank learned how to tell weather, and direction, and what to eat from the woods. He was like a regular Indian when he was out in the wild. Then Frank taught his brother Jesse how to do all these things."

Jabez and Queenie walked on toward the house.

# 9

## KANSAS AND THE UNION

Jabez Cooper: *As Pa predicted, the antislavery population of Kansas soon became the majority. They voted in a state constitution that forbid slavery, and they applied for admission to the Union as a new state. After seven years of struggles between Free-Staters and proslavers, Kansas became a state at the end of January 1861.*

*At the same time, the Union was splitting apart. Six states had already seceded, and other states of the South were headed that way. There were many here in Missouri who wanted our state to secede, and a Constitutional Convention was established to consider the matter. The Convention decided to keep Missouri in the Union, but soon after the war broke out, the state was split between pro-Union and pro-Confederate. A pro-Confederate army called the Missouri State Guard was organized under the leadership of a former governor, Price. The Union brought federal troops into the state and organized a pro-Union state militia also. The war had come to Missouri.*

# PART TWO
# WAR INSIDE WAR

# 10

## GOING TO WAR

May 4, 1861, Liberty, Clay County, northwestern Missouri
Jabez heard the ring of spurs. He raised his eyes from his anvil and saw his friend Frank James entering the blacksmith shop. "Frank, mighty good to see your ugly face. What brings you to Liberty today?"

"In about an hour you can call me Private James. I'll expect a salute. I'm mustering into the new Confederate army that's been organized to fight here in Missouri."

Jabez was surprised. "That's a big step, my friend."

"It's a natural step for me. We're Secesh to the bone. I was mad as a hornet when the politicians refused to secede Missouri from the Union. I figure if I want us to secede, I need to fight. We'll be fighting the Union troops that are here in the state, and the Unionists who are in the state militia. When we win, we'll secede. What about you? Don't you know there's a war on? Jefferson Davis needs you, son."

"Well, you know I joined the Self Defensive Association because I promised my pa that I would help in defending our border. It isn't a regular army outfit, but it's an important one. Jennison's and Lane's Jayhawkers are making as much trouble as they can, and they will be all over these western counties soon enough, now that the war is on. Best part about it is I can serve in that way and still run the forge. Another thing, I was in on the raid we made on the arsenal here in town just two weeks ago. We got over a thousand muskets then."

"All right, just so we're on the same side."

Jabez shot back, "You may be fighting soldiers that are Missouri Unionists, not just Yankees. Maybe some will be our neighbors. How are you gonna handle that?"

Frank picked up a horseshoe lying on the anvil and slapped it in his other hand. "Any friend of my enemy is an enemy to me is the way I look at it. You gotta be on one side or th'other. My father used to quote Jesus saying you are either for me or against me. If Missouri Unionists shoot at me, I'll be shooting back. Anyway, this thing will be over in a few more months. Yankees are no match for Southern boys."

"What guns are you takin' with you?" said Jabez.

"All I have now is my hunting rifle and a revolver. Hope they give me a better rifle."

"Maybe you'll get one from what we seized at the arsenal. Say, how'd you keep your brother Jesse from hitching up with you?"

"He wanted to come with me, I can assure you. They won't take someone that young, he's not even fourteen yet. He looks even younger, so he couldn't fool 'em if he lied. Anyway, my mother said he had to stay to help run the farm. Not to mention she's afraid he'll get killed."

# 11

## OSCEOLA

Jabez Cooper: *While General Price's men, including Frank, were fighting the Union troops in a series of battles in the western part of Missouri, the Jayhawkers from Kansas started to attack Missouri towns along the border. The worst of the Jayhawker raids was against the town of Osceola. By coincidence, that English journalist, Fielding—Pa and I met him back in 1856—had come back to our part of the world to write about the war here. He interviewed one of the Jayhawkers who was in the raid, and the interview got published in the London paper and also in a St. Louis newspaper, then re-published in local newspapers in western Missouri. I tell you one thing—this raid on Osceola and this interview riled up folks in Little Dixie more than anything the Union army had ever done to that point.*

*Here's what was in the papers:*

FIRST-HAND ACCOUNT OF INFAMOUS
JAYHAWKER RAID
Written by Edwin Fielding for *The Times of London*
(England)
*On September 22, 1861, the town of Osceola, Missouri, in St. Clair County on the western border of the state, was raided by the 3rd, 4th and 5th Kansas Volunteers, Union fighters better known in Kansas as Jim Lane's Kansas Brigade and in Missouri as Jim Lane's Jayhawkers. The attack resulted in the virtual destruction of the town's buildings and, it is alleged, the execution*

*of nine residents. To discuss the raid, I interviewed a captain of Lane's Kansas Brigade.*

Fielding: *Could you please tell my readers your name and background?*

Moonlight: *My name is Tom Moonlight. I was born in Scotland and came to the States as a young man, along with two of my cousins. I worked in farming in the East for a few years, and when I was twenty, I joined the army and served in Texas for a while. I settled in Kansas in 1860. When the war with the South began I joined the Union side, and I serve Jim Lane as captain of the battery of one of his regiments. Folks in Missouri call us one of the Jayhawker outfits. I don't think they mean that name as a compliment.*

Fielding: *Please tell us about Jim Lane.*

Moonlight: *Jim Lane is about the most famous man in all of Kansas. He's a warrior, a fighter in politics and in warfare. For the years before Kansas became a state, he had warred against the proslavery settlers in Kansas and the Border Ruffians from Missouri, and he's got a special distaste for them. To him they are all pukes with walnut-colored, tobacco-stained teeth. But, I'll have to tell you, it goes both ways—they hate him fiercely and consider him brother to the Devil. General Lane is one of the chief Free State leaders, and when Kansas joined the Union, he became our first U.S. Senator. He's a personal friend of President Abe Lincoln. So, he knows politics inside and out. He is a hell of a speaker, well I should say orator, because he is that good, and folks would follow him to the gates of Hell just because of his explosive and persuasive words. The General is intense, that's for certain. He's about six foot tall, skinny as a rail, tough as a hickory tree, his hair thick and wild and never seen a comb or brush, he has a gaunt face and eyes that bore right through you. He is a man of action, not just words.*

Fielding: *What was the reason for the raid on Osceola and the destruction of the town?*

Moonlight: *When war broke out, Lane was appointed*

*a Union general, and he organized his Kansas Brigade. The Union army in Missouri has been fighting the rebels led by General Price, and a few weeks ago, we battled Price too, down along the border in Vernon County, but we were badly outnumbered, and we retreated back to Kansas. Then, General Fremont asked General Lane to make a demonstration on the Missouri border, so we are roving to root out the main centers of disloyal Secesh, because they are giving traitorous support to the Confederacy. General Lane said, "There is no such thing as a Union man in border Missouri. They're all wolves, snakes and devils." The General went on to state his strategy. He said, 'I want to see them cast into a burning hell! We believe in a war of extermination. I want to see every foot of ground in Jackson, Cass, and Bates Counties burned over, everything laid waste. Everything disloyal from a Durham cow to a Shanghai chicken must be cleaned out.'*

Fielding: *Strong words. So, have you raided other towns in western Missouri?*

Moonlight:  *Yep, we cleaned out Butler, Harrisonville, West Point, Papinville and Morristown. Yesterday, it was Osceola's turn. It's about the biggest border town in western Missouri south of Kansas City. Orders from General Lane were to destroy everything we couldn't haul back to Kansas.*

Fielding: *Tell us how the raid began.*

Moonlight: *An hour before daybreak, Lane said to me, "Cap'n Moonlight, line up your artillery battery and bombard the courthouse yonder. Some rebel troops are camped in it." We lit up the sky with fire coughing from our cannons, and at dawn our troops entered the town. General Lane ordered that we should not harm the civilian population unless they resisted. We didn't expect much resistance, because most of the men of the town, of fighting age at least, had left and were fighting elsewhere with the Confederate guard. There were about fifteen hundred soldiers in our party, and we accomplished our mission in short order. As we entered the town, we met*

*resistance from a small band of Confederates, but we drove them back and then they disappeared. One of their men was killed.*
Fielding: *We've heard reports of the execution of nine residents of the town tried in a field court martial and hanged as disloyal traitors. Are these reports true?*
Moonlight: *Folks are confusing Osceola with Morristown. We did execute some residents in Morristown because they resisted us.*
Fielding: *Did your troops confiscate property in Osceola?*
Moonlight: *Why sure. That's what General Lane calls cleaning a town out. He is fond of crippling the rebel towns by emptying them of goods and supplies—it's part of his strategy, and it's effective. Since he believes every town in western Missouri is completely Secesh, we have a lot of cleaning out to do, and the prospect of acquiring the contents keeps many of our men keen for battle. We had many wagons in our train, and we planned to haul a lot of contents back to Kansas. In Osceola we found a large supply cache destined for the rebel army and confiscated it. Our men also removed livestock and all useable supplies from stores and homes as well as all the food and bottles of whiskey and beer we could get our hands on. We sought the contents of a bank, but the vault was empty—they'd hidden most of the cash. In total, our quartermaster reported we seized around $8,000 in cash money, three hundred fifty horses, four hundred cattle, many sheep and pigs, three thousand bags of flour, and five hundred pounds of sugar and molasses. We freed two hundred slaves.*
Fielding: *We've heard reports of widespread drunkenness among your troops. Can you comment?*
Moonlight: *Well, our boys found a warehouse full of whiskey barrels and they busted in the barrel heads and got into the liquid treasure, and some did become tipsy in celebration of the victory. Ha, some couldn't walk straight, and some couldn't even walk at all. So, when we departed Osceola we had to take a number of wagons*

*and carriages and their horses from the town as transport for these disabled gents. We needed to take a few wagons to carry the liberated slaves too.*
Fielding: *We've heard reports that the entire town was burned. Is that true?*
Moonlight: *You're damn right. We were under orders to do so. As we moved out of town, we torched the entire place, firing to the ground almost eight hundred buildings. Another thing is, we poured the remaining barrels of whiskey into a gulley leading to the river and ignited this stream too. I'll never forget that sight.*

# 12

## JABEZ AND FRANK

November 1861, Liberty, Clay County, Missouri

Frank James cracked open the front door of Jabez's blacksmith forge. "You got time to talk?"

"Well, I'll be damned. C'mon in. I always have time for you, pal. Take a seat."

Jabez removed his protective garb and joined his friend. "What are you doing back here? Tell me what happened."

Frank took a deep breath. "It's a long story, so right now I'll just give you the headlines. As you know, I went with General Price and his troops. We had some skirmishes and a big victory in Springfield. I'm sure you heard about it. Then, we moved on up this a-way, and we had another big fight in Lexington last September."

Jabez nodded. "Sure, I know about the Lexington battle. I helped get some of the volunteers across the Missouri."

"Did you fight in Lexington? Were we both together then?"

"No, I just helped those here in Clay County who were crossing the river to come and join you all."

Frank leaned back in his chair. "The Feds were well fortified. They had plenty of food, and they had better rifles. But we had them surrounded, and we cut off their access to water. They were desperate and tried to dig wells behind their fortifications, but they failed. We made a final push, using hemp bales for a sort of moving fortification. Some smart apple came up with the idea—brilliant idea—to soak the bales in water, and Yankee guns and cannons were useless against those soaked bales. That turned the trick, and we got an unconditional surrender out of the Feds."

Jabez grinned. "I hope the genius who came up with the hemp bale idea got a medal."

"I agree! Don't know if he did, but he shoulda."

"Well, how in hell did you wind up back in Clay County? Are you on leave?"

"No, toward the end of our battle in Lexington, I got to feeling poorly. By the time Price was leaving Lexington and taking his army back down south, I was sick. Felt like death warmed over. I had a case of measles, and I was in bed. When our men left, Union soldiers returned and found me in bed, and I had to surrender. I got paroled, I promised not to support the Confederates, and I was allowed to be at home. My ma had to put up a bond to secure my promise."

Jabez chuckled. "Do you feel lucky or unlucky?"

"C'mon. Unlucky! I want to get back into the war. I'll find a way. I just have to be very secretive."

# 13

## QUEENIE

Early January 1863, On the Road to the James's family farm, Clay County, northwest Missouri

Three slaves sat, side by side, on the wooden seat of a wagon pulled by two mules. They were heading to the farm of the family of brothers Frank and Jesse James. Two of the slaves, Queenie and Briggins, were from the James farm, and they were bringing to the farm a slave named Sissieretta, better known as Sissie, from the neighboring Mantooth family farm. The Mantooths had rented Sissie to Zerelda James Samuel and her third husband Reuben Samuel for work through the winter and spring seasons. Sissie had been purchased recently by the Mantooths from a farmer in southeast Missouri.

Briggins was driving the mule team. Queenie was excited to have a new acquaintance, and she was giving Sissie information about life on the farm.

"Missus Zerelda—she's called Zerel by the white folks, but we have to call her Missus Zerelda—is the ruler of our farm, and there ain't no joking around with her. I keep a sharp eye out for her moods. She whips us if she gets mad. She whips women just like she whips men. I got scars on my back from two whippings for lying to her about little things. She used a cat o' nine tails, but she's got a bull whip too. Says she will use it if we try to run away and the trackers don't catch us and hang us first. Her husband—that's her third husband Reuben Samu-el— doesn't do the whipping, just Missus Zerelda. Master

74

Reuben don't do much around the farm anyway."

Sissie squirmed in her seat. "Thank you for that warning. I'll be careful. How many coloreds on the farm?"

Queenie recited the facts. "Right now, we got seven colored folks. Charlotte, she's forty-three. She was a wedding present to the Missus. I still can't get over white folks giving a person to somebody for a wedding present—think about that. Charlotte is like a mother to me. I love her so much. I'm twenty-one, been on this place fourteen years. Then we got Nancy, she's nineteen. Briggins, he's eighteen. Delia, she's eleven. Shadrach, six. And David, he's just four.

"Missus Zerelda sells slaves, and she buys new ones. She sold four since I been on the place. When she sold little Hannah it like to have killed Charlotte, because Hannah is her daughter, and it about busted my heart too. Why do white folks want to tear up a family like that? Today, after all the selling and buying, we got about the same number we always had. Seven slaves seems about right for a place like this, two hundred acres. This ain't a Mississippi plantation."

Sissie said it was hard to remember all the people and their names. "You said the Missus has had three husbands. Tell me about them."

Queenie smiled. "Missus Zerelda's first husband was Robert James. Folks called him Bob. He's the father of Frank and Jesse and their sister Susie. He was a preacher. Southern Baptist. Preached at two churches. They say he baptized sixty people one Sunday at a place where they dam up the little creek close to the church and make a pool to do the baptizing. He would read to us from the Bible on Sundays after he did his duties at the white churches."

Sissie had a quizzical look. "A preacher with slaves?"

Queenie threw back her head and laughed. "Oh, yes, he believed very much in owning slaves. First of all, he wanted slaves to help with the crops and the house just as much as any farmer. And being a preacher didn't stop him from believing slavery was right. In fact, he believed it was God's plan."

Sissie interrupted, "God's plan?"

Queenie answered, "That's right. Master Bob said it's in the Bible that black people will always be slaves because of a curse. Said Noah put a curse on one of his grandsons named Canaan for something Canaan's daddy—name of Ham—did. It's called the Curse of Ham. The curse was that Canaan and all his line forever will be slaves. Master Bob said Canaan's line became black Africans, and we got the curse, and that means black people forever have to be slaves."

Sissie said she couldn't believe God would put a curse on an entire race of people. "What did they do to bring on the curse? What were their sins?"

Queenie continued. "Ham looked at his father Noah while Noah was sleeping naked. And it made Noah mad, and he put that curse on. But get this—he put it on Ham's son Canaan—not Ham, nor Ham's other boys."

Sissie burst in laughter, "Ha ha ha, ha ha, ha. Sorry to laugh when you're talking about the Bible, but all of this sounds crazy and just makes no sense."

"I know. It is crazy," said Queenie, but that's what Master Bob said, and he told us it's in the Bible. Genesis. He called it the sovereign word of God. I don't believe that's true. This curse story lets white people believe that the Good Lord has given them permission to own a colored person like owning a pig or a wagon. I can't believe God would do that to us because old Noah put a curse on one of his grandsons and on all us colored folks forever. Just because of Ham seeing Noah naked? Come on."

Sissie laughed and slapped her knee. "They had to find something in the Bible, didn't they? I will remember that story—Curse of Ham."

# QUEENIE

The wagon lumbered along. Sissie said, "I love the way you talk, Queenie. Tell me more about the farm."

"Happy to do so. I'll go back to my beginnings at this farm. Master Bob bought me at the auction in Kansas City when I was a little girl not yet seven. That auction is an awful mess. They look you over like you were a horse they're thinking of buying. They make you roll down a little hill. They look in your mouth. They make you take your clothes off. All that just to be sure you got nothing wrong with you. I tell you, I was a scared little girl, that is no secret. When I saw Master Bob looking around, I could tell he was gentle. He had a kind face, and he looked respectful. So, when he came to me, I said to him what an older slave had told me to say. 'Kind sir, I'm just a young'un so my price will be low, but I am already a good worker in the house. I am prime. I am likely.' It seemed to work, because when I got up on that block, he bought me."

Sissie grinned. "You are smart, girl."

Queenie continued, "If a slave can ever like a master, then I would say I liked Master Bob. He was a kind man, and he never whipped any of us. He never called us niggers, he called us colored, and he called us servants not slaves. Can't say the same for Missus Zerelda. She says nigger this and nigger that. We slaves are just property to her."

Sissie interrupted again. "What happened to Master Bob?"

Queenie's eyes narrowed. "About a year after he bought me, Master Bob went on a long trip, to California, on a wagon train to the gold rush. Nobody knows if he was going for gold or to bring Jesus to the miners, or just to get away for a while from the Missus, but they say it took him over three months on the wagons to get there, and then about a week after he was in California, he turned up sick and died. It was fever from the bad water at the gold miner camp."

"Aw, that's sad," said Sissie. "You say the Missus has a third husband now. Tell me about the second one."

Queenie collected her thoughts. "It was hard times without Master Bob. Shortly, the Missus married a rich man named Simms, but then in not two years Simms got tossed off his horse and busted his neck and died."

"Whoa," said Sissie. "She had a string of bad luck. Then what happened, and who is the third one?"

Queenie scratched her head. She knew she should be careful talking to this new person. No telling what Sissie might say to the Mantooths. She could sense that Briggins was uneasy about her openness. "Men tend to like Missus Zerelda. She has a lot of gumption and a lot of spirit—she likes to dance and ride horses. Anyway, it wasn't long before she married again, this time to Reuben Samuel, who was a doctor, but soon he stopped doctoring, and he spends his time here on the farm doing what the Missus tells him to and not much else.

"I got no idea about the age of Missus Zerelda and Master Reuben. They don't talk about it. I know she is not past the change of life. Even though she's got a grown boy, she's still makin' babies, and she's got one in the oven right now."

"Well, tell me about her children," said Sissie.

Queenie was enjoying being the fount of information. "Missus had three children by Master Bob. They are Frank, Jesse, and Susie James. She didn't have any by Simms. She has two little children by Master Reuben, Sarah Samuel and John Samuel. Like I said, she's got another coming. In about six months.

"Frank is turning twenty years in a few days. Jesse's fifteen. Susie's thirteen. Sarah just turned five. And John was born on Christmas Day in '61. Of all the Missus's children I like Frank the best. She calls him Mister Frank. Everybody says she's been doing so since he was a little boy. One day, I asked her why she calls him a Mister. She said because he's always been so grown up, from the day he was born. But I just call him Frank. He and I and Briggins grew up together. One time, Frank was talking with me, and he said, 'You and Briggins and Charlotte are like my family.' I thought to myself, 'How do white people twist things up so much in their minds that they can feel like family to us and at the same time own us and treat us like animals?' Maybe that's another trick that the white folks must play on their minds so that they don't feel guilty for keeping a person as a piece of property.

"Jesse don't pretend. He just tells us what to do, and he sure don't consider us family. Jesse can get wild, and he's got a temper. He and Frank are like opposites."

Queenie told Sissie about Frank fighting for the South, and how his fighting for slavery hurt her and made her mad. She told of Frank's being captured and how he now wanted to join the bushwhackers. "You know about bushwhackers, don't you?"

Sissie rolled her eyes. "Yes, we had them in our part of the state. They are like wild men. Not army, but fighting for the South against the Yankees, right?"

"That's right. They are tough boys who know how to ride and shoot, and they go after Union soldiers, Union militia, and even not-soldiers, if they are for the Union. I don't like it that Frank wants to join them."

The springtime beauty of Missouri was on full display, and Briggins began to point out features of the landscape as the wagon came closer to the destination. As soon as he finished talking, Sissie said, "Tell me more about the farm."

"Sure," said Queenie. "We grow t'bacca and hemp and wheat and corn, and we raise chickens, pigs, and cows. We grow a nice garden. We have six horses and these two mules called Banjo and Jeff Davis. They let me name Banjo, but Missus named Jeff Davis. The horses are fast, because Frank and Jesse love to ride, and they're good at it, and they always want fast horses.

"Colored women live in a little cabin—it's one room—and colored men in the other cabin, just a one-room shack too. The good earth is our floor. We eat mostly leavings that the white folks don't care for—sow belly, pigs feet, chitlins, sometimes a bit of chicken gizzard, and cornbread kush and molasses, and sometimes greens. When it's hunting time we can get a bit of possum and coon and rabbit and bird and deer, if Briggins shoots them."

Queenie paused, and the three sat in silence, gazing at the countryside while the wagon creaked along. After a while, Queenie turned again to Sissie. "I know you come from the eastern part of the state. I don't know what it's like there, but I tell you, things in these parts of Missouri and Kansas been in a fighting mess for years. Kansas is Union, and that's what the Jayhawkers are—Union. Kansas Jayhawkers come over here and raid farms and rob everything they can lay their hands on and burn the rest. They take slaves away to freedom too, and that riles the white folks here.

"Missus tries to scare us about escaping with Jayhawkers. She says trackers would catch us and hang us. She says it's crazy for slaves to try to go on the underground railroad to Canada. Says people tell her lots of coloreds die on the way up there, and even if they get there, it's winter all the time and black-skin people can't stand the cold since we are from Africa. She says anyway what we gonna do if we are free? She says we can't take care of ourselves, and slavery is natural and good for us. Ha ha, she expect me to believe all that? White people believe we slaves are ignorant because under the law we're not allowed to learn how to read and write, and so they think they can tell us any kind of lie to make us do what they want us to. But I got sense, and I know when someone is trying to pull wool over my eyes.

"We colored folks on this farm talk to each other

about freedom most every night. But we have to be careful as can be. We call freedom 'chitlins' so that the white people don't know what we are talking about. And we use a prayer kettle, so they think we're praying. We turn the big iron kettle upside down, put it on the ground, and prop the rim a tad off the ground with stones. Then we lie down on our stomachs with our faces just about touching the lip of that turned over kettle, and we talk to each other in that kettle, and it keeps the white people from hearing what we're saying. When we talk about the underground railroad, we call it 'pigs feet' so white folks won't know what we are saying."

Sissie leaned toward Queenie. "If you all are so keen on freedom, why does the Missus let you and Briggins come get me all by yourselves? She's not afraid you will run away? And me with you?"

Queenie lifted her forefinger. "I doubt she trusts me, but she trusts Briggins, because he and Frank are what you might call hunting pals. She thinks Briggins will never run."

No one spoke for almost a minute. "She's smart, I suppose," said Sissie.

"Unnnhuhhh," groaned Queenie.

# 14

## INTO THE BRUSH

Early May 1863, James family farm, Clay County, northwest Missouri

On a fresh May morning Frank James took the most momentous step in his young life. He was up at dawn, making final preparations to violate his parole and join the Secesh bushwhackers of his home county. The band was led by Fernando Scott, one of the lieutenants operating under the overall command of a guerrilla chief named William Clarke Quantrill.

Frank did not come to this decision rashly. His mother Zerelda's thousand-dollar bond to assure he kept his parole oath had restrained his desire to join Confederate guerrillas. He had given aid to the guerrillas during his parole, earning him two stints in the Clay County jail. He had just escaped from his second imprisonment, and he was a wanted man. Now, with Zerelda's blessing, he was ready to break his oath completely and go to the brush.

Frank cleaned his two Colt Navy revolvers and sharpened his big knife.  He filled leather pouches with gun powder, lead balls, and percussion caps. Loading a black-powder revolver was clumsy and time consuming, so in order to save time in a battle, Frank made ready-packets with powder and ball encased in paper cartridges that he would tear, pour the powder into a chamber and set the ball. Also, to deal with the difficulty of reloading, bushwhackers carried many loaded revolvers tucked into their belts, their coats, and their saddlebags. Two revolvers would be on the low side.

Frank stood in front of the mirror in the entry to the house. His lanky frame extended above the top of the mirror, so he moved back to get the full view. He pushed back his dark brown hair and gazed at his image. He didn't consider it an heroic image—just a farm boy with jug ears and a prominent nose, trying to look like a dashing soldier.

Frank considered his decision. He wondered if this would be the last time he saw his image. He knew guerrillas were criminals under the law, and he knew he would face death every day, either in battle or by execution if captured by the Federals. But he nodded at the mirror and committed himself to the brush.

Frank packed a bed roll and pulled out his saddlebags, and he loaded clothes and necessities for the trail, admiring the bushwhacker shirt his mother had told Charlotte to sew for him, with a flower and curlicue design on the front and forearms. From beneath his bed he pulled out the wooden case where he stored his library and removed his favorite, a thumb-worn volume containing the collected works of William Shakespeare.

*

By late afternoon, Frank reached the camp of Fernando Scott. Frank and Scott were friends from younger days, and Scott knew his friend could ride and shoot about as well as a Comanche. Frank said to Scott, "My belly is full of Union men. I'm here to join you."

As Frank wandered through the camp, he spied his friend Jabez Cooper. "Hey ho, Jabez, it's me, Frank. How do ye?"

"Tolerable," drawled Jabez. "But better now that I see you. I'm sure glad you are here."

Frank dropped his gear to the ground and shook his friend's hand. "Well, I just signed up. I have been helping bushwhackers as best I can, and I've been in jail twice for it. I broke out of the last jail, so the Federals are looking for me. Figured it was time to do some real fighting, and so here I am."

Jabez had a big smile. "We sure can use you."

Frank looked out at the camp. "How long you been with our friend Scott?"

"Not long. As you know, I closed my forge and went down to Arkansas. Then I came back and joined Scott. My work for him is mainly back here at camp, fixing things and taking care of horses. Not seen action yet, but I expect I will go on raids sometimes."

Frank asked, "How do you like living in caves and woods? Hard life?"

"Yeh, living in the brush is no fun."

The two men talked for a half hour, catching up on their lives over the past two years and the news from back home in Clay County.

Frank was preparing to leave, when he said, "Say, when I was with Price, we made blood oaths with fellow soldiers, so we would watch out for each other. Want to do that?"

Jabez had a puzzled look. "Watching out for each other sounds good, but what's a blood oath?"

Frank pulled out his knife. "We both make a small prick on the tip of a finger. Like this. Then we press our hands together, so the blood mingles. Like this. We are then blood brothers, each sworn to look out for the other. Before we go into a battle, we can remind each other of our oath by raising our right hand, with palm open toward our blood brother."

"Let's do it," said Jabez.


May 1863, Clay and Clinton Counties, Missouri
Fernando Scott gathered his gang on the morning of May 19 and sketched out an ambush. The militia and Union soldiers regularly searched the Fishing River in southern

Clay County for bushwhackers, and Scott said he knew that a search party was headed to the river that day. He said, "I'll use a Secesh sympathizer to get the searchers to ride into a trap we'll set."

Scott took Jabez aside and said, "I want you to come. This will be your first raid, I know, but we're going to move through a county or two and make a new camp. Pack your tools up, and we'll find ways to carry them."

In the afternoon, a group of five Federals rode into the guerrilla squad's ambush. Scott's men killed all five, including one attempting to surrender. The bushwhackers melted back into the woods. Frank and Jabez had their first taste of guerrilla warfare. Jabez didn't feel right. A shiver of guilt ran up his spine. He rode beside Frank and whispered, "Why did we have to kill the fella who was surrendering? Aren't we supposed to spare them if they surrender? I don't like what was done with him."

Frank reined his horse to a halt. "We had no choice. We can't deal with prisoners, so we would have had to parole them."

"What's wrong with paroling him, letting him go? It's not like we would be releasing a whole squad of Feds who would come back after us. Why'd we have to kill him?"

"They'd do the same to us. You know the Yankees are now not taking bushwhackers prisoner? They would probably shoot us upon capture, because they call us outlaws since we're not regular army."

Jabez shook his head. "Still don't like what we've done."

*

Later that evening, Scott's gang entered Missouri City in southern Clay County and robbed some known Unionist families. Over the next few days, the guerrillas moved on raids through Clinton County and then back to Clay County. In the countryside, their method was to commandeer a farm, hold the family as prisoners, rob them of money and small valuables, spend the night and replenish their food supplies, then move to another Unionist's farm the next day. Their parting words would always be, "If you tell anyone we were here, bushwhackers will kill you."

When Scott got word that Union soldiers were tracking his men, Frank James said, "Let's go to my farm. We can hide in the woods there for as long as we need, and my ma will feed us."

# 15

## PIG AND SNAKE

May 26, 1863, James Family Farm, Clay County, northwest Missouri

Zerelda Cole James Samuel swept her copious figure out the front door of the house. She removed the pipe gripped in her mouth and handed it back to her third husband, Reuben Samuel, while she kept her gaze forward. She lifted both arms and yelled to the dozen riders assembled in her yard, "Welcome men. Welcome. Frank will show you where there's water and where to set your camp. After you get settled, we'll give you some supper tonight. We have pork and chicken. Pone cornbread too. Charlotte, Queenie, and Easter will feed you about an hour before sundown."

Jabez elbowed Frank and whispered, "See, your ma is calling Maria by the Queenie name now," and then he chuckled. Frank smiled.

Fernando Scott walked up the path to the front of the house and removed his hat. "Thank you, Mizez Samuel, we sure 'preciate your Southern hospitality."

Zerelda moved to shake Scott's hand. "Well, we 'preciate what you men are doin' in the war. I see you have some Clay County boys with you. I see Jabez Cooper and others. Proud of all you Clay boys. But I want you to take care of Mr. Frank. You hear? He's my first born. You hear?"

Zerelda paused and raised a warning finger. "Let me tell you something. Mr. Frank says you all are headed across the Missouri. But my son Jesse has been there, and the ferries you all could use are heavily guarded. There's Federals all along the river. You better stay here in our woods for a few days until they drop their guard. Now you all go on and set up camp, and we'll make you some supper. Stay a while."

As Frank and Jesse started to lead Scott's troops to the camp site, Jesse yelled, "Look, come here, the pigs have cornered a snake. Hi yi, come and watch."

The men secured their horses and moved toward the hog pen. The snake was coiled tightly, backed up against a fence pole, its triangular head raised above the coil, in a cocked position, wavering in a nervous but graceful motion, and prepared to strike.

"Stay back," said Jesse. "Don't interrupt them. Don't let them know you're near."

The creatures in the pen appeared unaware of the crowd.

"Ain't you afraid it'll kill your pigs?" said a man.

"Not worried," said Frank, without explanation.

"Is that a copperhead?" asked one man, in a tone of apprehension.

"That's a rattlesnake," said Frank. He pointed in a casual wave. "Look at the rattles on his tail. Can't you hear them singing?"

"Yeh," said another. "And counting those rattles it looks like he must be at least seven or eight years old. He's got a load of poison for those pigs."

Three pigs moved nearer to the snake. They looked stupid, unaware of the snake's presence, moving close to the rattler's striking range, poking their snouts into the ground, snorting and grunting as they rooted for whatever food they could unearth.

"Which is the Yankee and which is the Rebel?" a voice said in a yell of a whisper.

"Don't you know the pig is always the Yankee?" said Jabez.

The snake's torso writhed in lubricated movement like a piece separate from its head and tail, both of which were fixed and taut. The torso was now as fluid as a piece of cloth or a worn leather belt as it slid its entire coil toward the right. But then it couldn't slide farther. It was now flush against the wide section of the water trough. The biggest pig, a black and white one with dry mud caked over its backside like brown armor, snorted closer to the snake.

"Hell, that pig sure-nuf is a Yankee," said someone. "Look how dumb the sonofabitch is. And look at how riled up that snake is. He's like a Secesh, and he's gonna take that pig down." The man spat tobacco juice into the dirt in punctuation. Some of the men laughed nervously.

Everyone went silent, waiting for the fatal moment. With lightning speed, the snake struck with its mouth gaping wide in a one hundred twenty degree spread, hit the pig on its face, and recoiled just as quickly. It happened so fast that no one could see its fangs or exactly where they struck the pig. The suddenness of the strike startled everyone. Many jumped or lurched backward, and some gasped or made yelps of surprise.

"Damn, did you see the speed of that rattler?" someone said.

"Shitfire," said Jabez.

The pig did not flinch, nor give any sign that it even knew it had been hit. It didn't quail nor attack. It just scooted closer to the snake, but in no way giving the impression that it was interested in or even aware of the reptile. The snake struck, hitting the pig's face. And again, the pig gave no more recognition to the bite than it would to a leaf falling on its head. The snake came closer and struck again.

Suddenly, the pig moved with purpose and stepped on the snake with its cloven feet in a clumsy shuffle, tearing at the flesh below, slicing a piece from the torso like a ribbon. The snake tried to escape but the pig had it pinned to the ground. The other two pigs moved in, and the crowd lost sight of the snake. Then, the first pig had the remains of the snake in its teeth, waving the creature above its head, and the others made short jumping movements with their front legs lifting a few inches, snapping their teeth at the rattler, trying to have their turn.

The snake was dead. The victorious pig pushed the reptile into the corner of the pen and, with its snout, scraped dust over the carcass. The pig then left its kill and resumed rooting the bare ground of the pen, continuing its search of food as if nothing had happened.

The crowd held their collective breath, waiting for the pig to collapse. "That pig is still alive?" one man asked. "How can that be? He's gonna die for sure any minute."

"No," Frank said in a confident, knowing voice. "It's a rare thing for a snake to kill a pig. Their hides are damn tough, and they've got lots of fat, and I suppose their blood vessels are buried down in their fat bodies."

"I damn sure don't want your ma serving that pig at tonight's supper," said Jabez, and everyone laughed and moved away from the pen.

"The Yankee won," said another, as they trailed toward the woods.

No one laughed.

# 16

## BETRAYAL


Jabez Cooper: *After supper, our unit set up a camp in the woods near the edge of the James farm. We felt safe in the thick brush. Miz Zerelda said no patrols ever came to the farm.*

May 27, 1863, James family farm, Clay County, northwest Missouri

Jesse was up before light to perform his chores so he could join the bushwhackers at the campsite. As the sun broke the crest of the horizon, he walked the path to the patch of tobacco seedlings, hoe in hand. His mind was not on hoeing but on Frank and the guerrillas.

An hour after sunrise, Jesse saw a cloud of dust kicked up by a band of riders approaching across the grassy plain. He was soon surrounded by the men and their horses. *There must be twenty or thirty*, he thought. The riders were a combined patrol of voluntary militia from Clay County and nearby Clinton County, both of which supplemented the Union troops in the area.

"Morning, boy," said the leader in salutation.

Jesse dropped the hoe and, shading his eyes with both hands, squinted up at the men on the horses now encircling him. He recognized two of the men, Brantley Bond, a neighbor, and Alvis Dagley, who lived not far away.

The horses trampled some of the tobacco plants under their hooves, and one emptied its bladder on a section of the field.

"Hey, your horses are tearing up my new plants," said Jesse. No one replied.

"We're huntin' bushwhackers. Seen any?"

Jesse shook his head. "Naw. Just my family and some slaves here. I ain't seen any bushwhackers."

"That's funny, people said yesterday about a dozen Secesh rode right up the lane to your house over there."

"Naw, that's a lie, or if they came they were here when we were in the fields working. We've not seen any."

The leader dismounted and pulled a Colt Navy 1851 revolver from his belt and smacked Jesse hard on the side of his face with the barrel. The gunsight raked across Jesse's cheek. "You're the one who is lying. Where is your brother Frank?"

"I ain't lying. He's with our relatives in Kansas City."

"Now I know you're lying. You're hiding something. C'mon boy, you better tell us, we don't want to have to kill you."

Jesse didn't speak, and the leader slapped him in the face and threw him to the ground. "All right, boy, if you can't help us we gonna see what your ma and pa have to say." He dragged Jesse to his feet and pushed him in a stumbling walk toward the house.

*

The riders identified themselves to Zerelda as Union militia. Zerelda stood in the doorway. She was three months pregnant and not feeling well, and she was in no mood for dealing with Union militia. She turned to look back inside the house and told Charlotte to take Susie, Sallie, and John back to the cornfield where the other slaves were working and stay until the militiamen left.

Zerelda rubbed the sheen of sweat from her brow and upper lip. She looked at Brantley Bond. "I know you, neighbor. You were in the old guard unit with Frank that fought for the South with General Price. Guess you switched sides."

# BETRAYAL

Brantley Bond looked away and spoke as if to no one in particular. "Is Frank here? We want to talk with him. People say bushwhackers came on your land yesterday. That gang has been raiding all through this part of Missouri. Last week, they ambushed our men on the Fishing River and killed two of 'em. Then, they raided Missouri City and attacked Union families there, and they plundered their way from Missouri City up to these parts. They are cold-blooded murderers and thieves. They will kill a civilian just as soon as they would a Union soldier. You can save Frank's life by getting him to surrender."

Zerelda turned as if she were heading back into the house. "Mr. Frank is not a bushwhacker, and he hasn't been in Missouri City. He's in Kansas City, been there a week."

"Hold on," said the leader, raising his right arm. "Woman, the truth is not in you. Where's your man?" What's his name? Get him out here."

Zerelda kept moving toward the door. "His name is Reuben Samuel, and he don't know anything that I don't. Y'all go on now."

One of the militia pushed past Zerelda, through the door, and in to the house and pulled Reuben Samuel out into the yard. Reuben's face was pale gray as cold ashes. The questions were posed to Reuben. He didn't respond, and he didn't move.

The leader jumped off his horse. "Reuben, speak dammit. I am going to count to five, and if you don't tell us where those men are camped, we're gonna string you from that tree over yonder."

"Leave him alone, you can't do that, you can't mob him, don't you dare touch him, there's nobody on our property except us," barked Zerelda. "You, neighbor Bond, stop these animals. I'm with child. Don't you have feelings for your neighbors?  Y'all get out of here." She was screaming now.

"Calm down, woman," said the leader. "Feelings don't have nothin' to do with this business."

The leader made the five-count.

Reuben said, "Zerel spoke the truth. No bushwhackers are on our land."

Then the leader said, "Reuben, that smells like a lie." He walked a slow circle around Reuben. "We gonna have to see if we can liberate a little truth from Mr. Reuben here." He walked slowly to his horse and removed a coil of hemp rope. His movements were slow and teasing.

Reuben was watching and sweating.

"Here now, Reuben, this is what we're gonna do. Hold on to this rope that I'll lay around your neck, and we'll just lift you up, and you can get a good view of your property, so you can see where those bushwhackers went and then you can educate us. The idea is to dangle you, not strangle you. But, if you dangle long enough, well, that will be very bad for you, because you can't hold the rope with your hands forever. Just soon as you are ready to tell us the truth, wave that right arm, and we'll let you down."

The leader slipped the rope around Reuben's neck, making a loop, and he tied a fixed knot, not a slip noose, so that the loop would not close on his neck. There was space enough for Reuben to grasp the rope with his hands and hold it away from his neck. He grabbed it immediately. In a slow, ceremonial movement, the leader took the other end of the rope to a limb and tossed it over. Alvis Dagley and Brantley Bond and another militiaman then pulled the rope to lift Reuben from the ground and tied it off. Reuben hung as a dead weight, but he held tight to the loop to keep it from choking him.

Zerelda and Jesse were screaming. "Stop, you will kill him."

"We're gonna take our time, Reuben, and just wait for you to tell us. We're in no hurry. After a while, your arms and hands are gonna get real tired. And weak. After a while, and it won't be long, they won't be able to keep that rope off your neck. That's when things get a little dicey. I know you don't want your body to hang like a sack of wheat with your Adam's apple 'gainst that rope. I sure know I wouldn't. After a short while you won't even be able to breathe. Now we ain't gonna lynch you, but you could wind up lynchin' yourself, if you don't speak the truth." He pulled a cigar butt from his pocket and lit it and leaned against the tree.

Zerelda ran towards the men, screaming, "Let him down, let my husband down, dammit, you'll kill him, that's murder. If you think he's done anything wrong, you have to arrest him, and a jury has to try him."

One of the men grabbed and restrained her.

"So, you are a lawyer?" the leader asked her. "Is that right? There's a war on, lady, and we are the officers of martial law, and we are the judge and jury when it comes to murderous raiders. You better calm yourself, or you can get some dangle time too. We have more than one rope."

Jesse ran toward the leader. "Let her go, leave my ma alone, and take him down."

One of the men cuffed Jesse. "Shut up boy."

Reuben had been very still, but his arms were quivering. He squirmed and flailed his legs, and this made the matter worse. Reuben let go of his right arm and waved it furiously as the signal. The left hand could not hold the loop away from his neck. He gasped and sputtered and made a ruckling sound. He waved his right arm more fervently and then grabbed the loop with both hands again. Then he repeated the waving, and the rope choked him again. The rope prevented any speech, and Reuben could only make a panicked squealing sound as he waved the arm. His pants were wet and dripping.

Jesse turned his head and gasped.

The leader smiled. "Well boys, looks like Mr. Reuben

has done some remembering. We can let him down now and we'll see what he has to say."

The release of the rope was like dropping the strings of a puppet. Reuben crumpled as his feet hit the ground. He coughed and sobbed and held his throat. Zerelda and Jesse ran to him, and helped him to the front door of the house. He tried to talk, but the trauma caused him to wheeze the words.

The leader let Reuben recover for a few minutes.

Everyone was silent except Zerelda who was screaming "Take him to a doctor. You choked his voice out. You almost killed him."

The leader took Reuben aside and they talked quietly, and then the leader said, "Come on boys, we are gonna take a little trip with Mr. Reuben to a campsite." He turned to Zerelda. "I'm leaving a guard here at the house to make sure you folks stay put. He will shoot you if you try to run off and warn the gang."

Zerelda was crazy distraught, now crying and shrieking and moaning. She was as unnerved by Reuben's betrayal as by the imminent danger to Frank. But the twinning of the two traumas unhinged her. She could not stop her keening.

In a half hour, they heard the pop, pop, pop sounds of gunfire, a deadly battle in the woods that sounded as innocuous as popcorn in a skillet. The guard mounted his horse and rode from the house to join his comrades.

Zerelda shook her fists at the sky. She said to Jesse, "This did not happen, Jesse, it did not happen. I don't want you to tell anyone in this world at any time that Reuben broke. You must say Reuben was a rock and didn't give them a damn thing, and I made them take him down. Say that. It's our secret. You promise? Promise me."

"Yes, ma. And I promise you we will have vengeance."

# 17

## SKIRMISH

Jabez Cooper: *At our campsite, we had taken breakfast and had just started a faro game. The men put on a blanket some of the plunder we had taken on our raids in these parts, like watches and rings and pocketknives, money, and so forth. Things you could carry on your person or in a kit on your horse. Plunder served as a pot for each game of faro or poker or seven up.*

*We dealt the cards, and I won the first pot, and we were just getting into the second game, when, all of a sudden, the Union militia were shooting into our camp. We always kept our guns close, and so we jumped up, scattered behind trees, and fired back, and the militia pulled back a bit. Then both sides went at it again, and the militia pulled back again. We grabbed our horses, which were already saddled, and beat a hasty path out of that camp.*

*Sadly, we left behind two of our boys killed by the militia. Boys who would be farming tobacco if not for this war. This was the first time I had seen any of our bushwhackers killed. It came as a shock, more so than I ever expected. Just thinking of those boys gone in a matter of minutes almost panicked me. There was nothing we could do to save them. We had to leave them there in the woods.*

*Three more of our group had been shot, but the wounds were minor. They were able to flee with us.*

*We scattered in small groups and headed south for the river, the Missouri. We knew we had to swim to cross it, but if we could get across before the Federals showed up, we knew they wouldn't cross, 'cause they would be like ducks on a pond. Like shooting practice. At a crossroad we made tracks in all directions to confuse the Federals. Frank had taught us this Indian trick. Later, we regrouped at the Taylor place, but the militia found us again and attacked. We lost three more boys before we made the Federals back off a short distance. We took several of them down. The Federals got off their horses to reload and take care of some wounded. We got a good start on them and made for the river.*

*When we got to the river, we crashed into the water at what seemed like full speed. Frank led us as we swam our horses across the Missouri and melted into the brush. I was scared in that crossing, because I didn't know how to swim. Also, I knew the militia was right behind us and might be shooting at us any second. I held tight to my horse's tail and tried to keep low in the water so they couldn't see me. The Federals came to the river. We had just made it to the other side, and they saw us and wouldn't get in the water— they knew they would be shot. We stood guard behind trees on our side until they turned around.*

# 18

## QUANTRILL

June 1863, Sni-a-Bar Wilderness, Jackson County, western Missouri

On June 17, Fernando Scott was killed in a raid. His death was a blow to the raiders. He was a fellow everybody liked. Jabez and Frank were especially touched, as they had known him since younger days. A few days later, Jabez and Frank left the group and joined William Quantrill at the leader's hideout in the wilds of the Sni.

Quantrill had a checkered past. He had lived in Lawrence, Kansas in the 1850s under the alias Charley Hart and had belonged to a gang that rustled cattle, horses, and mules. The gang also had plundered in Missouri, stealing slaves and selling them back to their masters. When the law in Lawrence issued a warrant for his arrest, he moved to Missouri and became a soldier in the rebel forces.

Like Frank, Quantrill had fought at the battle of Wilson's Creek in 1861 under the command of General Price. When Price's fighters were pushed out of Missouri later that year, Quantrill left the regular military and became a bushwhacker. Quickly he developed a reputation as the greatest of the guerrilla leaders in the state.

Jabez and Frank met Quantrill in his shelter along Blackwater Creek. Jabez was struck by the easy, fraternal manner of the leader. Quantrill went through a litany of questions about the backgrounds, skills, strengths, and weaknesses of the two men. Jabez thought Quantrill seemed like a farmer examining livestock.

Jabez didn't think of himself as much of a fighter, and he wanted to highlight his other talents. "My best role with other outfits has been around the camps. I'm a blacksmith and farrier. And I know a bit about taking care of sick or hurt horses. Since humans aren't much different from horses, in a pinch if there's not a doctor around, I can try to help put a wounded man back together."

Quantrill had no visible reaction. "That's fine. We need those skills. But I want you to join in the raids. Everyone in the outfit is a fighter. Can you do that?"

"Well, sure. I follow orders. I was on a few raids with Scott."

Quantrill smiled. "Welcome to our camp."

Jabez believed he had made a good impression on Quantrill. He already liked this leader. The three men walked from the shelter toward the tents, laughing and joking. Jabez was amused by Quantrill's flamboyant imperial mustache with its tips curling upward and across his cheeks, but he suppressed his impulse to ask about how a man could maintain such a look in battle.

At the end of their meeting, Quantrill said, "In a few days, we'll have some good work for you all. Meantime, I want you to get to know some of my lieutenants—George Todd, Bill Anderson, Arch Clement."

Jabez and Frank wandered among the makeshift nests of the raiders, unkempt and cluttered with the detritus of primitive camp life—food waste, bones of butchered animals, discarded plunder from raids, and droppings from horses.

Jabez scooted the mess out of his path. "This place obviously has no rules. And it stinks."

Frank laughed. "You got that right, it looks like a hell hole to live in."

They came upon Arch Clement's shelter, a tarp folded over a rope suspended between two trees and secured to the ground at the corners. Arch was chewing on an unlighted cigar as they approached. Jabez was surprised to see that Arch was very young for a lieutenant. *He can't be more than eighteen.* Jabez was struck also by Arch's small stature and mentally measured him. *Top to toe the boy isn't over five feet.*

Jabez introduced Frank and himself. "We joined up today. We're from Clay County. I'm a blacksmith and farrier, and Frank and his family have a good-sized farm and some slaves. All our people are full-on Secesh. My pa—rest his soul—rode with Atchison back in the Kansas troubles in the '50s. Frank is a top horseman and a hell of a shot. I repair things, do some metal work, and tend to the horses."

Arch slowly withdrew the cigar from his lips and grinned. "Well, y'all are exactly what we need. You seen any action?"

"I was with Price in a couple of the battles in '61," Frank said. "But came down with measles at Lexington, and the Feds captured me while I was in a sickbed. I took the parole oath, but I did so with a wink, and then I joined up with Scott, and we had some skirmishes before he was killed."

Jabez told Arch of his time with the border group defending against Jayhawkers, and his participation in the sack of Lawrence in '56 and the sack of St. Joseph in '61, as well as the seizure of the Liberty Arsenal in '61.

"Well then, y'all don't need no training. I know we can sure use your smithy talents, Jabez."

Frank asked Arch about Quantrill.

Arch removed the cigar again and put it in his pocket. "As you probably know, Quantrill spent a lot of time in Kansas. He knows both sides of the border. That's mighty helpful in dealing with Jayhawkers. Ever'body in the outfit likes him, and I know he will take a personal interest in you, just like he does with all of us. He's a fearless fighter and a fine horseman. He lives up to his reputation. One thing that's funny about him is that he sings during battles. Know that's hard for y'all to believe, but that's right, he sings! Says it calms his mind. And you'll see, he is cool in battle." Arch chewed on his cigar like he was in thought. "We don't have many rules in the outfit, but one rule is that once you're in, you're in for good. No sunny-day soldiers in this outfit. You'll have a chance for some time off, but once a bushwhacker always a bushwhacker.

"Another thing is that he sees this war in black and white. I ain't talking about race, I mean he doesn't believe there can be any middle ground in Missouri. I'm the same way. Either you're a Unionist or a Secesh. We don't put up with fence sitters. If you ain't a Secesh, you're a Unionist, subject to being killed by us. And fence sitters better watch out too. You're either for us or agin' us. Makes it simple. Quantrill has an oath you'll take, and in it you swear these words, 'I will kill those who support the Union.' So, it's more than just soldiers we're after."

# 19

## ESCAPE

August 1863, Clay County, northwestern Missouri

Pulled by the two mules Jeff Davis and Banjo, the wagon carrying Queenie and Briggins bumped along the dusty, rutted road past fields and open land and woods. To an observer, it would appear to be carrying a load of sticks for hanging harvested tobacco in barn rafters. But hidden underneath were panniers of bacon, beans, cornbread, hardtack, greens, sweet cakes and other victuals, and whiskey. The hidden space also contained a wheat sack filled with new bushwhacker shirts. In the toolbox the drivers had hidden gunpowder, balls, and percussion caps for revolvers.

Queenie's pulse was racing. She twisted her head, her eyes flitting rapidly back and forth, surveying the road ahead and behind. She feared they would be stopped and searched by Union militia. "They might throw us in jail or even shoot us if they see what's in this wagon. Why are we risking our lives helping these Secesh who are killing the soldiers who are trying to set us free?"

Briggins was driving, and he had his eyes fixed on the road. "You right, girl. Making us do this is like some cruel joke Zerel is playing on us. Maybe we should deliver this load to the Yankees."

Queenie grabbed his arm. "You want to get us killed? Every Secesh and guerrilla in this county would be looking for our blood."

"Well, maybe we should just drive this wagon north to

Iowa or west to Kansas and set ourselves free."

Queenie turned to him, holding her hands up, in a gesture of exasperation. "We can't do that, can't escape in this wagon in broad daylight. Can't cross the river, no ferryman would take us. Can't go to Iowa, that's a far piece, and we don't know the way. If we don't get back tonight, Missus will put out the alarm, and either trackers or bushwhackers will catch us before we get to freedom. Then we'll get shot or hanged by our catchers, or if they bring us back, we'll get lashed with that bullwhip.

Briggins had an irritated expression. "Yeh, you're right, but that's what I'd *like* to do. I'm itching to be free, and every day the itch grows," he said. "I'm ready to get outta Missouri and start a new life, a new me."

Queenie sighed. "We'll be free after the war because Lincoln says so. Also, I hear the North won some big battles last month, and that's a good sign."

Briggins looked straight ahead, avoiding eye contact with Queenie. "Don't count on it. I'm not. The war goes this way and then that. No telling who is gonna win. Listen to me, I talked with Alex, one of the field hands over at the Mantooth farm, and he said there is gonna be some pigs feet next week. Says it is all lined up with Jayhawkers and freedmen coming over from Kansas. Many of our people will escape. Says white folks call something like that a slave stampede. It'll be dangerous, I know, since someone may slip and tell, and the whole thing could blow up. I'm going on the stampede. You with me?"

"I'll think about it."

"Don't tell anybody, girl. 'Specially Charlotte. Ain't no way she would leave, and she might tell Missus."

"Uh huh."

The two lapsed into silence. Queenie was thinking about joining the stampede, but she wanted to change the subject to give her time to process the dangerous idea. "I'm so angry about Frank, fighting and killing to keep us in slavery. Jesse will join him soon, I know that. And Missus does everything she can to help the bushwhackers. I can't tell you how all that hurts me, I feel it down to my soul."

"You women always talk about feelings. I just wanna be free. Is that a feeling?"

"I expect it is. Something's a feeling if it hurts or makes you feel good. For me, I'm hurting from knowing we are trapped by a family that owns us and is making war to keep it that way."

Briggins reined the mules and pulled the wagon to a stop. He turned and looked into Queenie's eyes. "They're not gonna change. Frank, Jesse, Missus, and all of them, are doing what has already been set by hundreds of years of their blood, white blood from England, and by what their friends believe, and by what the preachers say at the white churches, and on and on and on and on. They could not think, they could not act, in any other way. At day's end they don't give a damn about colored people. White people are the kings in their world, and they ain't gonna do a damn thing to change that. Listen, we are money to them, that's all. They give us enough food and shelter to keep us alive and in working order, which is about the same as they do for their livestock. The sooner we get away from them the better. So, you better stop thinking about your feelings, and think about this opportunity to take the pigs feet."

Briggins started the mules again. Queenie didn't speak. The wagon creaked as it heaved over the contours of the eroded lane.

*

A week later, on August 13, under the black cape of night, Briggins and Queenie stole away to join the stampede with slaves from the neighboring farms heading for Kansas.

Queenie rubbed her hands and looked at Briggins.

"I'm scared. I don't know this area very well. I'm counting on you to guide us to the meeting place."

"You're in good hands, Queenie. I've been hunting with Frank and Jesse in the area before. First, we'll meet up with the folks from the Mantooth farm and the other runaways. Then we'll move on later to meet the Jayhawkers who will take us across the river to Kansas."

After walking through woods for an hour, they came to an opening in the forest, and Queenie sagged and dropped to one knee. "Lord, I'm tired, boy. We need to rest a bit."

Briggins found a place that would allow a wide view of the clear sky. They sat on the ground and then lay on their backs gazing upward.

The night of August 13 was the peak of the Perseid meteor shower, called the Tears of St. Lawrence for the mythical sparks of the fire that roasted Saint Lawrence alive. The Tears are an annual rain of space debris that traces across the sky in short bursts in the first couple weeks of August.

The sky was clear, and the moon was only a thin sliver, a waning crescent rising not until midnight, so the viewing conditions were perfect. As each meteor flashed across the visible sky, Queenie would say, "There goes one." Then, "There goes another!"

Briggins pulled himself up and stretched. "Those shooting stars are a good sign. We got to go, Queenie."

Despite the momentary rest, Queenie was still tired—scared too—and worrying whether they should continue. "Is this what we should be doing?" Are we crazy? What am I gonna do when I get to Kansas?" She began to cry.

Briggins put a hand softly on her shoulder. "Queenie, there is no turning back now. Come, dry your tears, we have to go. We will make it. And our lives in freedom will be so much better."

Queenie looked up, her face wet with the tears. "As

awful as slavery is, we are safe back at the farm. We can wait til this war's over. When the Yankees win, we'll be free without risking our lives."

"We never know how this war will turn out," he said. "And even if the Yankees win, we may not be freed. I don't want to spend any more days being owned by the Missus. Life is short, Queenie. Men and women are like those stars that are shooting tonight in the sky—one minute we're here, and then in a flash we're gone. Pigs feet is dangerous, yes, but Queenie, we can do it. You are a strong and brave woman. You've come this far. It is gonna take both of us to be alert and smart now. I need your help."

She said nothing, but she was thinking, *Briggins is right.*

Briggins stood motionless above her. After a while she stanched her tears, and he reached his hand toward her. She took it, and he raised her from the ground.

She looked into his calm face. "I'm over it now. I'm with you. Yes, we can do it."

They moved on to meet the runaways from the Mantooth farm. Other runaways soon joined, then the heavily armed Jayhawkers and freedmen from Kansas. They moved on to the banks of the Missouri River, then crossed by rafts and small boats to Kansas. Briggins left his slave name behind and became Abraham Douglass.

# 20

## THE WOMEN'S JAIL

June–August 1863, Kansas City, Jackson County, Missouri
On June 16, 1863, the day he assumed his new appointment as Brigadier General in command of Union forces in the area of eastern Kansas and western Missouri, Thomas Ewing, Jr. was alone in his office, writing in his notebook. He was listing the problems he must immediately address.

The District was boiling with guerrilla activity, both pro-Southern and pro-Union. Confederate bushwhacker gangs roamed both sides of the border, striking against Unionist families and farms as well as federal troops and Union militia. Murder, arson, robbery, and pillaging had become their trademarks. Their counterparts on the Union side were rogue bands of Kansas Jayhawkers that crossed into Missouri exacting reciprocal violence against Confederate sympathizers. Their reputation was more about their looting and pillaging. A small band of Jayhawkers known as the Red Legs emerged and looted and burned and killed without regard to the loyalties of their victims.

Because of repeated violence from bushwhackers, Jayhawkers and Red Legs, many families in the western counties of Missouri had pulled up stakes and left their land. For the same reason, certain counties in eastern Kansas south of the Kansas River were becoming virtually depopulated. It seemed that no one near the border was secure, whether Unionist or Secesh.

Trying to quell the cycle of violence, the Union army troops and militia had intensified their campaign against Missouri's Confederate guerrillas. But the violence continued.

Ewing had a difficult assignment and he had limited military experience. Nonetheless, he was a capable man. He was educated in the east and was one of the key Free State figures who helped bring Kansas into the Union, and he then served as its first Chief Justice. He was well connected. His father had served in the cabinet of Zachary Taylor. His foster brother, who became also his brother-in-law, was Union General William Tecumseh Sherman. Two of Ewing's brothers were also Union generals. Ewing was a personal friend of President Lincoln.

On the day after General Ewing assumed his official duties, a bushwhacker gang ambushed a one hundred fifty-man Federal cavalry detachment in Jackson County, western Missouri, killing fourteen. For several weeks General Ewing studied various alternative strategies for combatting the guerrilla problem. On July 6, he leaned back in his office chair so that the front legs of the chair lifted a few inches from the floor, crossed his feet and rested them on a low table, put his hands behind his head, and stared at the ceiling. His aide, Major Paul Craig, was taking notes as the General talked through a new plan he was considering.

"These guerrilla ambushes are playing hell with our troops," Ewing said. "Our men are so afraid of ambush that they have confined their patrols to open prairie. The bushwhackers can easily hide in forests and glens, and our men won't go in after them. Setting up classic battle lines with bushwhackers is not in the cards. If we could do that, we would easily put them down. But they're dictating the format of skirmish—it's close-up and on horseback—a format they are very talented at, and our men are just plain scared to go after them."

Craig rubbed his smooth, shaved head. "Bushwhackers are wild animals. They don't fight like regular army. And they're taking scalps and keeping count of 'em, I hear. Ha, I shaved my head so they won't be coming after me."

"Very funny." The General scowled. "Well, I'm thinking of a way to put pressure on them. We know the identity of many of the leaders. We know their families are helping them, spying and passing communications between the gangs. If we put pressure on their families, we put pressure on them. We need to start locking up their women—sisters, wives, girlfriends. We don't need proof of any specific crime of supporting the enemy, just being connected to the guerrillas is enough. Write an order to start the process of corralling. Wives of guerrillas can be exiled from the District. Sisters and girlfriends who are supporting them can be arrested. We can temporarily put them in a building I know about. It's a place where we can hold them in Kansas City until we ship them to St. Louis for trial. This will send a strong message."

"Are you sure, General? It's an unwritten rule here that women are exempt from the war. If Secesh women are jailed or exiled, soon Union women will be targeted by the rebels."

"Exempt? asked Ewing. "Well, they threw away their exemption by supplying the bushwhackers and spying."

Craig raised his eyebrows. "With all respect, sir, the temperature around here is hot with emotion, and each attack guarantees a violent response. It's just a never-ending cycle of revenge—blood for blood. Locking up women just because they are kin to bushwhackers will create a new cycle of hate and revenge. I would urge you to reconsider."

"Thank you for your view." Ewing had an edge to his voice. "We have to use pressure and force. We can't be passive in the face of these guerrilla attacks. We're not making progress in dealing with these gangs, and some-

thing's got to be done. Give the order to my provost marshal, Mr. Craig."

*

August 13, 1863, Kansas City, Missouri
Within a week, eight women were arrested and impris-
oned on the second floor of the recently constructed
three-story brick structure, the Thomas Building, on
Grand Avenue. All were sisters, cousins, or girlfriends
of bushwhackers. Ten-year-old Janie Anderson joined
the eight women, because her sisters, who cared for her,
were among those arrested, and she could not live on her
own. After a few days in the makeshift prison, Janie Anderson began to squall about the filthy conditions of their
incarceration and curse the jailers for detaining her sisters. The guards lost patience with the girl's tantrums and
chained her wrist to an iron ball next to her bed.

Adjoining the temporary prison was a house for the
guards. Union soldiers had revamped it by removing par-
titions and posts in the center section in order to provide
more room for the guard garrison, weakening the guardhouse to such an extent that it had begun to list against
the Thomas Building. In addition, the soldiers had cut
through a common wall between the guardhouse and the
Thomas Building, weakening both structures.

On August 13, a guard and a first-story tenant both no-
ticed that the pressure from the guardhouse was cracking
some parts of the Thomas Building. The tenant called for
an inspection. It was too late. The guardhouse collapsed,
triggering in turn the collapse of the Thomas Building in a
heap of brick and wood, burying the occupants of the jail.
Four women died immediately. One died later, and the
rest suffered serious injuries.

# 21

## THE LAWRENCE MASSACRE

Jabez Cooper: *For me, the war was about to take a mighty big turn. I don't mean to suggest we had any big impact on the war, because I came to know that we really did not. At best we were an irritant to the Feds. What I mean is that I was about to get thrown into situations I could never have imagined.*

August 10, 1863, Sni-A-Bar Wilderness, Jackson County, western Missouri

The plan had been inchoate for some time, slowly turning in the mind of William Quantrill. The destruction and looting of Osceola and other towns in western Missouri by Kansas Jayhawkers smoldered in the memories of all Secesh in Missouri. Quantrill wanted eye-for-eye revenge against Kansans. He was biding his time until an opportunity presented itself.

On August 10, Quantrill held a council with his top lieutenants at a Secesh farmhouse near Blue Springs, in Jackson County. He sensed the time was ripe for a major strike into the heart of anti-slavery Kansas on a scale that would sound throughout the entire nation and spread terror among Unionists on both sides of the state border. Lieutenants attending the meeting included George Todd, Cole Younger, Bill Anderson, John McCorkle, and Arch Clement.

Quantrill laid out his plan, a mounted strike against Lawrence, the most famous abolitionist town in Kansas and a sanctuary for Jayhawkers. "We will attack Lawrence. Satan himself lives there—Jim Lane. We need to take his ass prisoner and bring him back for execution here in the Sni. I'm tryin' to decide whether hanging or burning at the stake is the most appropriate punishment. Most of the Missouri property the Jayhawkers have stolen is located in Lawrence, in their fancy homes. Jim Lane's big home is full of plunder he took in Osceola. We need to take our property back to Missouri. Returning property is one thing, but the biggest thing is this list here in my hand of the worst Jayhawkers of Lawrence. I want to kill every one of them."

"I love it," said Arch, grinning like a possum. The others nodded their heads.

Quantrill spread a detailed map of the town. One of his spies had marked the homes of the prime targets, Union soldiers and Jayhawkers, most especially General Jim Lane. "At the houses on this map, take everything of value you can find. We'll liberate their horses to carry it all back. Do not harm the women or children—remember, we are Southerners. Burn every house."

"Lawrence is a far piece away, one lieutenant said. "We'll be mighty exposed. How long will we be in the saddle?"

Quantrill replied, "We can gather men from our western counties and mass near the border, then ride all night and arrive at Lawrence before dawn, finish our work there in less than a day, and return to Missouri in forty-eight hours. The whole operation will take no more than four or five days."

Another lieutenant said, "So, for up to five days we will be exposed to Federal troops. They may jump us before we get to Lawrence. Even if we get to Lawrence, they stand a good chance of jumping us on the return."

"Those are the risks. But we'll have surprise on our side. We'll avoid their stations, and there aren't so many folks living in eastern Kansas these days, they are so afraid of us. We may never be seen before we get to Lawrence."

The council discussed the details of the plan for hours, with many enthusiastic, but some deeply skeptical, about the chances of success. Refinements were made, and Quantrill's idea moved to the chrysalis stage.

*

August 15, 1863, Sni-A-Bar Wilderness

Quantrill called his lieutenants together for another meeting to review and refine the plan for the attack on Lawrence. "Y'all know now of the collapse of the Taylor Building jail in Kansas City. That was intentional and a cold-blooded murder of our women by the blue bellies. They have no idea how much hate they stirred up. We've now got hundreds of men already committing to join us in the raid, and I expect many more. This will be the largest guerrilla operation in the entire war."

Quantrill asked Bill Anderson to speak next and give his view. The leader believed Anderson would whip the gathered group to a frenzy. Anderson was twenty-three years old, and he was already a charismatic force among Quantrill's raiders.

Quantrill knew Anderson's history and believed he was the kind of reckless and bloody fighter he needed to persuade the others to make the raid on Lawrence. Like Quantrill, Anderson had previously lived in Kansas before the war. He and his brother were skilled horse thieves, operating on both sides of the border in the early years of the war. When their father was killed in Kansas in the summer of 1862, Anderson and his brother avenged the murder by wounding the killer, locking him in the cellar of his store, and burning the building. The two brothers fled to western Missouri, and in early 1863, they joined Quantrill's raiders.

Anderson had three sisters in the collapsed prison. One died, and two were grievously injured. He was already full of hate for the North, and the loss of his sister and the injuries to the other two flamed him to hysteria.

Anderson rose to his full height and scanned the room. His eyes were faintly gray like those of a wolf. He pushed back his long dark hair and with both hands smoothed his dark beard. "The goddamn Yankees have my sisters' blood on their hands, and we gotta strike them hard and fast. We can't let the filthy sonsabitches get away with murdering our women. I know they intentionally weakened the building so it would fall with our women inside. They killed my sister Jo. My sister Mollie was crippled for life. My little sister Janie, just ten years old, a mere child, was chained to a ball when it happened. She was covered with rubble. Both her legs were broke, and she has a busted back. It's a miracle she's living."

Anderson spoke faster and faster as he recounted the building's collapse and the death and injuries, not only to his sisters, but to other prisoners who were related to fellow bushwhackers. He was standing and swinging his arms and spitting the words. His eyes bulged. "Vengeance! Kill every damn male thing in Lawrence," he yelled. "No mercy."

Cole Younger leapt up. "You goddamn right, I lost two of my cousins. And McCorkle's sister Charity was killed too."

John McCorkle was now on his feet with Anderson and Younger, and they were all shouting for revenge.

Quantrill smiled. He had lit the fuse. "Yes, kill every male capable of carrying a gun."

*

August 21, 1863, Lawrence, Kansas
After two days on the trail, four hundred fifty horsemen under Quantrill's command gathered south of Lawrence as the sun rose.

The gang had started on the Blackwater River in Missouri on the morning of August 19. Tributaries of bushwhackers flowed from various hide-outs and converged into a surging river of horses and men. They camped on a farm outside Lone Jack that night and crossed the state line near Aubrey, Kansas on the next day. The raiders were spotted in the border crossing, and word was relayed to the small Federal post at Aubrey. Through a series of delays and mistakes, Union officers failed to notify any town in Kansas, and Federal cavalry lagged hours behind the invaders.

As the raiders proceeded in formation through the eastern Kansas countryside, they flew the Stars and Stripes of the Union flag as disguise. Those in front wore Union uniforms taken from the corpses of federal soldiers previously killed. They rode all night on August 20 and early the next day. Scores of men, including Jabez Cooper and Frank James, tied themselves to their saddles in case they fell asleep on the trail. There was no moon, and to assure they didn't make a disastrous wrong turn, the invaders forced a series of local farmers into guiding them through the Kansas countryside and then killed each impressed guide when they could no longer use him.

Now, at Lawrence, the men pulled off their Union jackets. No one wanted to risk being mistaken for a Yankee by another raider. The Union flag was lowered, and a new banner was raised—the black flag of no quarter. One of the female Secesh had sewn the name Quantrell—a common misspelling of the leader's name—in red across the face of the flag.

Scouts sent out by Quantrill had reported the town was asleep, with pickets nowhere in sight. Many of the raiders expressed their surprise, and some speculated that there had been so many false alarms that the town had developed a false sense of security.

Shortly before five o'clock in the morning, a crashing wave of four hundred fifty men on horseback galloped into the streets of Lawrence. The combined sounds of horses' hooves and of men screaming the rebel yell and shooting into houses sounded like a tornado. The rushing mass of horses tore through the tents of a makeshift camp of recruits of the Fourteenth Kansas Brigade. The raiders shot soldiers fleeing their trampled tents. Small groups of bushwhackers split from the main horde and raced down the side streets, shooting male residents.

Quantrill's lieutenants sent riders to the roads leading out of town to block residents attempting to escape. And they cut the cables of the ferry across the Kansas River. The raiders had pulled tight the strings of a deadly purse trap.

The main column rushed down the main street, Massachusetts Street, and turned toward the Eldridge House, the new hotel that had risen from the ashes of the former Free State Hotel torched by Sheriff Jones's posse in 1856. The guerrillas surrounded the hotel, then paused and went quiet as Quantrill dismounted.

A hotel guest waved a white sheet from his window in surrender. "What is your intention? Why are you here?"

Quantrill looked at the fluttering sheet and put both hands on his hips. "We're here for plunder," he lied.

"We are at your mercy," the guest said. We ask that you protect those in this hotel."

Quantrill ignored the plea and entered the hotel and spoke in a calm, business-like voice to the assembled guests. "As long as you offer no resistance, you'll be safe, because Lawrence is our target. But we need your contributions."

Two guerrillas walked among the crowd, collecting wallets, purses, watches, and rings as loot. Then a group of bushwhackers escorted the guests to another hotel run by an old friend of Quantrill.

The raiders poured through the lobby, dining area, and rooms of the Eldridge House, ripping curtains down, pocketing silverware, and gathering clothes as additional plunder. As if struck by lightning, the hotel was suddenly in flames, scorched by Missourians for the second time in its brief history.

*

Jabez led a group and set fire to the town's newspapers. While watching the flames, he saw a group of guerrillas looting a store, grabbing shirts and coats, and throwing them in the street to be picked up and put on packhorses. He joined them. A pair of black leather boots caught his eye, and he put them on.

Next door, the looters found whiskey, and began chanting, "Whiskey, whiskey, whiskey." They passed around the bottles. The drinkers were saying things like "down the creek," as they passed the bottles around. One man couldn't hold the bottle steady and spilled the brown liquor across his mouth and chin and onto his shirt. The drinkers laughed and passed the bottles for a second round. They had been in the saddle for so long, it didn't take many mouthfuls of whiskey to enhance their audacity.

The invaders were in complete control of the town, and they were in no hurry as they picked the downtown business district clean. The plunder lay on Massachusetts Street in large piles, and guerrillas loaded it on horses plucked from nearby stables. Many exchanged their jaded horses for stolen fresh mounts. Jabez put his saddle and kit on a black gelding he rustled. There was a lull, and the invaders stood as if frozen, waiting for the signal to resume the killing.

Quantrill rode along Massachusetts Street, parting his men to the sides of the wide avenue as they awaited his command. He lifted his hat and yelled "Kill, kill, kill," and spurred his horse. A roar of rebel yells rose as the guerrillas fanned out through the town. As they attacked, their war cry became, "Osceola!"

Jabez saw Arch shoot and wound two Lawrence men

trying to protect a store. Arch and three other raiders tied the hands of the wounded men and then roped the two together in the store and set the store ablaze. When the tied men struggled in an awkward stumble to escape, Arch kicked them back. They tried again to run out of the burning building, and Arch laughed and cursed, and kicked them back a second time. The two collapsed from their wounds and the effects of fire and smoke. Soon the small space was an oven. Jabez cringed and turned his head, but said nothing to Arch.

A resident ran into the street with a Sharps rifle and began firing at the guerrillas. Frank James rolled to the protected side of his horse and raced toward the shooter. Frank held his saddle horn with his left hand, leaned right, craned his head under the neck of the horse, reached his pistol under and dropped the man with a single shot. Jabez witnessed and thought, *Just like a Comanche. He learned that from his uncle Wild Bill.*

The raiders scattered through the residential streets of Lawrence, searching for the houses marked for death on Quantrill's map. At each residence, the men and boys were killed first. Then the victims were robbed and plunder was taken from the house, and then the house was burned. Men and boys were shot in front of their wives, daughters, sisters, mothers. One woman held her husband so tightly that the guerrillas couldn't pry her away as she begged for his life. They shot the man while she clutched him. She sobbed uncontrollably as she continued to hold him while the life bled from his body. As bushwhackers departed, they tipped their hats to the ladies of the house, as if they were Southern gentry paying a Sunday visit.

Someone told Jabez that the women of Lawrence were hiding their men in wells. He saw a group of raiders checking wells, and in one they found the town's mayor who had suffocated while hiding. A few minutes later, he saw a woman roll her husband in a rug and drag it outside the house and cover it with kitchen items the guerrillas wouldn't want. Jabez felt a wave of sympathy. He turned his head and told no one. He hoped her ruse would not be discovered.

Near the end of the rampage, Jabez and three others were ordered to put the courthouse to the torch. At this point, the whole town appeared ablaze. Jabez carried out his duty, but he was sick inside. *How can we do this to civilians—to an entire town? They are the same people as we are, just are on the other side of a war—a war about . . . what?*

*

Quantrill's spy had told him that General Jim Lane would be out of town on this day, but just in case the intelligence was flawed, Quantrill dispatched Bill Anderson—who in turn chose three others to ride with him—to Lane's home on the western edge of Lawrence. Before Anderson's group of four arrived at his door, Lane fled in his nightshirt to his cornfield and covered himself with fallen stalks. His wife convinced Anderson that Lane was out of town, and the raiders left, but not before torching the house. Jim Lane survived, but one hundred and eighty-four men and boys died in the massacre.

*

After Quantrill ordered his men to leave the burning town, Jim Lane cobbled together a small force, hastily armed with shotguns and corn knives, to pursue the guerrillas. Soon Lane's group met up with Federal troops dispatched from Kansas City, and the combined force made chase, but they failed to find a meaningful battle with the raiders. Quantrill and his bushwhackers crossed into Missouri and dispersed in rivulets of riders to familiar woods and caves and farms.

*

When they reached Missouri, Jabez rode beside Frank,

and the two discussed the raid.

"Anderson and Arch were out of control," Jabez said. "They love blood too much. Anderson says somebody gave him a silk cord from the plunder, and he's going to tie a knot for everyone he kills. I heard that today he put fifteen knots in it. Arch burned those men alive, and I saw Anderson shooting boys in front of their mothers. Anderson made one man get down in the dirt and crawl to him, and he made the fellow lick the dirt off his boots. Then he shot him in the back while the wife was begging and screaming. Anderson said to her, 'Woman, I'm here for revenge and I got it.' Frank, this isn't right. We're goin' to Hell. Can't Quantrill stop that crap?"

Frank wouldn't look at Jabez. "In a raid, our boys can get out of control. Only a shot from a Yankee gun can stop them. That's how war is done. War's about killing. Bad things are done on both sides."

# 22

# GENERAL ORDER NUMBER 11

August–October 1863, Kansas City, Missouri, Office of the
Commander of the Missouri-Kansas Border District of the
Union Army

Union General Thomas Ewing reeled from the shock of
the news about the Lawrence massacre, and he called his
aide Paul Craig to his office to help him develop a new
and sweeping order. "Paul, I haven't slept for days. This
Lawrence disaster may end my career. Folks in Kansas
are asking, 'Where was the defense? Why didn't Ewing
stop Quantrill at the border? Why were the Union troops
not able to intercept the raiders before they crossed back
into their Missouri hideouts? Why can't Ewing find their
hideouts and root them out?'"

Ewing was physically agitated and could not sit down
for more than a minute. He stalked around his office, circling Craig's chair. "Kansans are mad as hell. And they're
scared. There are daily rumor-panics that Quantrill will
return and wipe out whole towns. Lawrence was almost
emptied by a false alarm that the raiders were returning.
Kansas families are moving out of the border zone to the
interior until this Quantrill is brought to heel. Jim Lane is
saying I've been too soft, too many half-measures. He's
threatening to have me removed if I don't act strongly
against the bushwhackers. Missouri Unionists are mad
and scared too."

"I'm sorry General. I know this is a hell of a blow."

Ewing went to the window, looking out at nothing

in particular. "Making matters worse, the Jayhawkers and Red Legs from Kansas feel licensed to retaliate, and they're burning towns in Missouri, and looting everything they can get their hands on. The odd thing is they don't attack the Secesh bushwhackers. That would be a godsend if they did. But, no, that would be too dangerous for the Jayhawkers. They claim that everyone in western Missouri is a Secesh, and that they are helping the Union cause by raiding and looting Secesh towns and farms, but the Jayhawkers are driving Union supporters into the hands of the rebels."

"Right," Craig said. "What do you have in mind?"

Ewing returned to his desk. "We have little control over the Jayhawkers, so I think we should continue to focus on the Secesh. I want to drive a stake into the heart of the guerrillas. First step is to cut off all sources of their support. Then exterminate them."

Ewing pulled a map from a drawer. "Look at this map. I've outlined the heartland of disloyal supporters of Quantrill and his men. It covers the border counties that run from just south of Kansas City, on down through Jackson, Cass, and Bates counties and includes part of Vernon. I want to hollow out that area. Evacuate everyone in the rural area of that zone, move 'em out of our district. Even the Union loyalists must go—they will have to go to a Union military station or move to interior parts of Kansas. We will eliminate the support structure that the rebels are using, and we will eliminate the targets the Jayhawkers keep hitting. We will confiscate livestock and food supplies. We also will confiscate grain and hay, and what is left in the fields would be burned. After the war is over, the loyalists could come back and claim their land, and we could compensate them for what we confiscated. Jim Lane and I have discussed this plan, and after Lawrence happened, he told me if I don't do it, I'm a dead dog. What do you think?"

"Whew," exhaled Craig, "You sure have been thinking big. So, are you asking me what will be the downsides, or whether it will work?

"Just give me the downsides."

Craig squirmed in his chair. "Well sir, with all respect, I think this will inflame the civilian population on both sides of this war. What will happen to the abandoned properties? The bushwhackers will loot the farmhouses, the smokehouses, and the livestock. The Jayhawkers will come over from Kansas and do the same. The bushwhackers will have lots of empty territory where they can hide. Every family that is displaced will hate you and the Union Army with a passion. Those could be serious downsides."

Ewing threw his hands in the air. "But do you—does anyone—have a better plan? We need to get the rebel supporters out of this area. Without their support, we stand a better chance of getting rid of the bushwhackers. Another reason to get the rebel supporters out is that the Jayhawkers are talking about bringing five thousand men to the area to wipe out the Secesh. We need to remove their targets. We could have a full-scale war between the two states."

Craig was quiet, studying the plan in his mind. Then, he said, "You want to move Union loyalists out too and take their crops?"

Ewing was back on his feet, roaming the office, then abruptly sitting down again. "If we let the loyals stay in that zone, it would be like painting a sign on their barns saying 'Unionist,' and the rebels would attack and wipe them out. There would be no way we could defend those remote farms."

Craig rubbed his shaved head.

Ewing rose to leave the room. "I know this plan has risks in the short term, but I've made up my mind—we need to take a bold step, and now. Write it up."

"Yessir."

# GENERAL ORDER NUMBER 11

General Order No. 11.
Headquarters District of the Border,
Kansas City, August 25, 1863.

1. All persons living in Jackson, Cass, and Bates counties, Missouri, and in that part of Vernon included in this district, except those living within one mile of the limits of Independence, Hickman's Mills, Pleasant Hill, and Harrisonville, and except those in that part of Kaw Township, Jackson County, north of Brush Creek and west of Big Blue, are hereby ordered to remove from their present places of residence within fifteen days from the date hereof.

Those who within that time establish their loyalty to the satisfaction of the commanding officer of the military station near their present place of residence will receive from him a certificate stating the fact of their loyalty, and the names of the witnesses by whom it can be shown. All who receive such certificates will be permitted to remove to any military station in this district, or to any part of the State of Kansas, except the counties of the eastern border of the State. All others shall remove out of the district. Officers commanding companies and detachments serving in the counties named will see that this paragraph is promptly obeyed.

2. All grain and hay in the field or under shelter, in the district from which inhabitants are required to remove, within reach of military stations after the 9th day of September next, will be taken to such stations and turned over to the proper officers there and report of the amount so turned over made to district headquarters, specifying the names of all loyal owners and amount of such product taken from them. All grain and hay found in such district after the 9th day of September next, not convenient to such stations, will be destroyed. . . .

By order of Brigadier General Thomas Ewing.

# WAR INSIDE WAR

In coerced compliance, over twenty-five thousand residents in precarious conditions moved out in wagon trains miles long, or on foot, carrying what they could of their domestic possessions. Many had no idea of where they would end their journey. A woman gave birth roadside during the march. A number fell ill or were injured from the stress of the evacuation. Union troops and Jayhawkers burned the buildings and the crops that hadn't been confiscated. A shroud of smoke hung over the counties that became known as the Burnt District.

*

In late October, Ewing and Craig discussed the impact of the Order.

Ewing said, "Order Eleven has been a calamity. We've—I've—managed to make everybody on both sides of the border spitting mad. The only winners have been the very elements we were trying to weaken. I wanted to destroy the support given by the Secesh population to bushwhackers, but the opposite happened. They're calling the area the Burnt District, and from reports it sounds like almost all the buildings in the entire area, as well as fields, were put to the torch. After the counties were emptied, bushwhackers had easy access to the livestock, chickens, hams, and other stores on the farms, and so they got more food support than they had ever received from the Secesh. And bushwhackers had plenty of space in which to hide. The Order didn't stop the Jayhawkers either, as they too were busy looting the empty houses and barns and stores and then burning them. Even residents who were Union loyalists rage against the heavy hand of the army and how this order caused the loss of their buildings and crops and in the long run will only incite further attacks from the rebels. I know, I know, you're thinking *I told you so.* But do you have any ideas about what we could do to salvage this disaster?"

Craig rubbed his shaved head. He had predicted this

outcome. "While the deed is done and you can't get the evil genie back in the bottle, maybe at least you could allow proven loyalists to return to their farms and businesses. They'll have to rebuild, but it will send the message that loyalty to the Union has its rewards. Problem is, like you said back in September, the returning Unionists will be clear targets for the bushwhackers."

"Well, that is a downside, but I think your idea is a good one. Let's do a new order allowing the return of those who can prove their loyalty. But not the Secesh."

*

The new order came too late. Quantrill and his bushwhackers knew how to make the most of the tragedy of mass removal. "General Order No. 11" was now a rallying cry to the residents of western Missouri as powerful as "Osceola."

# 23

## THE PROMISE

Late September 1863, James family farm, Clay County, northwestern Missouri

Frank James was yelling "I'm back!" when he and Jabez came to the gate. Jesse ran hard toward the figures on horseback, scattering chickens. "Ma, Susie, everybody, it's Frank, he's home. Jabez is with him." Jesse waved his arms in wild windmills.

When Zerelda walked out to greet them. Frank cried, "Look at you, ma! "You're as big as a harvest pumpkin. When's that baby coming?"

"Could be a week or so. And guess what, no matter if it's a boy or a girl do you know what its middle name is going to be?"

Frank laughed. "Noooo, how could I know? I been in the brush."

"Quantrill." Zerelda cocked her head and put her fists on her waist. "If a boy it will be William Quantrill Samuel, and if a girl Fannie Quantrill Samuel. The most famous name in these parts is Quantrill, he's my hero, and that name is going to be in our family."

"Ha, that's gonna make the captain happy and proud," said Frank.

Frank slipped his lanky body off his horse and handed the reins to Charlotte. "It's so good to be home, even if just for three nights."

"Aw Mr. Frank, just three nights?" said Zerelda.

"Yeh, I'm going with Quantrill down to Texas for the

winter. When these leaves finish falling in the next few days we won't have cover, and it's too dangerous to live in the brush without cover. Plus, it's warmer down there in winter. I have to meet up with some men along the Fishing, then we go to join Quantrill."

"Charlotte, put on a big supper for Mr. Frank and Jabez tonight," Zerelda commanded. Reuben and the other family members and the slaves gathered around Frank.

Frank bent down on a knee and hugged the little ones. "I need a bath first, got so much grit and grime on me from the trail. But where is Queenie? I want to see that girl."

There was a long silence, each waiting for somebody else to give Frank the bad news. "She ain't with us no more," said Jesse. "She ran off in a slave stampede last month with Briggins and a bunch of slaves from the Mantooth farm and other farms around here. I s'pose she's alive, but if she is, she's in Yankee land now."

Jabez asked, "Briggins? She ran off with Briggins? Were they secretly married?"

"We don't think they eloped," said Charlotte. "We think it wasn't love but freedom she wanted. That's what the coloreds at the Mantooth place who stayed behind said. Queenie didn't tell me nothin' about them leavin'."

Frank kicked the ground and slapped his leg with his slouch hat. "God Damn it, what is she gonna do with freedom? She had a good life here."

No one spoke. Charlotte and Easter went to make supper.

*

Over the meal, Frank and Jabez recounted life in the Sni, the skirmishes, and the big raid on Lawrence. Each downplayed his role. Frank couldn't quit talking about Quantrill—about what a friendly fellow he was at camp and what a warrior in battle. The family hung on every word, most especially Jesse.

Reuben asked, "How is the war going back east?"

Frank grunted. "I dunno. Jabez keeps up with war news. Let him tell you."

Jabez pushed back from the table. "Lee had a big setback at Gettysburg and about the same time Vicksburg fell to Grant. We lost a lot of Missouri boys last year in the battles of Iuka and Corinth down in Mississippi, but I haven't heard whether we had Missouri boys in Vicksburg. I hear that the South is running low on money and materials, not to mention food. The Yankees are going to use their wealth and their factories and their farms and their numbers to grind us down."

Frank cut in, "Another thing, the Feds are now recruiting coloreds to fight in the Union Army. We sure as hell don't need that."

Reuben continued, "Well, what can Missouri bushwhackers do? What's y'all's strategy?"

Frank shot back, "Our strategy? We don't have a strategy. Or maybe we do, and it's called pain. We want to inflict pain and terror. We want to hurt and scare  the Unionists in this state until they say enough is enough."

"Seems like the more hurt you cause, the more hurt the Yankees throw back on us," said Reuben. "You heard about Ewing's General Order Eleven? Look at Jackson, Cass, Bates, and north Vernon. It's ghost country. I hear there ain't hardly a soul left living there."

"Yeh, I know about General Order Eleven. It's awful," said Frank, omitting that the guerrillas had taken all they could in the Burnt District and were using the empty space for hideouts.

Reuben reached across the table and took another piece of cornbread. "It will be merciful to end this war. I'm at the point where I don't care which side wins, I just want this misery to be over."

Frank forcefully pushed his chair back as if he were going to stand. "What the goddamn hell are you saying, Reuben? You might think this is misery now, but if the North wins this war, what we are going through now will be like a Christmas party. I'll be lynched. We will lose all of our slaves, maybe this farm too. We can't quit. It's war to the knife, as long as it takes."

Reuben didn't look at Frank but wouldn't let go. "It was a mistake for us to get involved in this mess. This is a war for the benefit of the planters in Virginia, the Carolinas, Mississippi, Georgia. It is not for the benefit of people here."

Zerelda put her hand on Frank's arm. "Well, honey, don't pay no attention to Reuben. He's not been right since the militia tried to lynch him. I'm proud of what you and the bushwhackers are doing. You don't need a strategy. You are standing up for our way of life, and that's strategy enough for me. The more pain and fear you all put on the goddamn Yankees and Unionists the better. Wipe 'em out."

Frank knitted his brow. "What do you mean? Reuben lynched? When was that?"

Zerelda fidgeted and looked at Jesse. "Aw, it was when those militia attacked you at the camp here on the farm back in May. Someone had seen you all coming on to the farm, and the militia tried to make Jesse and Reuben tell them your location. Neither one of them would talk, and so they hauled Reuben up on a rope and tried to get him to talk, but he wouldn't, and then they rode out to try to find you. I cut the rope and let Reuben down."

Frank looked stunned. "Why didn't you tell me?"

"We haven't seen you since that time."

Frank slammed his hand on the table. "Well, somebody must have told them where we were camped, 'cause they sure found us over in the woods. Who told?"

Reuben wouldn't look at him. "Frank, this farm is only two hundred acres, they didn't need anyone to help locate you. They just rode to the most likely spots where bushwhackers would be camping."

Frank was breathing hard and staring at Reuben. This time he rose from his chair, his hands clenched into fists.

Jesse interrupted. "Frank, I hate the Yankees so bad I can taste it. I wanna join you and your company. I want Union blood on my knife, some of it from our neighbors, and I've got a long list of names. The first two names on that list are men I recognized in that militia outfit that attacked you here, Alvin Dagley and Brantley Bond."

"Shit," said Frank, "Were they in that militia squad? Brantley is one of our neighbors, and he served with me at Wilson's Creek. He's now a traitor fighting on the Union side?"

"That's right," said Jesse.

Frank exploded, yelling and storming about the house. He left the house and walked in circles outside.

In time, tempers cooled, and after Frank returned, he and Jabez talked with Jesse about joining Quantrill's raiders. Frank said the time wasn't right, that Jesse had just turned sixteen, and anyway the guerrillas were going to Texas for the winter. Next spring, he said, after the leaves are on the trees, would be a time for Jesse to join the bushwhackers when they come back to Missouri. Jabez nodded in agreement.

Reuben had been listening. He raised his hand. "That's good timing. Jesse has to move the tobacco from the plant bed to the field by about that time."

Frank blurted, "Well you and the slaves can tend the tobacco, Reuben. A war's on, and you don't seem to know that."

Jesse turned to his mother. "I'm goin' with Frank as soon as he comes back."

# THE PROMISE

Zerelda said, "This time, I say yes. But it hurts to think of both you boys in constant danger."

Jesse turned to Frank, "You promise me you'll come get me when y'all return to Missouri?"

"I promise."

# 24

## BAXTER SPRINGS

Jabez Cooper: *Captain Quantrill passed the word that we should all be moving toward Texas and meet up near the southwestern border of Missouri. My options were limited. Either I would go to Texas for the winter, or I would join the regular Confederate Army and fight in the east. Both options were awful to me, but I chose Texas.*

October 5, 1863, Baxter Springs, Cherokee County, southeast Kansas

Heading southward toward a winter home in Texas, four hundred bushwhackers moved in small groups from their various nests in Missouri. After a week in the saddle, the threads of Quantrill's raiders collected near the southern corner where Kansas meets Missouri. Most were veterans of the Lawrence massacre, hardened now in body and in hatred of Unionists, and they included lieutenants Bill Anderson, Arch Clement, Dave Pool, George Todd, and Fletch Taylor. Frank James and Jabez Cooper rode with Clement. In the advance guard the guerrillas were dressed in Union uniforms and flew the Union flag.

Along the way, Quantrill's men had encountered small groups of federal soldiers whom they quickly dispatched. At the southeast corner of Kansas the bushwhackers hanged several Federal soldiers. Before hanging one, the guerrillas interrogated him. Vainly believing that candor would save his life, the soldier revealed the details of a new federal fort nearby.

The fort was manned by a combination of Negro soldiers from the Kansas Second Colored Infantry and whites from the Wisconsin Third Cavalry. About one hundred sixty troops in total were stationed at the fort, and sixty had departed that morning on a foraging assignment. Officially named Fort Blair but known as Fort Baxter, the fort was a circle of four-foot-high earthworks, open at one end, enclosing a large field with a log blockhouse in the middle that served as barracks for the Negro soldiers. Outside the fort were various log structures as well as tents for the white Wisconsin soldiers.

The guerrillas despised the Union's colored troops, and the idea of destroying a Union fort combined with the prospect of dispatching Negro soldiers made an attack on the garrison irresistible. Quantrill's lieutenant, Dave Pool, arrayed his horsemen along the edge of a wood, and while the distracted Feds were taking their midday meal at a makeshift kitchen outside the fort without the protection of their rifles and pistols, the guerrillas launched a screaming attack.

Some of the Union soldiers fled into the woods, but most were led into the fort by first lieutenant, James Pond. A group of the guerrillas followed on horseback through the open end of the enclosure, firing their pistols and stampeding Union horses in the enclosure, but the raiders were driven back outside. As the bushwhackers were preparing a second assault, Pond grabbed a mountain howitzer and asked for help in firing it, but his soldiers were shaken by the attack, and he had to operate the weapon single-handedly. He fired three rounds, decapitating one of the rebels. It was enough to move Pool's men away from the fort, and they turned their attention to killing soldiers who had fled to the woods.

Quantrill and the main column of the raiders had been lagging behind Pool and the other attackers, and they now joined Pool's men in the woods. Several of Quantrill's lieutenants, including Anderson, urged a second attack on the fort. Quantrill demurred.

As if in a dream, a column of Federal troops appeared, led by Union General James G. Blunt, the Union commander of the District of the Frontier. Blunt was riding in a buggy, with his horse tied behind, saddled and bridled. He was leading about one hundred cavalry and infantry men from Fort Scott, Kansas to Fort Smith, Arkansas, accompanied by a fourteen-piece brass band. As the column neared the fort, those on horseback dismounted. The band struck up the tune "Yankee Doodle."

Horsemen clad in Union uniforms and bearing the Union flag emerged from the woods. One of Blunt's aides rode to meet the soldiers.

The aide turned and raced back yelling, "It's not our troops, it's Quantrill!  I recognize him!"

Blunt leapt from the buggy and called his men into an infantry formation. Quantrill led his raiders as they walked their horses double-quick toward the Federal formation, then burst into full gallop, screaming the rebel yell. The Union soldiers fired off an ineffective volley. To a man they began to break formation and run across the open plain, some to the fort, others struggling across the exposed prairie. Blunt mounted his horse and rode hard in an escape to safety.

The running soldiers were attacked at close range by the rebel horsemen. Eighty Union soldiers died, mainly by shots to the head, so their uniforms could be stripped unsoiled for future use by the raiders. Then the guerrillas set about the business of scalping.

The bushwhackers had lost two men, the one by the howitzer shell and another by gunshot. Arch made a captured servant of General Blunt dig the graves for the two dead, then dig a grave for himself. Arch then shot the man in the head, stripped off his Union jacket and shoved his body into the grave.

After the uniforms and weapons were collected, Arch rode up to Anderson. "You got some more vengeance today, Bill, and we got rid of some nigger soldiers too. He laughed in a high-pitched staccato. "Those Yankees ain't got shit for brains. They are under orders to kill us if they capture us, but when we get the drop on them they pull out their flimsy white handkerchiefs and wave them and say 'I'm a prisoner of war, don't shoot.' What the hell do they think I'm going to do? Carry them all the way down to Andersonville Prison?" He laughed again.

"Yeh, we had a great day," said Anderson. "Did you see that General running like a scared rabbit? We whipped him good. I just wish I had caught his ass as he fled. I wanted his scalp."

The two men rode to talk with Quantrill. Anderson said to the leader, "Let's take the fort down now. Let's finish this job."

Quantrill smoothed his imperial mustache. "Nah, we don't need to put any of our men in danger at this point. Anyway, we need to get out of here before Union reinforcements show up. We had a great victory. Now, let's move on."

Anderson shot back. "We need to wipe this fort off the face of Kansas and kill every goddamn Yankee soldier in there. You know there are still some nigger soldiers in there, and we should kill every one of them as a lesson to all blacks who are joining the Union army."

Quantrill said cooly, "No, Bill, you heard me give an order. Are you going to follow it?"

Anderson wheeled his horse around and rode off, with Arch following.

*

Quantrill's raiders continued their march around four o'clock that afternoon and filed down the Texas Road.

Jabez rode alongside Frank James. "Frank, this is bloody business, awful business." Frank did not reply.

Jabez was conflicted. Once again, he had participated in a victorious battle but was sick at heart from the brutal actions of some of his comrades. "Frank, I'm having a hard time with this. Why did we have to kill all those boys in the brass band? They weren't soldiers. One of 'em was a drummer boy, just a kid, couldn't ha' been more than twelve years old. Arch was about to scalp that little boy, 'til I stopped him."

Frank slowed his horse to a walk. "Well, this is war. There's bad on both sides. If we don't kill them, they will kill us. That's the way it is."

"C'mon Frank. Those boys were just sittin' in the wagon, not even close to the Yankee soldiers. They waved white handkerchiefs, crying out "We surrender, don't shoot us, we are just the band." We could have just left them alone with their horns and drums. They weren't ever going to make war. Arch and his men ignored the handkerchiefs. They attacked the wagon and shot every one of them in cold blood. Scalped some of them. Then they dragged all their bodies under the bandwagon and burned it. Fourteen of them! Fourteen! Why? Why? I thought we are supposed to be Christians."

"Jabez, come on. You're wearing my patience. We're Christian, yes. This is war. You just need to keep in mind that we have God on our side."

"Sure 'bout that? You talkin' to God?"

After the two rode in a sulking silence for a half hour, Jabez finally spoke. "Another thing I need to tell you. One of those colored soldiers we killed was Briggins."

Jabez saw Frank's mouth open in stunned disbelief.

"That can't be right. Briggins would not ever fight for the Union."

Jabez thought that Frank had finally seen the cost of war. He looked Frank in the eyes. "I got a good look at his face after the battle, and I am certain I'm right."

"How do you know it was Briggins?"

"Well, I had seen him several times at my forge, and also at your farm, like when we all went hunting together. I remember he had that big scar under his right eye. This dead soldier had that same scar, and I recognized his face too."

"That's like we killed a member of my family. I loved Briggins. We spent so many good times together hunting and working. Goddamn it, why did he have to go and join the Union army? And why did he take Queenie and run away from our farm in the first place? She's like family too. Now for all that, Briggins is dead. We took good care of our slaves. I don't understand why those two left us."

Jabez couldn't believe Frank's lack of awareness. He looked directly at his friend. "Are you kidding? Do slaves want freedom or to remain in bondage? That's an easy question. They are answering it with their feet all over Missouri and the entire South. Sure, they face a lot of risks when they run away, but that tells you how much they hate being slaves."

Frank wore a peeved expression. "Well, I dunno. Here's another thing, something you probably don't appreciate because you don't own slaves. I will tell you that they cost us a lot when they ran away. They were good workers, and they were worth a lot of money if we ever wanted to sell them."

Jabez thought about what Frank said. *I don't get it. Briggins was like a member of his family? He would sell a member of his family?*

# 25

## THE FISSURE

Jabez Cooper: *The winter of 1863–1864 we spent around Sherman, Texas, just over the border from Indian Territory, was damn miserable. For one thing, the news of the war was a long string of bad. On top of their victories earlier in the year at Gettysburg and Vicksburg, the Yankees were driving the Confederate army south toward Atlanta.*

*Another thing was that Quantrill lost a lot of men. He reorganized our guerrillas, which had been about four hundred when we got to Texas, and he transferred all but about eighty-five to the regular army. I think Confederate brass made him do it. He said it didn't weaken us, because we do better in small groups. But that didn't persuade me. He claimed that Lawrence and Baxter Springs were our big victories, and we had over four hundred men in both of those raids. Bigger is better. Then, on top of those transfers, a bunch of men transferred to the regular army because they were sick from what they had seen in Lawrence and Baxter Springs. I almost quit bushwhacking to go to the regular army too. I couldn't get over the killing and mutilating done in those two battles.*

*Another bad thing that winter was that we all felt cooped up. There was nothing to do in Texas. We had spent the spring and summer and early fall in some exciting raids. Now, for over five months, we didn't have nothing to do but sit on our tails. Boys got antsy, and they were drinking a lot of whiskey, shots at breakfast and elevens, more in the afternoon and night. They were fistfighting and wrestling. They loved to fight the local fellas. And chase the local women. They did some pilfering too, claiming plunder was a tax the people had to pay us to fight for them.*

*But the most miserable things that happened in Texas had to do with Bill Anderson and George Todd and Quantrill. Let me explain. I'll start first with Anderson. It goes back to Baxter Springs, when Anderson wanted to strike the killing blow to that fort in a second attack, and Quantrill refused. For me, that was a good decision, because we'd already done enough cold-blooded killing—we had won the battle, a huge victory. But in Anderson's view, Quantrill's decision was the act of a coward. Anderson just can't get enough revenge, and he wanted to kill every last soldier in the fort, especially the colored ones. So, when Quantrill stopped Anderson from making the second attack, it must'a' been the last straw for Anderson.*

*When we got to Texas, Anderson spread the word around that Quantrill was too damn shy in battle. Went as far to say the Captain was yellow. Todd took it up too, and he was bad-mouthing Quantrill about as much as Anderson was. We could see that somebody would try to take the command from Quantrill. Todd and Anderson were just biding their time.*

*Down at Sherman, Anderson's men, who probably sensed the tension and wanted to push it, would just ignore Quantrill's orders about discipline. Finally, one of them killed a farmer, and Quantrill had the killer tried on the spot and convicted and shot. Anderson was in a fury, or least he acted that way, and we thought he would kill Quantrill. Anderson seemed always to act before thinking, but this time he stopped himself.*

*Then, next day, Anderson went to Brigadier General McCulloch, the commander of the Confederate regulars, camped at Sherman. McCulloch was plenty mad about all the robberies and other wild rioting our boys were doing, and Anderson told him a whopper of a lie—said Quan-*

*trill was responsible for it all. Fancy that! Next thing you know, General McCulloch had Quantrill arrested, but then Quantrill escaped and lit off toward Indian Territory with his men, including Frank James and me. For some reason, George Todd and his squad joined us. The regular Confederate troops were chasing us. And Anderson and his men were chasing us too, and then of a sudden, Anderson's men started a shootout in the woods with Todd's men. It made no sense. I tell you, it was wild. It didn't last long, and nobody was hit, just a lot of trees got splintered, but for a short time there was a civil war going on between our own raiders.*

*I admit I was more scared by our internal skirmish than by our fights with the Federals.*

*

*Eventually, we made it into Indian Territory, and in April we moved on up to Missouri. Well, the old Quantrill Country, as we called it, meaning Jackson, Cass, and Bates Counties, had been cleaned out by Order No. 11, so we moved about forty or so miles east of Kansas City.*

*Not long after we set up a camp, Quantrill and Todd were playing a game of seven up, with a hundred-dollar pot. Todd was cheating in the most obvious way. Quantrill could see it. Some of the fellows also saw what was happening and went silent. They crowded around the table, their eyes on the two men. One of the boys said, "Y'all come over here and look. Todd is cheating Quantrill, and it's flagrant." Some smart-aleck said, "Flagrant? Hey that's a big word, a half-dollar word," and he tossed a New Orleans half-dollar coin to the fella who said it. It was a kind of joke those two boys play, so I know he got that coin back— that's a lot of money for a word.*

*Well, anyway, Quantrill could see that they were making fun of him, and he pushed his chair back and said to Todd, "George, you goddamn cheater, this game's over, and that pot belongs to me." Todd pushed his chair back too, and said, "Those are fighting words, and I wouldn't expect them from someone who seems so afraid of everything." Things were getting hot, and Quantrill said, "I ain't afraid of nothing." Whereupon Todd pulled his Colt out of his belt and pointed it straight at Quantrill's face—not more than two feet away from his nose—and Todd said in a teasing way, "Are you afraid of me?"" Everybody went stone silent. Nobody moved. All eyes were on Quantrill, and his eyes were on that Colt. He stared down the barrel of the revolver for what seemed like forever. Then he said, "Yes, George, I am afraid of you." He didn't try to put any barbs on those words. He just said them like he had given up and was whipped. He lifted his hands up above his shoulders, palms forward, got out of the chair, and walked out the door.*

*About an hour later, Quantrill and ten of his men rode away. We didn't see him again for quite a while.*

# 26

## THE INITIATION OF JESSE JAMES

May 1864, Clay County, northwestern Missouri
Jesse awoke from the sound of horses whinnying. He grabbed his pistol and ran to the door. It was around midnight, and he couldn't make out who had ridden close to the house. Then, Jesse yelled, "Frank!  Frank is back!"

The entire household threw off bedcovers and ran to the porch.

"Frank, we've not heard from you for months," Zerelda said. "Didn't know if you was dead or in prison."

"Well, here I am—alive and well and free. But, I tell you, it's good to be back from Texas. I don't want to spend another winter there."

Jesse was jumping with excitement. "You are damn lucky I didn't blow your head off—you comin' here in the middle of the night."

"Well, little brother, I'm a wanted man around here, and I have to travel at night."

Zerelda was smiling too. "Tell us all about Texas."

Frank said, "We'll catch up after breakfast." Everyone went to bed, except Frank and Jesse.

Over the winter, Jesse had dreamed about joining the guerrillas, and at last Frank would be able to make the introduction. Now, he wanted to hear every detail of life in with Quantrill. "I heard about what y'all did after you left here last fall—destroying the Feds at Baxter Springs. That battle on top of Lawrence makes Quantrill's Raiders about the most famous raiders in the whole war," said

# THE INITIATION OF JESSE JAMES

Jesse. "Tell me all about it. Tell me all about Texas too."

For the next couple of hours, Frank filled Jesse's ears with tales of the guerrilla trail. Jesse hung on every word.

"I'm ready to go, Frank. Remember, you promised me. Even if Quantrill is not with y'all, I want to go."

Frank said, "After Quantrill left, I joined up with Fletch Taylor and Arch Clement. Jabez joined too. We all are under Bill Anderson's overall command. Tomorrow we can go to the camp. I don't know if they will take you, due to your age. Fletch says that a chain is only as strong as its weakest link, and he won't take any weak links in his troops."

"C'mon Frank. Don't pull my leg. You know I can ride and shoot as good as any bushwhacker. And I'm tough as nails."

Although Jesse was sixteen years old, he looked even younger. His delicate, smooth, almost feminine face showed only a trace of the sandy fuzz he was trying to make into a beard.

The next evening, Frank and Jesse James mounted the two best horses on the farm and slipped through the cover of night down to the camp of raiders led by Fletch and Arch. Clouds obscured any light from the moon, but both knew the route well and did not need moonlight. The two reached the camp on the Fishing River, slipping off the road and down animal tracks into woods now green and thick with spring leaves. They came upon a picket, Frank gave the password, and the brothers slipped quietly into the camp.

*

The next morning, Frank introduced Jesse around, and Jesse underwent a questioning by Arch Clement about his political views and his skills as a horseman and a shooter. Arch, often called Little Archie because of his diminutive size, was eighteen years old, but already a veteran lieutenant.

Arch was chewing on a stubby cigar that rolled from side to side in his mouth as he talked. "We don't take child soldiers in this outfit."

Jesse shot back, "Well, you made it in, and you don't look any older than me. Look, I'm plenty tough."

Arch chuckled and made a half smile while his cigar covered the rest of his open mouth. "I reckon we'll give you a try."

After administering the bushwhacker oath, Arch asked Jesse, "What's happening in the rest of this war?"

"We don't go to town much, try to stay out of the way of the Union patrols, so I ain't up to date. One big piece of news I know is, Lincoln appointed a new General in charge of all the Yankee armies, Ulysses Grant. But you know a Confederate soldier is equal to about three Union, and Grant ain't gettin' much done in Virginia so far. So, I'd say, while it may take a while, we're gonna win this war."

"Hope that's so," said Arch. "We're doing our part here in Missouri, and we're glad to add you on. We're ir-regulars, and we don't have many rules. But, on each raid, we have one chief. You'll get the hang of it soon enough."

"Fine. What's next on your schedule?"

"I think you need some of what we call initiation. Just so you can see if this war life is gonna work for you. It's not for everyone. After breakfast tomorrow, we'll put a squad together and go find us some Union men."

"I don't think I'm gonna need much training, Arch. I'm loaded and cocked, ready to go now. I've got a list of my own, starting with two men who tried to lynch my stepfather and kill Frank.

Arch pulled the cigar from his mouth and grinned. "Glad to hear that. We'll look at your list and head out tomorrow and be in the field for about three or four days."

*

The next morning was clear and warm, a day a farmer would work his crops. The rich smell of plowed earth filled the air. Arch, Fletch, Jabez, Jesse, and three other new recruits rode north toward Jesse's familiar Clay County homeland. All six wore Union military uniforms stolen from dead enemies. Along the way, they spotted an elderly farmer in a field, close to the road. The riders pulled to a stop and waved to the man. He came over, smiling. He appeared eager for a break in his work and a chance to talk.

"Hidy," said Arch, "you seen any bushwhackers in these parts? They's hit some farm families, and we've been sent out to get information."

"Can't say that I have," said the farmer. "But they're spread all over the map of this county. Glad to see you all are on their trail."

"I bet you are," said Fletch. "You Union, ain't you?"

"Damn right," said the man.

Arch slipped his hand inside his Union coat and in one fluid motion whipped out his revolver. He held the gun as though it were a separate living thing, a serpent. The cocking of the hammer was like the opening of a snake's hinged mouth, the powder and ball were the poison coiled in the body of the weapon. Before the man could move, Arch shot him in the face.

"What do you think of that, Jesse?" said Arch.

Jesse was charged with adrenaline, but he tried to appear cool and worldly. "Well, it was quick. How did you know enough to kill him?"

"You're a smart one, just don't be a smart-aleck. There's a lot we don't know, but we can't take chances. If a man says he is Union, we have to take him at his word. And you know what our oath says, we swear to kill Unionists. That's the way this system works. A man is either for us or he's an enemy. You can be damned sure the Union army and militia are out to kill us, so it's kill or be killed."

Fletch commanded the other recruits to search the corpse for valuables and drag it to the field. After this was done, Fletch said to Jesse and the other recruits, "Do you have a problem with killing a man on suspicion of being a Unionist? Can you do that?"

Jesse blurted, "If that's what it takes to be in this company, yes I can." The others nodded in agreement. Jesse added, "I've got a list of men I know to be Unionist. I want them."

Jabez had remained quiet during the episode, despite feeling guilt for their squad's killing an innocent farmer for no reason other than to test the recruits' appetite for senseless violence. Afterwards, he said nothing and rode at the back of the group.

*

The next day was the first of June, a warm spring day with a soft breeze from the northwest. Early on, the squad was on its way to the two targets chosen by Jesse.

Jabez rode close to Jesse. "You sure you want to kill these men?"

"They're enemy combatants, Jabez. They beat me, they almost lynched Reuben, and they attacked my brother and you and the other raiders the same day. Need any more reasons?"

Jabez saw that dissuading Jesse was not possible, and he drifted to the back of the group once again.

The first target was the James family's neighbor, Brantley Bond. The riders pulled in front of the man's house, and Jesse stayed at the rear with his hat pulled down to hide his face. Jabez did the same, but for a reason different from Jesse's—he was trying to distance himself physically and emotionally from what was to come.

Mrs. Bond came out, drying her hands with a kitchen towel. "Good morning fellows. What can I do for you?"

"Good morning to you, ma'am," Arch said. "May we speak with the man of the house?"

"Yes of course, and would you boys like some spring water?" When they declined, she returned inside.

Soon, Brantley Bond appeared and greeted the riders.

Arch took off his hat in a feigned gesture of respect and said in a pleasant tone, "Good morning, sir, are you Mr. Brantley Bond, the owner of this farm?"

"That's me," said Bond.

"You are in the Union militia, no?"

"I served for a couple years, but now I'm just farming."

Jesse pushed his hat back, loosed the reins, and edged his horse up to the porch steps. "Remember me?"

Bond squinted. "Not sure. Reckon I don't."

"Well, I remember you. I remember when you came to our farm and hit me and kicked me around and almost lynched my step-daddy Reuben Samuel and . . . ." Jesse cut off at that point and jerked his revolver from his belt and shot Bond in the chest.

Bond fell like a sack of coal and writhed on the porch.

Jesse dismounted and slowly walked up the steps and put a bullet into Bond's forehead. He remounted, and the riders wheeled and raced away.

Mrs. Bond ran to the porch, crying "Oh God, oh God, oh Godddddd!"

*

The next stop was the farm of Alvin Dagley, who along with Bond was a member of the militia that swung Reuben and extracted the location of Frank's camp. Dagley was out in his tobacco patch, and the riders walked their horses slowly over to Dagley, who gave them a friendly wave.

Jesse wanted to be the spokesman this time. Again, he had pulled his hat down low on his brow. "Good afternoon. You Mr. Dagley?"

"That's me, Alvin Dagley. What can I do for you soldiers?"

"You're in the Union militia, right?"

"Was," said Dagley. "I ain't now, but I was."

Jesse opened his coat and pushed his hat up. "Remember me?" "Remember when you strung up Reuben Samuel?"

"What's that?" Dagley cocked his head and leaned forward to hear better and get a good look. Dagley barely got those words out of his mouth before Jesse fired his Colt revolver into the man's forehead.

Fletch said to Jesse, "Give me his mule. I'll take it back to his woman and let her know where to find her husband's body."

Jabez was heartsick. He said to himself silently, *I've never felt so trapped in my life. Made to be an accomplice to the most ruthless murders. The only good thing is they didn't make Jesse scalp these men.*

# 27

## FISHING RIVER CAMP

May 1864, Fishing River, Ray County, western Missouri

"Where you headed?" the picket on the chestnut mare asked.

"To the castle," said a young blonde woman in the carriage, giving the password.

"Goooood," said the rider with a laugh. "Who goes?"

"Amanda Thomas. You all call me Rebel. And this is my friend Cait O'Kelly. She's on our side." Amanda reined the two horses pulling the carriage. Cait pulled off her hat, pushed her long red hair away from her eyes, and smiled at the rider. He couldn't find words, yet his mouth was agog. He blushed a bright red. Amanda knew he was gawking at both women.

"Come with me," said the man.

Amanda drove the carriage and followed the rider along a faint roadway until it ended in the woods. Then she moved it into some brush and locked the brake. Amanda and Cait walked behind the rider, dropping down into a wooded hollow and through a stand of blooming downy-white serviceberry and reddish redbud, scattering the blossoms of the serviceberries and redbuds. Wildflowers were in bloom, scattered across the forest floor. They came to a camp in the wilderness, near the point where the Fishing River joins the Missouri, and they entered what looked to be a small cave along the bank of the tributary, formed by a fold in the rock. It was more of a depression than a cave but it was shelter. A group of men slipped out of the woods to greet them.

"I've got some information," Amanda said. "Where's your captain?"

A man took her through the woods to the tent of Fletch Taylor. He greeted them. "We 'preciate you gathering information for us. We know that's dangerous work. You were taking a chance today, just coming over here. The Federals are on the roads."

Amanda said, "My grandparents live not far from here, they're elderly, and I have cause to visit them. I don't believe the Federals would be thinking of me as trouble."

Amanda told Fletch that Cait had come along for other purposes, to meet an old friend. "I hear you have a blacksmith named Jabez Cooper in your unit. Could you ask him to join us?"

Fletch and Amanda retired to their meeting after he sent for Jabez.

*

While Cait waited, she was wondering how Jabez would receive her, given the the way their past relationship had ended. *Does he still think about me? Maybe he hates me, and he'll be annoyed to see me. But maybe he will be happy I came, and he'll want to reconnect too?* She felt nervous and tense. She paced back and forth, chewing on her lower lip. She was irritated with herself for having these nerves.

Meantime, a throng of bushwhackers surrounded her. Women in camp were a magnet, especially beautiful ones like these two. She tried to shed her anxiety in chatter with them and in bursts of loud laughter. Still, she felt on edge.

Shortly, a tall man with brown hair and thick beard and a hat with a feather in the band appeared.

"Is this Jabez?" Cait whooped. "Didn't recognize you with that beard, 'til I saw the feather."

"Yep, Cait, I'm me all right," he replied. "I'm in disguise—it's called bushwhacker fashion."

The other men understood the situation, and they drifted away, some making theatrical whining sounds.

Amanda and Fletch had taken a break from their meeting, and Cait waived her arm toward Amanda. "Come and meet the old friend I told you about."

Cait turned to Jabez. "This is my friend, Amanda Thomas. Bushwhackers call her Rebel. She brings information."

Jabez turned to Amanda. "Well, that's good to know, Rebel. If you were called Yankee we'd have to shoot you."

"Don't shoot! I'm on your side, working in bushwhacker support."

Everyone was laughing.

Amanda and Fletch returned to their meeting, and Jabez found a private place at the edge of camp where he and Cait could talk.

Cait looked at the ground. "Amanda—or should I say Rebel—heard you were with Fletch and his raiders, and when she told me she was coming today, I had to come along. It's been a long time."

"Too long. It's been almost four years since you moved from Liberty. I can remember the exact day you left. You look same as you did that day."

Cait felt her pulse quicken. Her face flushed. She wanted to appear natural, but words were not coming easily. "That was long ago. I live over near Richmond now, and it's not so far from here."

Cait thought Jabez looked nervous too. His voice had a strained sound, and he wasn't making eye contact. Then, smiling, he said, "Cait, I am happy to see you."

Cait puffed her cheeks and made a deep exhale.

Jabez moved closer to her and continued. "But tell me something—I would like to ask you what happened. Why did those letters stop?"

Cait was stunned by his direct question. She looked at the ground, took a deep breath and cleared her throat.

"Jabez, I really don't have a good answer. We were young, I . . . I . . . was immature. I didn't know how to handle a situation like we faced. The distance between Liberty and Columbia was too great, and we never were able to get together." She swept her red hair from her face and looked into his eyes. "I still had feelings for you, but it wasn't working."

Jabez came closer. "You could have told me that, Cait, and as painful as such words are, I would have understood. It woulda been far better than just waiting and not hearing."

She gave a pained look. "I'm sorry," she whispered.

Jabez grinned and stepped back. "I won't hold it against you. I'm just happy to see you again. Will you stay a while? Let me show you around the camp?

Cait felt a surge of relief. "Yes, sure, I can stay to visit with you until we have to leave. You're the reason I came here—I'm not a spy like Amanda. And yes, I would like to get a tour of your camp."

Cait saw Jabez's shoulders drop, and she thought he looked more relaxed.

He smiled. "Good. First, I'd like to show you my forge. My pa made a traveling one back in the time of the Kansas troubles, and me and a few of the boys sneaked it here by wagon in several loads. At some of our camps I have to do my smithing with a campfire and use light tools, but here I have a real forge and real tools, just more compact than what I had back in Liberty."

*

After visiting the forge, Jabez and Cait began a walk through the camp. Jabez was smiling and pointing out features of the hide-out. "Do you have a code name like Rebel?"

She laughed. "No, I'm not a spy—at least not yet. I'm still just Cait."

Jabez made a quizzical, impish face and raised an eyebrow. "Your surname still O'Kelly?"

She laughed again. "Do you mean, am I married now?"

Jabez took off his hat and fingered the feather in its band. "Ha, you got me on that one. Are you married now? You are such a catch, I bet you are. But I don't see a ring."

"Nope. What about you?"

"Naw, who would marry an ugly, filthy bushwhacker?"

"Well, you bushwhackers do seem to need a bath. How long have you been in the brush?"

Jabez made a theatrical count on his fingers. "A bit more than a year."

Cait looked at Jabez as they walked. "That's a long time to be living this way and fighting. Come to think of it, you've been fighting for even longer. I remember you were in the posse at Lawrence back in '56."

"Yeh, well that was mild compared to the raid we made against Lawrence last August. In '56 it was kinda fun. The raid last year was damn bloody and awful."

"But that's war. It's sad, but that's what it takes. Right?"

"I suppose. Let's stop talking about war and take a tour of our camp. You'll need a man like me to protect you from these wolves."

They walked through the woods where men had rigged makeshift tents or simple beds on the ground with their saddles for pillows. After a while Cait pointed to clothes drying on tree limbs and to scattered heaps of food waste. "Y'all need a female touch. This place is an awful mess."

Jabez pointed a finger at her and laughed. "You got that right. Discipline is not our strong point. We're better at chaos. Why don't you move in and get this place in order?"

Cait blushed and looked away.

After the tour of the camp, two men approached. One was a good-looking, slender boy. He had sandy hair, ice-blue eyes, nose turned up at the tip, and an attempt at a new beard. The other, a few years older, was not as striking as the first, but handsome in a rough way. He had long, dark brown hair and a full beard, with a set of jug ears and a nose that occupied considerable territory on his face. The boy was natty, with his clean bushwhacker shirt and combed hair. The other seemed careless in his appearance, made even more so by the wind tousling his long hair.

Jabez hollered, "Ho there, Frank and Jesse, do you remember Cait O'Kelly from years ago back at Liberty? She's come here for a visit. She came with one of our lady spies who is a friend of hers."

Frank threw up his hands. "Cait!—it's been a while. Sure, I remember you. Of course, I know you moved away. Glad you are with us."

Cait smiled. "Frank, it's good to see you again, and I remember Jesse too. He's grown up in the meantime. Jesse, are you fighting or just helping in support?"

"C'mon," Frank said. "He's fighting, and he is a tiger. 'Fraid of nothing and can ride and shoot—almost as good as I can."

Jesse pushed Frank aside. "I joined up to save these old men from the Federals. Things are beginning to look up for the South here in Missouri since I became a bushwhacker."

Frank rolled his eyes and drawled, "Shurrr."

"Say, we're eating blues for supper," said Jesse. "Corn is gonna noodle a few now, and we're going to watch him."

Jabez tugged at Cait's arm. "You want to watch, Cait?"

Cait was puzzled, and she asked, "What does noodling mean? I have no idea." She looked at Jesse. "And who is Corn?"

"You'll see," said Jabez. "Corn is one of the most famous noodlers in western Missouri."

Cait grabbed Jabez by the arm and punched him lightly in the chest. "You all are fooling me. C'mon, what's a noodle? Like Dutch food?"

"Takes too long to explain. You just have to see it for yourself," Jabez said in a teasing tone.

The four walked along the riverbank for about a quarter mile. Jabez pointed to the figure standing on the opposite bank. "There he is. Corn." Jabez called to Corn Thompson, who waved back.

Jabez picked out a flat rock to sit and watch. Frank and Jesse moved down the bank a short distance. The sun had warmed the rock, and Jabez stretched his legs out and balanced on a forearm beside Cait. She bent toward him, and Jabez scooted closer, lightly touching his shoulder against the sleeve of her blouse. Her pulse raced, and she wondered if he had acted accidentally or unconsciously, but then he scooted again, a few inches. Cait felt a sweet, hollow feeling, a light frisson of reconnected attraction. She tilted her head and swung her long red hair faintly against him.

Then she laughed and pushed away. "Where's the noodle."

Jabez pointed toward the stream. "Just watch."

Corn glided into the water near the riverbank.

Jabez said, "We have to be quiet and whisper." He moved close to Cait and bent toward her ear. He whispered, "Now here it comes. You gotta watch what he does in the water."

Corn had moved to the shallows along the bank. He had a long stick in his right hand. His left arm was wrapped in a cloth, with a glove on the hand. He was otherwise naked except for a black fabric around his privates fashioned like an Indian breechcloth. He was moving slowly now along the water's edge, facing the bank, and working the stick under the water's surface, prodding and poking, feeling with the stick.

The catfish, called blues in these parts, were prized food. But a big blue caught by hand-grappling, or noodling as they called it, was the biggest prize. It could be larger than anything you could bring in on a pole, and the catching of it by hand gave the meat entertainment value in table conversation.

Cait whispered to Jabez, "Tell me what's going on." Their faces were almost touching.

Jabez nodded toward the stream. "During the spring the female catfish lays her eggs in the river's hollows and the snags along the bank. The male chases her away, and he settles into guard duty for the eggs. When an intruder comes close to the nest, the male defends by snapping or trying to swallow it. Corn's hand and arm can't be swallowed, but it can be ripped by bony ridges in the catfish's mouth—they're kinda like teeth. That's why Corn is wearing a glove. When the fish clamps on the hand, Corn grips the jaw and pulls the fish out of the water."

Cait's eyes grew, and she shook her head. "I wouldn't put my hand in a hole in the river."

Jabez nodded in the affirmative. "I am with you. Corn says a noodler doesn't always find a catfish back in those holes. Snapping turtles are around. Every now and then some noodler loses a finger to a snapper. Corn uses his stick to probe the creatures in a hole. If he detects a slick surface, it's a turtle. If it feels rough, it's a blue."

Corn signaled by raising his gloved left hand. He moved closer to the hole and crouched. He was a short man, and he was squatting, so only his head and shoulders were above the water's surface. He was moving his covered left arm and gloved hand into the underwater hole. Then his head disappeared.

Cait grabbed Jabez' arm. "Did that fish get him?"

Corn exploded to the surface and sucked in a deep breath. "Look a-here." Corn had his gloved hand in the throat of the fish, pulling it out of the water and holding it tight. He threw on the bank the big, violent thing with whiskers, a wide gasping mouth, and bug eyes. "Supper."

Jabez clapped his hands. "You're a hell of a man, Corn."

Cait laughed and rolled against Jabez. She put her mouth close to his ear and whispered, "You still haven't told me why y'all call this noodling."

Jabez turned and whispered in her ear, lightly brushing it with his beard. "That's a secret in this camp. Sorry, I can't tell you now. Maybe I can give you the secret later. You may wake up one day, and I'll be knockin' on your door."

Cait's heart surged. She could barely breathe. She whispered back, "I'd be pleased to hear that sound."

*

Later, Jabez and Cait walked into the woods and stopped at a small clearing.

"Tell me about your life in Richmond," said Jabez. "How long have you been there? And how's your folks."

"Don't live in Richmond. My place is about half mile west of the town. Not really my place—it's my father's farm he bought just before the war started. About a year later, he and mother decided to move away until the war's over, to his brother's farm in Kentucky. Father said they were too old to tolerate living in a battlefield. Of course, they expected me to go with them, but I said I wanted to stay and take care of the farm. My father and I had a terrible fight about my staying. He said it wasn't safe for a young woman to be living out in the country in the middle of a war. But eventually, he gave in. I think the reasons he agreed were because he knows I can run the farm and because we have hired hands to do the hard physical work. He knows I can take care of myself. Also, I think he was comforted because I persuaded my friend Amanda to share the house with me.”

Jabez lifted his eyebrows. “Aren’t you women scared, living alone in the country? I see your pa’s point.”

“I can handle a gun every bit as well as a man, and Amanda can too. Even if my father was still living there, he wouldn’t be much protection. He’s up in years, as you know.”

Jabez dropped the subject. He gave her a hand while they forded a small creek. They walked silently through the green envelope of trees lining the river’s banks, and he didn’t release her hand.

The two entered the space where the saddles and bridles were arrayed. “What is this? Cait asked, poking her finger on a pelt. “I see it on lots of bridles here.”

Jabez said, “Don’t ask.”

“I’m serious, is that what I think it is?”

He didn’t respond. They stood for a long silence.

“Jabez, are these human scalps?”

His continued silence gave her the answer.

“Do you do that?”

“No, and I never will. And I’ll tell you, it’s eating me up. It’s one of too many awful parts of this war.”

# 28

## O'KELLY FARM

Two weeks later, near Richmond, Ray County, western Missouri

Jabez made certain no one was watching and then slipped from his horse and cut a rose from a garden and stuck it in the band of his hat. He chuckled at the thought that he had taken plunder. A quarter hour later he knocked on a farmhouse door.

"Who's there?"

"Just a bird, a crazy jay."

The door flung open, and Cait screamed, "Jabez! I can't believe it's you. What brings you here? Oh, wait, is this really Jabez? What's that in your hat? Not a bird feather but a flower. You can't really be the Jabez I know."

"Plucked this one for you.

"You are as crazy as ever."

He was laughing, and he pointed a finger at her. "I told you someday I might be knocking on your door."

"Well, come on in. I like this rose bouquet of one. So thoughtful of you. What are you doing now? Have you quit working with Fletch?"

"Just taking a little break to come see you. We have to get out of camp for breaks or we'd go crazy. I don't have to be back for some days."

"Are you staying in Richmond?"

"Well, no, well, uh, I was wondering if you had some place I could lay my head." He held a steady gaze into her eyes.

She didn't look away or blink. She was quiet and didn't

move, a neutral expression on her face. "Might be able to put you up in the pig pen."

"That might be a step up from the camp."

"Based on what I saw on my visit I would agree with you. But now that I'm thinking about it, we do have some space in our hayloft where you could stay. You'll have to do some chores to pay for your lodging. Maybe help my hired hands."

"I can do any needed work on your horses."

She extended her hand. "Sounds like we've struck a bargain."

Jabez shook her hand in agreement. "Are meals included too?"

"Amanda and I are great cooks. This is your lucky day."

"You can say that again."

Cait smiled. "Put your horse in the barn. I'll draw you some water for a bath. You're a sight."

At supper that evening, the two reminisced about their years together in Clay County and their separate histories after Cait and her parents moved away. Jabez was tempted to ask her about her romances, but he restrained the impulse. He was feeling a strong attraction, and he didn't want to ruin the feeling with that kind of talk.

Amanda joined them at the table, and Jabez asked her about her people. Amanda's folks had moved to Texas, to escape the turmoil in western Missouri, and she stayed behind to help in support of the bushwhackers. She said she still had kin in the area, her grandparents lived not far from the camp, and she also had an aunt and uncle who lived in the river town of Glasgow, a few counties to the east.

Jabez was surprised to hear that the aunt's husband was a wealthy Unionist. He teased, "I can't believe two things. First, you have Unionists in your family, and second, you haven't had them shot."

Amanda laughed. "I know, I know.  But they are the kindest folks, have always been so sweet to me and my whole family. And probably they can't believe I am Secesh."

Jabez rubbed his beard. "Let me ask you, why are you a Secesh? And why are you helpin' us bushwhackers?" He often wondered why people wound up on one side or the other of this war.

Amanda said, "I believe people really and truly don't understand what makes them what they are. Maybe we are stamped at birth. Or by our folks. I suppose I'm for the South because my parents and friends are for the South. We don't have slaves, and we don't want to own people. But I like the Southern way of life. It's my known world. Yankees are like foreigners to me."

Jabez turned to Cait. "Why are you a Secesh?"

She rubbed her chin. "I believe we are free to choose, and those choices make us what we are. In this war situation, I chose the side of the world I know, the people I know. I'm a Southern girl. Maybe we should ask you the same question. What about you?"

Jabez laughed at his question circling back to him. "I think I was stamped at birth. As you know, Cait, when the Kansas troubles began, my pa was one of the leaders of the Ruffians. He made me promise to join the Self Defensive Association and fight against the Jayhawkers. Then the war came along. A man had to choose his side. But it was like I didn't make a choice—it was made for me—it was like a giant wind was sweeping me and all my friends into the war and there was only one side to be on, the Southern side. For the reasons you all said."

Cait pressed on, "If the choice was made for you, are you happy with that choice? Would you make a different choice today?"

Jabez flinched inside from the pressure of the question. He felt uncomfortable with the conflicts he had begun to feel, and he was afraid that being honest about those conflicts might endanger the possibility of starting anew with Cait. Worse, he feared Amanda might reveal his thoughts to Fletch.

"I'm not big on war. But yeah, if I have to be in a war, I suppose the only way is to be on the South's side. The thing that I have a hard time with is needless killing. I tell you, there is nothing more dangerous and violent than a pack of twenty-year-old boys with their belts full of revolvers. All of a sudden, farm boys from good families are killing people, not just soldiers but many innocent civilians who are for the other side. Some are neighbors of our boys.

"Life is no longer black and white to me, there's a lot of gray and many shades of that color. And that's odd, because you would think the fighting would make me more of a black and white fella, more of an us versus them fella."

Amanda collected the dishes and went to the kitchen. Cait moved her hand on to Jabez's arm. "I see this is troubling you. I could see it at the camp when we talked about those scalps."

Jabez took a deep breath. "This bushwhacking—it's not like regular army fightin'. It's not battles that are fought by rules, with winners and losers that will decide the outcome of the war. We are just an assassination squad, going around the countryside killing anyone who is loyal to the Union. Sometimes killing fence sitters."

"Doesn't your work help the South to win the war? We think it does."

Jabez worried that he had gone too far. *Cait and Amanda think bushwhackers are heroes. Why do I need to be talking this way? I could lose Cait again.*

But Jabez couldn't dam his feelings. He continued, "I can't see that it does. There's no strategy other than to raise hell, spread terror, and kill Unionists—whether they are soldiers or not."

Cait tightened her hand on Jabez' arm. "Is there something more?"

Jabez looked away and didn't speak for a while. "I keep having these dreams about the men our squad kills. In the regular army part of this war the two sides line up and start firing. They don't hardly aim, they just shoot, and with everybody shootin' at once, it creates a storm of bullets. Yes, people die, but they may be hundreds of feet away. It's army to army. Here, it's killing face to face, and the other face is only a foot or two away. Bam, shoot 'em right in that face. You see their face as it is shocked, as it dies."

Cait rubbed his arm. Despite the comforting touch, Jabez worried again that his revelations would turn her away from him. Still, he continued.

"I had this dream. I was walking into a cave. It was daytime, and the light at the opening faded behind me as I walked deeper into the darkness. Then there was a fluttering like bats flyin' around, but it wasn't bats, it was faces of men and boys our squads have shot on the roadsides and in fields and at their homes or in raids like Lawrence and Baxter Springs. At Baxter Springs, our men killed some young boys in a brass band. For God's sake, they were no threat to us or to the South. Our men scalped some of them. In my dream, I saw some of their faces flying about the cave. This dream has a powerful hold on me. I don't usually have nightmares."

Cait didn't respond, and Jabez looked into her eyes for signs of her thoughts. She rubbed his arm again.

"Worst part is, I can't deal with killing civilians. Like an old farmer just plowing his field, minding his own business, and we come upon him, and we're wearing Federal uniforms, and we ask the man if he is for the Union. What's he gonna say? Of course, he's not gonna say he is Secesh, he's not that stupid. So, he says he is a Lincoln man, and that just signs his death warrant. One of our boys shoots him, or Arch Clement cuts his throat. Why? Because he says he is for the other side, not because he is trying to kill us. And anyway, we don't really know he is for the Union."

Cait had a shocked look. "Good Lord."

The words and emotions tumbled from Jabez. "Just the other day, we ran across a fellow who told us he was getting married the next week, and we asked him who he was for, and of course he said Union, and I know he said so because we had on the blue uniforms, and our men killed him right then and there. I think about his woman, a widow before she is a bride."

Cait groaned. "That's awful, not what I thought our boys were capable of."

Cait rose from the table. "You need some rest to settle your mind and get the old Jabez back. Stay here for a week. It might help you get rid of those worries.

"I'll take you up on that invite.  If anything can get rid of war dreams, I expect a week with you would do it."

# 29

## BLOODY BILL ANDERSON'S GANG

July–August 1864, Platte and Clay Counties, northwestern Missouri

Arch Clement left Fletch Taylor's raiders to join the band of raiders led by his hero Bill Anderson. On July 10, Fletch and his men broke camp on the Fishing River and moved due west to Platte County, north of Kansas City. They murdered an abolitionist minister of the Northern Methodist Church and joined forces with a rebel leader named Coon Thornton to invade Platte City. They met no resistance, as the local branch of the militia mutinied and welcomed the bushwhackers. The raiders looted Unionist shops and rained havoc on the town.

Fletch stabbed a Unionist in the heart and displayed the bloody knife to roars of approval from his men. Jesse James found time to pose for photos in the local photography studio, brandishing his revolvers and striking a pose fit for the theatre. Jabez lay back at the rear of the raiding party. He couldn't stomach another episode of excessively cruel violence against civilians.

In retribution for the bushwhackers' raid and the mutiny of the local militia, Union and Jayhawker forces flooded the Platte City area and burned the town on July 12. Fletch was badly outnumbered, and he instructed his men to scatter and to either rejoin him later or join up with Bill Anderson. Fletch headed south of the Missouri River.

*

Jabez and Frank and Jesse slipped back to the James's family farm in Clay County. At the farm, Frank, Jesse, and Jabez were taking supper when Zerelda showed them a published letter to the editors of the two newspapers in Lexington. Both papers had called on citizens to resist the violence and looting of the bushwhackers, and Bill Anderson had penned the following letter in response:

> Mr. Editors: In reading both your papers I see you urge the policy of the citizens taking up arms to defend their persons and property. You are only asking them to sign their death warrants. Do you not know, sirs, that you have some of Missouri's proudest, best, and noblest sons to cope with? Listen to me, fellow citizens; do not obey this last order. Do not take up arms if you value your lives and property. It is not in my power to save your lives if you do. If you proclaim to be in arms against guerrillas, I will kill you. I will hunt you down like wolves and murder you. You cannot escape. I have chosen guerrilla warfare to revenge myself for the wrongs that I could not honorably avenge otherwise. I have fully glutted my vengeance. I have killed many. I am a guerrilla. I have never belonged to the Confederate Army, nor do my men. Be careful how you act, for my eyes are upon you.
>
> W. Anderson

Jesse read the letter to Jabez and Frank, and said, "We know Anderson. He has balls. He's the worst devil of all of us as far as the Yankees are concerned. That makes him a hero in my eyes. Arch is with him. Let's join his outfit."

Frank had a less than enthusiastic expression on his face. "Anderson turned on Quantrill down in Texas. I don't know if I want to hitch up with a snake."

Jesse pressed the case, noting that they had to join a guerrilla band, because they were wanted men and needed the protection of a gang. He said, "We oughta go with the one who is the strongest and is more likely to fight off Yankees."

Frank shook his head at first, but came around to Jesse's logic. "I'll go with you, but I will keep my eyes on that man."

Jabez thought, *Feels like I go from one trap to another, and I can't seem to break out. Anderson is a devil, evil. He's a cold-blooded killer dyed in the wool.*

Jesse said, "What about you, 'Bez? You with us?"

Jabez looked at the ceiling. "I'm in too." But he realized he agreed because he was afraid to be the odd man out, and he felt a pang of shame. He thought, *There I go again. I can't seem to choose for myself.*

*

Frank, Jesse and Jabez met Anderson in a wooded area near Liberty. It was raining hard, and the four men sat on their horses with their coats pulled tight. Frank said, "As you know, the three of us have been with Fletch Taylor after Quantrill split off. After the Platte raid, Fletch thought things were too hot in our area, and he moved farther south and scattered his band. We'd like to join up with you. You know from Quantrill days that I'm a good fighter and that Jabez here is a blacksmith and farrier, not to mention he's an all-round fixer of broke things. Jesse is a good shooter and rider, as good as the Comanches, and he got some bushwhacker initiation and experience with Fletch. He took the bushwhacker oath and fulfilled it right away."

Anderson looked at Jesse. "Glad you and Jabez are with us, Frank. But I don't know about you, Jesse. How old are you?"

Jesse stood up in his stirrups. "I'll be seventeen in a few weeks. Like Frank said, I'm already a veteran. Arch Clement can speak for me. He's seen me work."

"Little Archie is now my chief devil and the brains of my outfit," said Anderson. "If he says yes, then you're in."

Frank shook hands with Anderson. Then he said, "Why don't you bring your men to my farm?"

"Good idea. That's a deal."

*

The next day, Anderson and his bushwhackers arrived at the James farm. Anderson was wearing all black with yellow piping on his shirt cuffs. Anderson's long, wild, black hair spilled out the back and sides of his black hat. He rode a large black horse.

Bill Anderson was a compulsive counter, measuring brief events, like dressing or loading his pistol, in counts he ticked in his head. He could count off a minute as accurately as a stopwatch. He had a fascination with the number four and tried to arrange matters in groups of that number. He felt an inner pleasure and strength when the afternoon clock reached the fourth hour. He tried to regulate his breathing in measured four second sequences of inhales and exhales. Anderson was driven by emotion and impulse, and he needed a thinker as a minder. His lieutenant, Arch Clement, was that minder.

Anderson, Jesse, and Arch met to discuss the issue of Jesse's joining the Anderson gang. Arch pulled some dry, hairy flaps from his saddlebag.

"Whatcha got?" said Jesse.

"Union scalps. I took all of 'em—with my own knife."

Anderson turned to Jesse. "Could you do that, boy?"

Jesse didn't hesitate. "Damn right."

Arch stuffed the scalps back in his saddlebag and smiled at Jesse. "Jesse's a tiger, Captain. I've seen him work. We can sure use him."

Anderson said, "Well, I'll give you a try, Jesse. We'll make a raid on Tuesday. Be prepared to leave after breakfast. Tell Frank and Jabez too."

August 9, 1864, Platte County, northwestern Missouri
Wearing Federal uniforms, Bill Anderson and his gang

swept like a storm from the James farm, raiding, looting and killing. Approaching a town, they came upon a militia man also dressed in Federal blue walking the road on his way to find a doctor for his mother. Seeing the Federal uniforms, he called out to the disguised raiders. Jesse moved forward of the guerrillas, pulled his revolver and shot the man in the neck and then the face. Anderson tipped his hat to Jesse. The raiders stripped the body of the uniform and left the half-naked corpse beside the road.

The gang surprised a German farmer riding a mule and after learning of his Union sympathies made him serve as a guide to Unionist dwellings. After his men executed three Unionists so identified, Anderson took the farmer into the woods. Anderson asked Jesse to accompany him. The other raiders pushed close to watch.

Anderson directed Jesse to tie the man's hands and commanded the man to fall to his knees. "You are a good fighter, so far, boy. Have you got a strong stomach? We need to deal with this Yankee-loving Dutch. Will you?"

"Sure." Jesse fired his revolver into the farmer's skull. Anderson mounted his black horse to lead the gang back to Clay County.

Jabez turned his head to hide his disgust.

# 30

## JABEZ AND PREACHER



August 1864, O'Kelly farm near Richmond, Ray County,
western Missouri

Jabez had taken leave again, and he was back at Cait's
farm. He and Cait were up early. The day was already hot
and humid. Jabez said these were the dog days of summer. To explain, he said the expression came from the
beliefs of the ancients about a star called the Dog Star.
Greeks and Romans believed this star, the brightest star
in the heavens, was responsible for the heat, humidity,
thunderstorms, and mad dogs of some forty days in July
and August during which the star rises and sets with our
sun, supposedly adding to sun's heat.

"How do you know *that*?" asked Cait.

"My pa," he said, smiling. "He knew so many things.
The moon and the stars included."

The two left the house and wandered the fields and
woods on the farm for an hour or so, talking without
pause. Later in the morning, rain started to fall as a fine
mist. They sat propped against the lee side of a sycamore
tree. The sycamore had a large trunk they both could
lean against, and then the base of the trunk split into twin
pillars rising as if two trees. The two pillars supported a
wide crown and an umbrella of leaves, catching the rain.
The base had taupe-colored bark, but the outer bark on
the limbs above had peeled away, leaving only an under-
skin of white—it was a classic sycamore. Jabez put his
arm around Cait, and she buried her head between his

coat and shirt. He rubbed her neck, and neither spoke for minutes. There was only the sound of the fine rain on the broad sycamore leaves.

"What are you thinking?" said Cait.

Jabez pulled away, and words came streaming. "I have to clear my head. On that last raid I told you about, I knew what was happening to Jesse—he had to show he was as hard and desperate as the devil himself. Anderson raised the bar mighty high for Jesse to jump over and prove he will be a warrior, but I hope Anderson don't make him jump any higher, because Jesse would. He is smitten. And look at Frank, he is so proud of Jesse. I know where this is going, and it is not good.

"To boot, Jesse's best friend now is Little Archie. Arch is as bad as Anderson, maybe worse. He told Jesse that he only feels truly alive when he is fighting. How about that—he only feels alive when he is taking life. Worse, Arch loves playing with that Arkansas Toothpick of a knife he carries. He cuts throats from ear to ear, and he whips off a scalp faster'n a Comanche could. He's got so many scalps on his bridle and saddle bow that he's run out of room and now is passing them out to the other fellas. You know, my blacksmith duties include knife-smithing and keeping knives in good order, and every time I touch Arch's knife, I feel like vomiting."

Cait raised her right hand and interrupted, "No more. I can't take it. So primitive, so savage. Why do they do it?"

Jabez didn't answer her question. "Arch likes the loot too. He said when he was with Anderson's men in Huntsville over in Randolph County last month, they collected over $50,000 in greenbacks and a wagon full of plunder. Every time we shoot someone, even a soldier, Arch makes sure to clean out the wallet. Blood and money! What about the Southern cause? Isn't that supposed to be what this is all about? And it's not just Yankee soldiers and Unionists they take the money from. Anderson has something he calls the contributory tax. It's for protection—he has tax collectors who go to homes and farms and shops of Secesh and ask them to contribute to keeping us in the saddle. Anderson says it's voluntary, meaning you can choose to pay or choose to have your house burned. Guess who Anderson wants to do the burning? You're looking at him."

Cait didn't respond for a while. Then she spoke slowly and in a soft tone. "Well, we always have the freedom to choose. You can quit being a bushwhacker."

Jabez looked away. "A man doesn't have freedom if he's trapped, and I'm feeling trapped right now. Where would I go and what would I do if I quit? All guerrillas, including ex-guerrillas, are subject to being shot on sight or hanged by the Federals. Staying with bushwhackers gives me some amount of protection from the Federals. If I quit, Anderson would have me shot as a deserter. I'm trapped between the Federals and Anderson."

Jabez looked at the ground. He made a fist with his right hand and rubbed it hard with his left. Like before, he was nervous about revealing his feelings to Cait. He thought, *Will she ditch me now?*

But he couldn't stop. "I hate all this killing and butchery and stealing. It's like a stone in my boot that I feel with every step. I don't want any more of it. It took everything in my will power to keep from deserting when I saw Anderson and Jesse shooting a Dutch man, a civilian whose only wrong was that he came from Germany. For God's sake, how is that going to win a war?"

Jabez realized he may have gone too far this time. *But if she leaves me, that's just the way it is. She has to know about these feelings.* So, he continued spilling forth. "I figured I needed to talk to somebody in the outfit about killing and scalping and so forth, so I got some private time with one of the boys in the outfit who is a preacher. He had a little church—Southern Baptist—over in Lafayette

County before he went to the brush. Everybody in the outfit calls him Preacher. Our men think by his being a man of God, he brings us good luck, like a guardian angel sort of thing. Like he keeps God on our side. So, I wanted to ask him, as a man of the Gospel, what did he think about all the killing and mutilating.

"He said he was happy to discuss. It was a sunny day at camp, so he and I went for a long walk. After a while I said, 'Preacher, you are a man of the Bible, what does it tell us about killing in a war?  I know what the Commandment says.'

"He didn't give me a knee-jerk answer, but also I could tell right away this wasn't the first time the question had crossed his mind. He had a big red beard, and he stroked it while he was collecting his thoughts, and then he said, 'Let's sit down on that rock and talk about it.'

"'Jaybird,' he said—he always called me by that nickname—'you ask a very important question. I tell you the truth, I have killed Yankees, yes, and Missouri Unionists, yes, because they are our enemies. This is war. They seek to kill us. Before I joined this outfit, I had to convince myself that God wouldn't punish me for killing them. This is the way I figure it—killing takes place in the Bible. God was on the side of the Israelites, and he commanded them to kill many peoples, many tribes. God was with them when they took down Jericho, for example, and God commanded them to kill all the men and boys and married women in Jericho.'

"I said to Preacher, 'God told them to do *that*? I can't believe he did.' Preacher didn't like being pressed and said something about it being part of a bigger plan—the Jews were God's chosen people.

Once again, Jabez felt doubts about the wisdom of his revelations, and he was looking for signs of approval from Cait. She didn't speak. Just listened.

"Then I asked Preacher, 'Do you think God is on our

side? Does he want us to kill all the Yankees and those here in Missouri that support them?' Before he could answer, I said, 'There are thousands of abolitionist preachers who claim that God is on *their* side.'

"Preacher said he believed the Yankees are the aggressors, and we are just seeking to keep our way of life, so he said yes he believed God was on our side.

"I said, 'But what about the Commandment against killing?'

He said, 'Jaybird, the proper interpretation of the Sixth Commandment is that thou shalt not murder and that's different from killing in war.'

"Then I said, 'But did Jesus ever kill anyone? Or command his disciples to kill anyone? They had enemies.'

Cait interrupted. "What did Preacher say to that?"

"Well, he acted like he didn't hear me. He started to walk away, but I said to Preacher, 'There's another thing I would like to ask. What does the Bible say about scalping and cutting off ears and noses and such in a war?'

"Preacher stopped and turned around. For a long time, he didn't say anything. Then he stroked that red beard and said 'Jaybird, I do not do those things.' That's all he said."

Jabez looked away. "I may have aggravated Preacher by pressing that last question, but his answer told me something I needed to know."

Jabez paused. Neither he nor Cait said a word. She just put her arm around him and kissed his forehead and made a fuss over his getting wet from the rain now coming harder and how he should put his hat on.

Jabez stirred. "Rain's picked up. Let's crawl under that wagon over yonder. Looks dry underneath."

They lay beneath the wagon, curling together, listening to the rain splattering on the wood, and inhaling the rich smell of wet earth. Jabez caressed her cheek and traced his finger around her eyes and along her nose and lips. "I like the way your skin feels. It's like touching velvet."

Cait smiled. "I love your touch."

After a while, Jabez asked, "What are you thinking?" He was almost afraid to hear the answer.

Cait rested her head on his chest. "What am I thinking? I'm thinking about your hurting heart my cheek is against. I know the conflict in your mind and feelings. You are probably not the only bushwhacker who feels the way you do. And I know you are in a trap that you can't escape, at least not now. I'm feeling for you."

Jabez mumbled, "I 'preciate that."

Cait cleared her throat. "I see that you have to make a choice. You know, people are both blessed and cursed with the freedom to choose. We can't not have the freedom to choose. We may choose one thing or another as a way out of a trap, or we may also choose to do nothing, choose not to choose. Have you been choosing not to choose?"

Jabez knew she was right. *Smart woman*, he mused. He couldn't respond for almost a minute, trying to find the words. "If you put a gun to my head today and said 'choose or die' I would choose to quit this war. But, to tell the truth, I can't bring myself to make that choice. Maybe I'm afraid of the consequences. Maybe I feel loyalty to my fellow bushwhackers. Loyalty to my friends. Loyalty to Pa. Loyalty to the South. Maybe the most important reason I can't bring myself to quit is because I'm afraid if I do, I'll lose you."

After Jabez spoke the last sentence, there was an awkward silence. He scanned her face to try to read her thoughts. He thought, *Damn. I shouldn't a-said that.* He held his breath.

Cait finally spoke. "What will it take for me to show you I'm with you whatever you decide?"

Jabez exhaled. *Fine woman, I'm a lucky man.*

The rain came harder, and the two stayed under the wagon for a time. Then they got up and made their way toward the farmhouse.

"What's for supper?" he asked. "Fried chicken, I hope. I can almost taste it."

"We can do that."

Jabez spun in a circle. "I'll sing you all some songs for my supper."

"I love your singing. Amanda will too. You're so good at it. Especially those ballads. I remember you sang a lot back in Liberty."

"I miss those days."

She smiled. "Do you know what I'm thinking now?"

"Nope. Tell me." He pushed his face to hers, their lips brushing.

She kissed him. "I'm thinking I'll start calling you Jaybird."

Jabez pulled off his hat and swatted at Cait. "Get outta here."

# 31

## JESSE TAKES A BULLET

Jabez Cooper: *In August of '64, we—Frank, Jesse, and I—were on the move with Bill Anderson and his raiders. August had been a month of raiding in Platte, Clay, and Ray Counties, with no meaningful resistance from Yankee soldiers or Union militia. Jesse was developing a reputation as one of the best fighters in our outfit, and Anderson and Little Arch gave him special praise. Anderson called him the cleanest fighter in the bunch. Compliments like that from Clement and Anderson usually meant that a fighter was a brutal killer who would go out of his way to kill any Union supporters, soldier or civilian, and I found such fighting behavior to be disgusting, if not immoral. But I was still a member of the Anderson gang.*

*So that Jesse wouldn't get a big head from all that praise from our leaders, everyone joked him about how he was too young to grow a real beard. Not to mention he looked way younger than his age, and his voice was high-pitched.*

*Late in the month we were slashing through Ray County, and for a day or two after one of our raids, we broke into small groups like as usual, with plans to meet at a designated site. Frank, Jesse, and I were traveling along together, in no special hurry. Jesse spied a saddle sitting on a fence, and he said to me 'I like the looks of that saddle. It's like new and way better'n the one I got. Think it's time for a swap.' And in a flash he unhitched his saddle and slid it on the fence rail and swapped it for the new one.*

*As Jesse cinched the new saddle and remounted, I heard a musket crack and saw Jesse pitch to the side. Frank propped him up in the saddle, and I looked toward the sound and saw an old fellow running into his cornfield. It musta been his saddle. Frank saw him too and fired his revolver toward the man, but didn't hit him, and the man kept running. Frank was calling him a sonofabitch and tried to ride after him, but Jesse needed care right away, so I called Frank back to help Jesse.*

*Jesse said, 'I've been hit in the chest, but I can ride. Let's get the hell out of here, there may be others.'*

*I pulled his coat and shirt back and saw that a ball had entered just outside and above his right nipple and had passed clean through his chest and out his back. We were in the middle of nowhere, and we needed to get medical help right away. We rode side by side, with me holding him up straight in that new saddle, that cursed saddle. There was blood but not too much, and at first Jesse didn't seem to be in pain. We went about a mile or so before the sharp pain set in, and he was moaning bad. I was giving him water, and saying he was going to be just fine, and I tell you that boy of not yet seventeen was strong as iron.*

*We must have gone about three more miles total when some of our outfit came along in a wagon. Jesse said he didn't care if he died, the pain was so bad. We took Jesse by wagon to the farm of a Secesh that one of the boys knew. They hid Jesse in the attic. The farm was on the Missouri River, and Frank went by boat to Kansas City to get a doctor who came to see Jesse after a few days and said the ball sure enough did go through the lung and out. He told us the lungs can heal and thank goodness the ball was not a Minié ball, because a Minié makes a terrible wound.*

# JESSE TAKES A BULLET

*The doctor did all he could, but it was mainly to put poultices on the entry and exit wounds. Frank and I came back to stay with Jesse, and within a month he had recovered enough to join up with Anderson again.*

*It was like a miracle.*

# 32

## A CIRCLE OF FIRE

August 1864, Cooper County, central Missouri

The ferry at the Boonville crossing of the Missouri was packed with the horses and men of a Union militia patrol. As the troops disembarked, the leader tipped his hat to the ferry operator. "You're a great and loyal friend of the Union. We'll bring you some demijohns of whiskey when this war's over."

The operator smiled and waved his hat. "Good hunting!"

The patrol was part of the Fourth Missouri State Militia, and they were searching for Bill Anderson and his guerrillas. Anderson, now a terrifying presence in central as well as western Missouri, was wanted by the military leadership, dead or alive, but preferably dead. The patrol headed north toward Fayette and the Federal garrison there.

Shortly, the road narrowed, hemmed in by thickets on both sides. After a bend in the road, the militiamen saw two horsemen wearing bushwhacker-style shirts, and the leader called the riders to halt. The two spurred their horses forward, and the Federals made hot pursuit. It was a decoy trap, an ambush. From the woods exploded Anderson and his men, racing toward the patrol, screeching the rebel yell and firing their revolvers. Before the militiamen could turn around and retreat back down the road toward the river, the raiders were on them, dropping a dozen or more with pistol shots at close range.

Seven of the militiamen were still alive and writhing on the ground, and the raiders circled them, then dismounted.

"Take their uniforms," ordered Anderson.

His men stripped both the dead and the injured and pulled their bodies into a collected mass in the middle of the road. Anderson tied his black horse and walked over to the half-naked bodies. Sweat dripped from his beard, and he paused to look each of the injured in the eyes. "All right, Arch, go to work."

Arch slipped out his long knife and grabbed the hair of a dead soldier and quickly scalped him. Then Arch said to the other injured soldiers, "That's gonna be you."

The living injured screamed and yelled, some struggled to their feet and tried to run, and Anderson's men shot them. Arch then went one by one to those who were too injured to struggle and cut their throats. Then he and another guerrilla finished the task of taking scalps, and they hanged a scalped victim from a tree and attached a scribbled note, Clement skalpt me.

Anderson divided his troops and sent all but twenty-eight scattering into the nearby hills. He took the twenty-eight east to the river town of Rocheport, a Secesh stronghold fifteen miles from Columbia, where he was warmly greeted. Anderson proclaimed the town his capital and settled in for a two-week respite from the war.

*

September 12, 1864, near Rocheport, Boone County, Missouri
Five raiders were designated as collectors of Anderson's contributory tax, and during the pause at Rocheport they worked the town and countryside. Rain set in during the morning of September 12, and it was obvious that it would last all day if not longer. The five took shelter in the barn of a Secesh widow, where they took the opportunity to clean their weapons and curry their horses. Saddles, blan-

kets, bedrolls, and revolvers were spread over the barn floor.

Nobody expected the Federals would be on patrol in this weather. But they were wrong—a militia patrol of twenty-five men had picked up the guerrillas' muddy trail, following them to the barn. The militia burst in on the unprepared men and in a firefight killed all of the raiders.

The militia leader commanded his men to saddle the bushwhackers' horses and lead them back to Columbia. One of the men dealing with the horses shouted, "My God, look at this." He pointed to the scalps dangling from the bridles.

September 21, 1864, Rocheport, Boone County, Missouri
When Jesse James walked into Anderson's camp, the raiders surrounded him and crowded close.

"We thought you was a goner," said one.

"Are you a ghost?" asked another.

"We heard that musket ball went clear through your lungs and out the other side. Is that true?" said a third.

Jesse was smiling and parading around the group, his shoulders thrown back, his head high. "It hurt like hell, but I ain't gonna let a goddamn Unionist stop me."

Anderson walked up to the circle, which parted to allow him to approach Jesse. He put his arm around the boy's shoulder. "You're a tough boy. And what's this I see on your face? Is that a beard?"

The raiders laughed, and Jesse did too.

"Not only did this wound make me tougher, I turned seventeen while I was recuperating. I'm ready for anything the Federals dish out," squeaked Jesse in his high voice.

Anderson looked at the crowd that had formed around Jesse. "Well, we are gonna put you to work, boy. Those bluecoats killed our tax collectors. Sombitches just left them in a widow's barn for her to bury. They were some of our finest men. We'll have vengeance, and soon."

September 23, 1864, Boone County, central Missouri
A supply train of eighteen wagons filed up the road between Columbia and Fayette, guarded by eighty Union militiamen. From the woods burst Anderson's men. The militiamen wheeled in confusion. Some dropped from wounds as the bushwhackers fired on them, but most fled in panic. Twelve militiamen and three teamsters raised their hands in surrender. Then, a quiet fell.

Jabez grimaced at what he knew would come. Arch turned to the surrendered. "Remove your uniforms and stand in line on the roadside."

The men complied, sobbing for their lives. The raiders, some on horseback some on foot, pressed close to the fifteen surrendered men.

Jabez tightened every fiber in his body. He wished he could stop time, freeze the action. But he knew he had no power to stop the scene to come. Anderson ordered Jabez to organize some men to burn the wagon and supplies, and Jabez was relieved to get the assignment to deal with property rather than humans.

Anderson walked to the surrendered. He spoke softly, "Gentlemen, we fly the black flag—we don't take prisoners," and at that signal the raiders shot all fifteen prisoners.

Arch and two others made quick work of the scalping. Jabez and his group proceeded with burning the wagon train.

*

After the killing and was burning finished, the raiders split into small groups on a signal from Anderson and headed in various directions, some took the road and some fled into the woods. Cave Wyatt, Anderson's "sergeant," led a splinter group of eight that chose to take the road toward

Fayette. It was an unfortunate choice, because the Union militia based in Fayette had learned of the massacre and had sent a detachment to the scene. When they met the bushwhacker group, they overwhelmed Cave and his men. Cave was wounded and taken prisoner, and six of his men were killed.

The militia leader said, "Men, it's time to take our revenge. Eye for an eye, scalp for a scalp. Scalp those criminals." As the militiamen obeyed the order, someone grabbed Cave, but the militia leader said, "Don't harm him. I want him alive and as a prisoner."

One of Cave's men, a bushwhacker named Albert, had slipped into the woods during the skirmish, and he watched the scene unfold.

*

September 23–26, 1864, A Circle of Counties: Boone, Howard, Randolph

Bill Anderson and the strands of his scattered bushwhackers collected back at their camp near Rocheport. In the late afternoon, Albert, the survivor of the skirmish with the Union militia from Fayette, rode into the camp and sent word to Anderson that he had information about the skirmish.

"It was awful," Albert said. We were headed up the road in the direction of Fayette. We were going to take the first side road back to Rocheport, but then this troop of militia came in the opposite direction, I suppose from Fayette. Those goddamn bluebellies killed and scalped every one of our fellows, except me and Cave. I escaped. They took Cave prisoner."

Anderson walked through camp and to the tent of Arch. He relayed the account he had heard from Albert and slapped his hand against a tree. "I'm taking this news hard. First they murdered our tax collectors, now these men. And they're taking scalps now. We have to take our vengeance. I want to strike them at their base in Fayette."

Arch said, "Let's think this out. They've got a big garrison at Fayette. It's well fortified, and we might run into a wall of fire. A fight like that is not our style. We can do vengeance better by ambush."

Anderson was agitated and in no mood to think anything out. "No, I'm madder'n hell. I want to hit 'em hard, wipe 'em out, send a big message to Washington."

*

The next morning was clear and cool, good weather for a fight. After a sunrise breakfast, Anderson's gang of some two hundred dressed in Union uniforms, decamped and rode toward Fayette, thirteen miles to the northwest.

Nearing Fayette, Anderson and his men saw a cloud of dust and heard the loud thumping of hooves. It was a group of over a hundred mounted men. Many wore Federal uniforms.

Arch was looking through field glasses. "They're either Federals or guerrillas in blue uniforms." The riders came closer. Arch confirmed that they were bushwhackers. He rode over and spoke to the leaders. He returned and said, "That's George Todd, and he has pulled in Pool and Thrailkill. And even—can you believe it?—Quantrill and about a dozen of his men."

Anderson asked the chieftains to meet with him and Arch. In the meeting, Anderson started with the basics, "What are y'all doing here?"

Todd laughed. "What are we doing? We're doing the same thing you are—looking for Yankees to hit."

Anderson was annoyed and smirked his response, "Smart ass."

Todd laughed again. "All right then, General Price is marching his army up from Arkansas to liberate Missouri. Price is headed to St. Louis, and then he'll turn west to take Jefferson City, which officially will add Missouri to the Confederacy, and then he'll cross the state to Kansas City. Price wants us guerrillas to tear up the railroads, rip down telegraph lines, and tie up Yankee troops on the north side of the Missouri. Price's troops are a scraggly bunch—poorly equipped and many unarmed—and Price hopes we and other irregulars will join him as he plows through the state. When he comes past Jefferson City, we can cross the Missouri and join him."

Anderson said it made sense for his men and Todd's to join forces to carry out Price's instructions, and then meet up with Price when he comes past the capital. Todd agreed.

Anderson smiled and lifted a finger. "I don't know what you fellas had planned today, but if you are not otherwise engaged, I've got an idea to occupy your time. We can take that Union militia garrison at Fayette. I've got a special bone to pick with the Federals based there. I think it will not be difficult—most of their men are out in the field looking for me. My band can go in first. We have Federal uniforms and can practically walk into their headquarters. Easy. We'll start things off, and then you all can come along and add the finishing touch. The town will be ours."

Todd grinned. "I like it."

Quantrill rose and said, "I disagree. After the first, shot the militia will jump behind brick and stone. They'll be protected by the brick courthouse and the stone bank building. That's not our kind of fight. We fight close-up with revolvers, which are just pea-shooters against fortifications at distance."

Anderson walked up to Quantrill and stood inches from him. "There you go again. Captain Over-cautious."

A heated argument followed. Arch supported the Quantrill view, noting that ambush was the most effective way to attack Union forces. But Anderson and Todd were the principals, and it was clear that their plan would go forward.

Anderson sneered to Quantrill, "You're welcome to join us, but we don't need you."

     *

Late in the morning, Anderson and his blue-uniformed men walked their horses into the streets of Fayette, as if they were a returning Union patrol. Nearing the Federal garrison, one of the guerrillas in the lead spotted a black man wearing a Union uniform. He pulled his revolver and shot the man. The unmistakable sound of the firing revolver sparked an immediate response by the small contingent of militiamen who were downtown. Twenty militiamen ran into the courthouse, bolted the doors, and the battle was on. The militia was well protected by the bricks, and after a half hour of futile attempts, Anderson and Arch agreed that they should quit this skirmish and attack the militia camp on the edge of town, where the main militia force was likely to be—in tents.

As the guerrillas migrated towards the tent camp, word passed quickly to the militia troops that the attack was coming, and they sprinted from their tents to large cabins they had recently built from thick logs and railroad ties. The troops pushed out chinking here and there from the walls to make gunports. Enfield rifles protruded like porcupine quills from the holes. From a distance, the guerrillas' revolvers were again useless, and the attackers were being torn to pieces by rifle fire.

Jabez, Frank, and Jesse crawled to fallen guerrillas and wrapped them in blankets to drag them out of the line of fire.

A momentary pause in the shooting gave the rescuers a break, and they rested in a grove of trees. Pulling the injured to safety was frightening and exhausting for Jabez. "This is the worst fight I've ever seen," Jabez said. We should have listened to Arch. He's got brains. Anderson's just got balls. Anderson only knows one command, and that's Kill!"

Jesse said, "Why the hell did Sam shoot that nigger soldier? We would have taken the garrison if that fool had not lost his head."

Jabez thought of the Negro soldiers killed at Baxter Springs. He pictured Briggins's corpse. Why do our men want to kill colored soldiers more than they want to kill white soldiers? I don't get it.

Then, Quantrill pulled out, took his men, and left the Anderson and Todd bands on the field. Shortly after, Anderson and Todd withdrew their men too and moved some miles to a secluded wood where they bivouacked.

*

The next day, the 25th, Anderson and Todd moved their guerrillas to a nearby town, Huntsville, the site of another Union garrison. Anderson sent a demand for surrender to the commander of the garrison, but the commandant refused.

Todd said to Anderson, "If you want a repeat of Fayette go ahead and attack, but you're gonna have to do it without me and my men."

Anderson backed down, but he was bitter that Todd had made his threat to the Federals into a bluff, and that the bluff was called. The two bands moved east toward another Union garrison—this one at the town of Paris. Soon the men learned that the garrison was formidable, so they abandoned that plan. The next day, they headed south to make camp at a farm a few miles from the small town of Centralia. They were back in Boone County again after making a frustrating circle. Anderson's anger simmered.

# 33

## CAMPFIRE

September 26, 1864, near Centralia, Boone County, central Missouri

The night of September 26, more than three hundred raiders under the commands of Anderson and Todd camped at a Secesh farm along Young's Creek, a few miles southeast of the town of Centralia. Campfires burned in the evening twilight. The men were generally in a bad mood. Their combined forces had showed poorly at Fayette, where they lost five men dead and a score injured without any result, and then they had backed down from attacking the garrisons at Huntsville and Paris.

At a private meeting, Anderson and Todd discussed next steps with Arch Clement, Si Gordon, John Thrailkill, Dave Pool, and Preacher Tom Todd (no kin to George). The foul mood of the assembled men had erased any semblance of camaraderie.

On top of the failed campaign of the last few days, the recent scalping of Anderson's tax collectors had rubbed salt in the psychic wounds. As the men milled around, Arch Clement said to Anderson, "We're supposed to be the scalpers."

Anderson looked away and muttered, "Go to hell."

Talk turned to the news of the war in other regions. The fall of Atlanta was another depressing factor souring the mood of the assembly.

George Todd said, "It's bad that we lost Atlanta—sure. But we need to focus on what lies ahead. Lee is holding strong in Virginia. General Price invaded Missouri from his base in Arkansas a week ago. Southern victory here in Missouri will make the Yankees wish for an end to this war. Maybe they'll be so sick of fighting that Lincoln will lose the election."

Arch said, "Yeh. We can do some good work tomorrow in Centralia. They just built a depot at the station, and every supply train on the North Missouri line between St. Louis and Kansas City stops there. The town is easy pickings for plunder, and we can burn the depot and knock off a train or two. All we need is about fifty or sixty men. Then the Federals will come after us, but they don't stand a chance against all the bushwhackers here. The Federals won't know what hit them."

Todd said, "You can have the plunder in Centralia. You and Anderson use *your* men. I'm more interested in the fight with the Yankees when they come after you. My men can join you when you all come back. What I want you to find out in Centralia is where Price is now and how he is doing. Maybe someone on the train will have a newspaper."

*

After supper, Arch Clement went to the campfires of Anderson guerrillas to sketch the plan. "Tomorrow we go to Centralia, just Anderson men. It's about five miles down the pike, and we'll learn what is happening with Price and his men. While we're there we can raise some hell. We'll take over the town, cut telegraph wires, wreck the depot, and take down any trains coming through. If the trains have passengers, we'll collect greenbacks and jewelry. We're gonna raise so much hell that the Federals will be coming after us. They're stationed not far away, in Sturgeon. If we draw them out, all of our bands will join together to take them on. We can whip their ass and help relieve the pressure on Price a bit. We don't need our entire company.  I'll choose who goes."

# CAMPFIRE

Jesse James said, "Count me in for that trip."  He tapped the broad blade of his Bowie knife flat against his palm in rapid beats. "Never been to Centralia before."

Brother Frank didn't volunteer.

Arch said, "Jabez we'll need you to go along, to fire that depot."

*

Later, at one of the campfires where Anderson men were taking whiskey and swapping tales, several men asked Jabez to sing. He was the best singer in the bunch, and he knew many of the ballads that had come from the British Isles.

"Sing us a ballad, Jaybird," said Preacher.

Jabez never passed on an opportunity to show off his tenor voice. "What about that old Scottish ballad, Barb'ra Allen?" Whether the men accepted or not, that was the song he was going to sing.

Jabez cleared his throat, breathed deeply, vibrated his vocal cords in preparation and lilted,

In Scarlet Town, where I was born,
There was a fair maid dwellin',
Made ev'ry youth cry "Well-a-day!"
Her name was Barb'ra Allen.

All in the merry month of May
When green buds they were swellin',
Young Jemmy Grove on his death-bed lay
For love of Barb'ra Allen.

Then slowly, slowly she came up,
And slowly she came nigh him,
And all she said when there she came,
"Young man, I think you're dying."

As she was walking o'er the fields

She heard the dead-bell knellin',
And ev'ry stroke the dead-bell gave
Cried "Woe to Barb'ra Allen!"

When he was dead and laid in grave
Her heart was struck with sorrow.
"O mother, mother, make my bed,
For I shall die tomorrow."

"Farewell," she said, "ye virgins all,
And shun the fault I fell in;
Henceforth take warning by the fall
Of cruel Barb'ra Allen.

The men clapped. The dark mood was lifting. Someone said, "Wha'd she do?" There was no answer, and the mood dropped again.

Arch rose and circled the fire, pacing slowly, and all eyes were glued to his diminutive figure. The shadow cast by the fire, and the effects of whiskey on the men, seemed to enlarge Arch's size. "Frank, I heard you're a Shakespeare scholar. That true? You been in the brush now for over a year. Why didn't you tell us?"

Frank was leaning back against the pillow he had made of his saddle, with his hands behind his head, and he drawled, "I reckon I've read a lot of Shakespeare, that's true, and even seen some of his plays in Kansas City, but I don't know about being a scholar."

Jesse said, "Everybody in Clay County knows Frank can recite over a thousand lines of Shakespeare from memory."

Arch came near Frank. "That true, Frank?"

"I don't know. I don't count 'em. But I do know by heart some of my favorites."

Arch spoke in a loud voice so all around the fire could hear. "Tell us some Shakespeare. I know he wrote about a lot of battles. What's your favorite battle scene?"

Frank sat up, put his chin in his hand and looked down at the ground. "Well, I would say that the scene on the eve of the battle at Agincourt is my favorite."

Arch rushed toward Frank and bent to his face. "Tell us about it. C'mon. We'll have some Shakespeare tonight." Arch turned to the men around the fire. "Y'all tell the boys at the campfires over yonder to come and listen to Frank."

Men from several fires drifted over.

Frank rose and took his book of Shakespeare's plays from his saddlebag. He walked to a corner of the fire, standing tall in its orange glow. "All right. This is from a play called *Henry V*. I know some of this speech by heart but not all. So, I'm going to read it.

"In the play the English army under King Henry defeats the French army at a place in France called Agincourt. Most of the English soldiers at Agincourt are longbow archers."

Jesse blurted, "Frank and I can handle a bow."

Frank continued, "There's this scene before the Agincourt battle. The French army greatly outnumbers the English army, and the battle is going to be on French soil, so the chances of death are very high. To get his men ready for a bloody fight that was likely gonna be fatal, King Henry gives this speech. It's sometimes called the St. Crispin speech because it was given on St. Crispin's Day. . . ."

Frank paused. "Whatever in the hell St. Crispin's Day is."

The crowd laughed.

"Well, I should be serious. This speech is mighty. People say it will live forever."

Frank thumbed through the pages of the book to find the passage. "I said the English were outnumbered. I mean it was something like five or six to one. There was a good chance the English army would be destroyed, and

King Henry would be killed or captured."

Frank moved close to the fire so he could read in the dim light. "It's in old English, so I'm gonna say the words slow." He held the book in his left hand and flung his right arm in gestures matching the words, cupping his hand and then gripping the fingers into a fist.

"King Henry's cousin Westmoreland speaks, and he says he wishes that they had more men, a fraction of the men taking their rest in England on St. Crispin's Day. The King brushes off that wish and makes this speech to his soldiers in answer."

What's he that wishes so?
My cousin, Westmorland? No, my fair cousin;
If we are mark'd to die, we are enough
To do our country loss; and if to live,
The fewer men, the greater share of honour.
God's will! I pray thee, wish not one man more.
By Jove, I am not covetous for gold,
Nor care I who doth feed upon my cost;
It yearns me not if men my garments wear;
Such outward things dwell not in my desires.
But if it be a sin to covet honour,
I am the most offending soul alive.
No, faith, my coz, wish not a man from England.
God's peace! I would not lose so great an honour
As one man more methinks would share from me
For the best hope I have. O, do not wish one more!
Rather proclaim it, Westmorland, through my host,
That he which hath no stomach to this fight,
Let him depart; his passport shall be made,
And crowns for convoy put into his purse;
We would not die in that man's company
That fears his fellowship to die with us.
This day is call'd the feast of Crispian.

# CAMPFIRE

He that outlives this day, and comes safe home,
Will stand a tip-toe when this day is nam'd,
And rouse him at the name of Crispian.
He that shall live this day, and see old age,
Will yearly on the vigil feast his neighbours,
And say "To-morrow is Saint Crispian."
Then will he strip his sleeve and show his scars,
And say "These wounds I had on Crispin's day."
Old men forget; yet all shall be forgot,
But he'll remember, with advantages,
What feats he did that day. Then shall our names,
Familiar in his mouth as household words—
Harry the King, Bedford and Exeter, Warwick
and Talbot, Salisbury and Gloucester—
Be in their flowing cups freshly rememb'red.
This story shall the good man teach his son;
And Crispin Crispian shall ne'er go by,
From this day to the ending of the world,
But we in it shall be rememberèd—
We few, we happy few, we band of brothers;
For he to-day that sheds his blood with me
Shall be my brother; be he ne'er so vile,
This day shall gentle his condition;
And gentlemen in England now a-bed
Shall think themselves accurs'd they were not here,
And hold their manhoods cheap whiles any speaks
That fought with us upon Saint Crispin's day.

The men gawked silently at Frank until they could see
it was finished, and then one said, "Shitfire, Frank, that
was beautiful," and a cheer went up. Whiskey jugs were
passed around again.

Jabez was thinking, *What makes such a man as Frank?
He is a complicated fella, quiet and kind, fun to be around,
and he knows a lot about Shakespeare, but he can shoot an*

*innocent man between the eyes. Maybe those opposites ain't so unusual in people. Or maybe it's the tragedy that this war does to a good man.*

Arch Clement came beside Frank and spoke in a voice so all could hear, "You sure know your Shakespeare, Frank. Now I ask you this, what is the cruelest scene in Shakespeare?"

Frank put a hand to his chin. "There are so many bloody scenes in Shakespeare. He was blood and guts in so many plays. But maybe the cruelest scene I can think of is from *King Lear*."

"C'mon fellows, listen here. Tell us, Frank."

"*King Lear* is a play about an old king named Lear who decides to give away his kingdom to his three daughters. He sets up a test to see which daughter loves him the most, and the winner will get the biggest share. But one of them—who really does love him the most—refuses to play that game. Old Lear thinks that's a sign she doesn't love him, and he doesn't give her anything. The other two daughters actually hate him, and after the two get hold of the kingdom, they and their husbands turn old Lear out."

Frank paused to get his breath and clear his throat. "Old Lear winds up wandering in a wilderness with brambles and thickets. At this point, he's a raving madman because of what his daughters have done to him. King Lear has this friend, a nobleman, name of Gloucester, who is taking up for Lear and trying to save him. The evil daughters and their husbands arrest Gloucester, accuse him of treason, and bind him up with a rope. They can't kill Gloucester without a trial, so at the command of one of the evil daughters, her husband rips out one of Gloucester's eyes, throws it on the floor and stomps it. Then, he plucks Gloucester's other eye out."

"What?!" cried someone. "That's horrible."

"Remember, this was hundreds of years ago. Life was brutal."

Frank recalled his chain of thought that had been interrupted, then continued, "They cast this poor blind man out into the countryside. The play gets even bloodier after that scene, and just about everyone in the play dies. It's a very sad play. But the scene of old Gloucester getting his eyeballs gouged out, thanks to Lear's daughters, is—to me—the cruelest of all scenes in Shakespeare.

Cries rose from the audience—"Oh God, that's awful!" "Bitches!" "Witches!" "God Damn them to hell!"

"What was Shakespeare's point?" asked Arch.

"I can't rightly say," said Frank. "Maybe it was don't give your property to your children while you're still alive."

Everyone laughed.

Arch said, "Maybe. Or maybe the point was you need to be cruel sometimes to get what you want."

# 34

## CENTRALIA

September 27, 1864, Centralia, Boone County, central Missouri
A white-oak barrel of whiskey rested in the early morning shadows of the baggage porch beside the new depot at the railroad station in Centralia, Missouri, awaiting transport to Kansas City on the next train. The porch provided cool shade from the Indian-summer sun that was already beginning to heat the cloudless morning. The barrel stood thirty-five inches tall, with a twenty-one inch diameter at top and bottom and a center diameter of twenty-four inches. It was banded in three places by metal straps four inches wide. Empty, it weighed about a hundred twenty pounds, and now full of the brown liquid it weighed over five hundred. It held fifty-three gallons of corn whiskey aged three years. The mark of the distiller had been burned into the wood.

An axe split and slivered the cover boards of the barrel, sloshing a small bit over the side and onto the floor. The man who wielded the axe lifted the tool above his head and spun around, grinning through the beard that framed his round face. A cheer rose, and a flock of guerrillas rushed the porch.

John the Baptist Oliver, called Jack, was first to the open barrel. He pushed his face above the liquid, inhaled deeply, drew back, looked to the sky, spread his arms, and  burst out with utter joy. "Damn, we got a barrel of fine stuff, this ain't no bust-head." He dipped his face into the liquid and sucked in a mouthful.

The man with the axe grabbed Jack's collar and pulled him back. "Dammit, Jack don't you defile this booty. You're drinking this stuff like an animal." As he reeled backward, Jack cupped his hands together and lifted a puddle to his mouth.

Others crowded around the barrel. The man with the axe made them line up. A bushwhacker who got the third place in line said he didn't want to lose his proximity to the barrel, and he let go his water beside the cask. The crowd moaned "Awwww" and pushed him off the porch, his piss spraying wildly as he stumbled.

Men ran whooping to the general merchandise store and the two hotels to find vessels for the whiskey. Some ran into houses demanding cups or glasses.

A man unfurled the Black Flag and hung it on the boarding platform of the depot.

Bill Anderson and Arch Clement entered the Eldorado Hotel. Arch opened his coat to display the two revolvers and the Bowie knife tucked in his belt. The proprietor gave them seats at a table in the dining area. Anderson demanded a whiskey. Four guerrillas entered the hotel and went to the corner rooms on the top story to keep an eye out for signs of approaching Federals.

Guerrillas dressed in Federal uniforms fanned out in the town. One group began to loot the general merchandise store, and they strew ladies' undergarments and bolts of cloth in the streets. A guerrilla discovered three cases of new boots at the depot. He cracked open the cases and rushed armloads of the boots to the whiskey barrel to be filled with the dark liquor and tied to saddle horns for transport back to camp. Another found a supply of bottled whiskey in the store and passed the bottles around to the pillagers.

The area was a flat plain, and the second story of the Eldorado Hotel provided a full view of the surroundings. The lookouts saw a cloud of dust approaching town—a stagecoach—and eight of the guerrillas rode out and stopped it. One of the guerrillas said, "If anyone has a gun, tell me now, or you may be in your last moments." A passenger handed over his revolver. No one else moved.

"Get out your pocketbooks, gentlemen, it's time to pay for the protection we're giving to this fair state."

"But we're *for* the South," said a passenger.

"Why you not fightin' then? If you not fight, you must pay tax."

"I'm a preacher. For the *Southern* Methodist Church," said the passenger.

"Well now, Brother, I'm glad you are preaching for the South, since God is on our side, but you know, preachers need protection too. We're just collecting the tax, that's all."

All pocketbooks were taken, and the stagecoach slowly entered Centralia, where the whiskey-stimulated guerrillas were running through yards and houses, yelling about killing Unionists. Two men removed the horses from the stagecoach for future use by the raiders.

Three men on horseback trailed bolts of calico behind them in a cascading stream of color as they raced through the main street. A group of horsemen rode off to the guerrilla camp with loads of the barrel whiskey bucketed in the stolen boots. They stashed in their saddlebags some of the found bottles of whiskey.

*

Jabez Cooper and Jesse James milled about the depot. Jabez didn't participate in the whiskey drinking—he was a teetotaler. His assignment was to burn the depot when Anderson signaled. "I'm nervous as a barn cat, Jesse. There's gonna be a big fight to come out of this. Federals are all over this part of Missouri. What if the blue coats come in now, with over half our men stupid drunk?"

"Calm yourself," said Jesse. This is mighty flat land,

and we've got lookouts on the top floor of the hotel. They can see forever across this flat land."

"Spotting the Federals won't help. These men can't sober up in time for the fight. And you know that Anderson is drinking. That's a given fact. We'd just take on the Yankees like the drunk side of a drunken brawl. I don't want to be part of that. Don't want to be on the whipped side again. Fayette was bad enough."

Jesse said nothing. Jabez drifted aimlessly away and spoke to other guerrillas within earshot. "Say, has anyone gotten the news of the whereabouts of Price's army?" When no one responded, Jabez went inside the depot and spoke to the operator. "What do you hear about General Price?"

"He's in the southeast, near Ironton. They say he's headed to St. Louis, and a Union army has come down to try to stop him."

"When's the next train?"

"Arrives at 11:50."

Jabez went to the Eldorado and passed the information to Anderson and Arch. Anderson downed his third shot of morning whiskey. He left the hotel and gave orders to the men—move to the depot and prepare to take the train that's coming in.

Eight guerrillas on horseback rode east to escort the train in its approach. Back at the depot, teams of men lifted spare railroad ties on top of the rails to form a barricade. Jabez was alone, standing between the hotel and the depot, watching.

*

Close to noon, the train approached Centralia. Though the pile of ties on the tracks was clearly visible, the train lurched forward with increased speed as it neared the depot. One of the guerrillas said, "Damn, he's gonna try to bust through. The throttle must be full open." But the brakeman had already set the brakes, and the wheels screeched in an explosion of metal friction from the push of the throttle and the pull of the brakes. The train ground to a halt, and the engineer closed the throttle. Guerrillas jumped into the locomotive and shoved revolvers against the engineer and the fireman.

The riders were shooting into the cars, and the passengers fell to the floors in panic amid shouts and screams. Guerrillas entered the train. Some went to the express car, and the agent handed them the key to the safe, where they found thousands of dollars in greenbacks. They plunged into valises and suitcases in the baggage car, fishing out more money and some jewelry.

A group swept through the three passenger cars, yelling, shooting their guns into the ceilings, and demanding money and jewelry. As the men entered the last passenger car, they saw a huddled group of Union soldiers.

The soldiers threw up their hands. "Don't shoot, we are unarmed, we surrender."

One of the guerrillas shouted, "Keep your hands over your heads. You'll be treated as prisoners of war."

Anderson was outside the train when he learned of the soldiers. He ordered the civilian passengers to exit and line up on the depot side of the cars, where a more orderly search for their valuables could be made. He summoned Jabez and said, "Torch this train while I deal with these Yankee soldiers." He told Arch to take the soldiers to the other side of the train.

Anderson commanded Jesse and six other guerrillas to go through the line of civilian passengers, some one hundred twenty-five men, women, and children, making a careful search of their clothes and handbags. The passengers were frozen in fear, but some could not suppress their sobs and moans. Two fainted. A woman traveling with her child protested that she was for the South and her husband was fighting in the Confederate army. A guerrilla, stinking of sweat and whiskey, sneered. "That's what everybody claims." The guerrillas made everybody take off their shoes to be searched for hidden money and jewels. One man had hidden money in his shoe, and when a searcher discovered the stash, he shot the man in the face.

*

Anderson walked between the barricade and the train, over to the other side where Arch had collected the soldiers. "You boys take off your clothes, everything but your long johns. Put your money beside your clothes."

As they were stripping, one of the soldiers said, "Sir, we're not armed. We're not soldiers in these parts. We've been in Georgia, and some of us are finished with the war, and some of us are going home on furlough. We're headed to see our families."

Anderson said, "Georgia? Were you with Sherman in Atlanta?"

No one replied.

"Soldiers, attention! Answer me!" shouted Anderson.

"Yes," came a weak reply.

"That goddamn sonofabitch Sherman. You boys are scum to fight for that man."

Jabez had finished with putting flame to the interiors of the passenger cars, and he came to where the soldiers were being questioned by Anderson. He saw the shocked looks on the faces of the prisoners.

"Are you going to treat us as prisoners of war, like your men promised?" blurted a soldier whose face had gone pale.

Jabez could see an irritated expression on the chieftain's face. Anderson said, "I don't know what was said about prisoners of war. I'll ask my lieutenant."

Anderson called to Arch, "Come here, Archie, and tell me what we should do with Sherman's men."

Jabez had a sinking feeling. He sensed what was to come.

Arch walked the space between Anderson and the soldiers, back and forth, back and forth, surveying the nearly naked figures. "Oh, so they come from Atlanta? Captain, I think we should parole them," drawling out "pah-row-le." He turned so the soldiers couldn't see his face and winked at Anderson.

Jabez saw the wink, and his heart sank. *Don't,* he whispered to himself, *for God's sake don't.*

Anderson did not respond for several minutes. He walked around in a display of contemplation.

Jabez thought, *He's just playing with them. What a cruel sonofabitch.*

Anderson faced the soldiers. "Recommendation accepted, Archie. Now boys, we gonna parole you. You all go over and line up in front of the store."

"What are you going do with us there?" asked a soldier. "Can't we go now that we're paroled?" His eyes were wide and his mouth open.

Anderson said nothing.

Jabez believed the soldiers were beginning to see what Anderson was up to.

"Don't shoot us, Sir. We aren't fightin' you all," said the soldier. "We were going home. We want to see our families."

More guerrillas drifted from the depot to join those guarding the soldiers.

Arch came beside Anderson to talk. Jabez moved close so he could hear Arch, who was whispering, "Why don't we keep some of them for a prisoner swap for Cave?"

Anderson mumbled, "More than one prisoner will take too much time and trouble to deal with while we're on the move. I can agree to only one. Anyway, one's all we'll need to swap for Cave."

Jabez thought, *I knew it; these boys are doomed.*

Anderson held up a Union jacket with sergeant stripes. "Which of you boys is the sergeant?" No one moved.

"C'mon, who's a sergeant? I ain't gonna ask again."

A tall, burly man with a brush of a mustache raised his right hand. "Me. I'm a sergeant. Headed to see my family just across the border in Iowa."

"Step forward, sergeant. What's your name?"

"Ted Goodman."

"Well, my *Good Man*, come over here by me."

Ted Goodman moved alongside Anderson, and he was seized by two men. Anderson directed the two and Jabez to guard the sergeant.

Anderson wanted a count and had the other soldiers form a line. "I want you to go down the line and count off." There were twenty-two, not including Ted Goodman.

Anderson walked a few steps forward and turned around, his back to the soldiers. He spoke to the bushwhackers who had gathered. "Now y'all count off."

Anderson's men responded left to right with the consecutive numbers. Anderson positioned himself so that he would be number four. Then he said, "Those Yankee soldiers also have numbers from your left to right. You know your assignment now."

Anderson spun to face the soldiers. "You Federals have just killed six of my men and scalped them. I'm gonna send you all to hell."

"No, we were in Georgia. We have not killed your men!"

"All Federals are one. Federals killed my men, and you are Federals."

Jabez heard some of the soldiers sobbing, moaning, begging for their lives, some praying. He thought, *I'll live with those screams forever.*

Then, one of the Union soldiers ran, and the others began to run, ruining the shooting protocol Anderson had dictated, and guerrillas started firing randomly into the mass of Federals. Bodies fell to the dirt.

In the chaos, one of the soldiers, a bear of a man,

rushed to the space between the train and the barricade of ties. Jabez secretly hoped the soldier could escape.

A guerrilla stepped toward the fleeing soldier, about to shoot, but the soldier punched the man in the face and ran toward the depot and managed to dive into the crawl-space under the building. Guerrillas followed and yelled to the passengers to move away.

Anderson ordered Jabez to burn the building and smoke the man out. Jabez's heart sank again. *Oh no*, he thought, *no, don't make me do this.*

Jabez pulled some of the still-burning materials from the torched train cars, and he got several men to help him gather fuel. It took a while for Jabez to organize the burning. He felt that time was standing still—he wished it would. No one moved. The spectators were frozen. The Union soldiers were dead or dying. The guerrillas were waiting for Jabez to burn the soldier out of his refuge in the crawlspace.

Soon a rope of black smoke hung over the station. The soldier crawled from under the burning wood, coughing and trying to gain his footing. A guerrilla knocked him to the ground with the butt end of a rifle and shot him dead.

The guerrillas then walked to each soldier's body on the ground and either shot the man's skull, crushed it with a rifle butt, or cut his throat. Arch and another guer-rilla each took a scalp. Blood splattered the dusty ground, the dead soldiers and the living killers.

Passengers screamed. Jabez looked at Ted Goodman and saw the sergeant had buried his face in his hands, his shoulders heaving.

Anderson walked away from the site of the massacre. He asked for one of the whiskey bottles and took a swal-low. "Federals will be here soon. They got a garrison in Sturgeon. We'll need to leave.

"Jabez, get him a horse." Anderson spoke more loudly to the mass of guerrillas, "I do not want anyone to harm this man, y'all hear me? Unless he attempts to escape. That's an order to you all."

Anderson walked to the train. He had a wide grin. Jabez could not believe Anderson was capable of joy in a moment such as this.

Anderson said, "Before we leave this fine town, we're gonna have some fun, boys. Clear the track, so we can send this burning pile of railroad crap on down the track to Sturgeon. Engineer, fireman—y'all come here. Your locomotive ain't burned. It's in good shape. Fire up the goddamn engine, then open the throttle and tie open the whistle." Shortly, the empty and burning train puttered westward down the track, whistle screaming. A thin stream of smoke from the ebbing fires drifted out of the open windows and doors in the passenger cars.

Jabez stole a john mule from one of Centralia's citizens and stuck Ted Goodman on it, clad only in his underwear, riding bareback, his hands tied and holding the mane. As the guerrillas galloped southeast toward camp, the prisoner and his guards slowly followed, one guard riding in front leading the mule with a rope, and another guard in the rear. Jabez lagged along behind them, quiet in his thoughts about what he had witnessed, wondering what he would say to Cait about this day.

# 35

## BLOOD

When Jabez, the other guards, and the prisoner entered the camp outside Centralia, Anderson's guerrillas were boasting about their exploits. Many were still drunk. Some of the men who stayed behind were doing their best to catch up on the drinking, passing around the boots of whiskey from the town.

"Here comes that goddamn Yankee. Don't know his name. I'll just call him Sergeant Prisoner," yelled one of Anderson's men. "Sergeant Prisoner ain't gonna live long in this camp."

"Our boys put him on a mule. Shoulda found a donkey. An ass is the right thing for a Yankee to ride," said another.

"Well, he's an ass-*wipe!*"

The bushwhackers crowded about Goodman, greeting him with slaps or spit.

"Kill the bastard," said one. "Send him to hell with the others."

"No telling how many rebels he killed in Georgia. Now it's his time to die."

"I'm first in line," slobbered a tottering drunk. He waved his revolver above his head. "My gun's cocked. Get outta the way, so I can shoot him."

"You men back off!" Jabez stepped forward and shoved his own pistol in the man's face. "Put that gun down. Captain Anderson left strict orders not to harm this man, and I'll shoot anybody who violates his order."

Jabez knew the greatest danger would come from those who were too drunk to understand the order. He and the two other guards and the prisoner pushed ahead toward Anderson's tent as fast as possible through the boiling swarm of angry men.

Once they had delivered their prisoner, Jabez pulled Frank aside. "Frank, I know you weren't at the town, so I have to tell you what happened." Jabez gave a summary. Tears moistened his eyes as he wiped his nose on the back of a shaky hand. "I'm most torn up about me burning the depot to smoke out that Yankee so our boys could put a bullet in his head."

Frank stood. He was quiet and looked away. "This reminds me of a play by Shakespeare, called *Macbeth*."

"Wha? Whaddya mean, Frank?"

"Macbeth was trying to become king of Scotland. He hired assassins to murder his rival, while Macbeth was elsewhere. Afterwards, the ghost of his dead rival haunted him, and Macbeth said to the ghost, 'Thou canst not say I did it. Never shake thy gory locks at me.' I know that I can say those same words about Centralia—'cause I wasn't there. I think you can say them too. You didn't shoot any of those Yankees. You just did as you were told and fired the depot.'

Jabez looked at the ground. "I don't know, Frank. We're all in this. I feel as guilty as those who did the killing."

*

Deep in troubled thought, Jabez wandered down to a nearby creek to clean the body, if not the mind. He'd scarcely pulled his shirt over his head when word came that Todd, Anderson, and the other chiefs were collecting in a clearing.

When Jabez arrived, the bushwhackers had gathered about Todd and the other leaders, who stood in a cleared area on the ground. Todd was speaking. "Here's what I heard from our scouts. The Federal garrison at Sturgeon, 'bout ten miles west a-here is on the move. They're a company of new Union militia recruits led by a Major Johnston, mounted infantry riding farm horses, draft horses— and mules." Todd's wide grin drew snickers that were quickly snuffed as he raised his hands. "They left thirty or forty men in Centralia to clean up our little mess"— Todd whisked his hat off to cover his chest and bowed his head for a brief moment of mock reverence without breaking his sentence—"then left with about a hundred men mounted on those farm creatures."

Todd took a stick from Anderson's hand and looked around the tight circle, studying the eager faces. "Boys, we've got them outnumbered, and we can do a straight up fight. They probably don't know how many we have, or they wouldn't be chasing us. This is where I want to fight them." He pointed to a spot on a rough map he scratched in the dirt. "Here, between the main road on the west and Youngs Creek on its east. You know the big meadow that comes down to the creek with sloughs along each of its sides?" He drew a big "U" in the dirt. "The woods along the creek and the sloughs form kind of a horseshoe. We'll put Anderson at the toe of the horseshoe, in front of the creek. Pool's men can hide on the other side of the creek, behind Anderson, in the woods along the creek. My boys, along with Si's, will hide in the woods of the ravine on the south side of the horseshoe, and the boys of Preacher and Thrailkill will hide in the woods on the north side of the horseshoe. And we'll guide our prey to the top of a little hill, really no more than a rise, on the open side of the horseshoe, the west side, facing Anderson. We'll have over two hundred men hidden. The Federals'll see Anderson lined up and think they have to fight only about seventy or eighty."

"I like the looks of your trap," said Anderson. "How do we get the Federals into it?"

# BLOOD

Todd traced the ground with the stick to indicate the west side of the meadow. "I want Pool to send a few men as decoys and lead the Federals from the road into this place. And here's the sugar for your coffee boys; the Federals are armed with muzzle-loading rifles. To fight, they'll have to dismount. When they dismount, they'll have to assign men to hold their horses and mules or let them go. And once they fire that first round, they'll not have time to reload. After they fire that first round, I want them right here," Todd stabbed his stick into the ground, "atop this little hill—on foot, with empty rifles, in front of our cavalry.

"When they fire their round, the riders in the woods on the flanks can come forth while the Federals are reloading. We'll shock 'em and have them in a pinch."

All were waiting for Anderson's reaction. He stroked his beard and studied the crude map. "Let's do it."

Anderson turned to Jabez and the other guards. "Put Sgt. Good Man on that gray horse, and you all come with us—but stay at the back. You need to be in the charge, in case we need you to fight, but I want to protect the prisoner if we can. Tie his hands. If he tries to escape, shoot him at once. Otherwise, protect him."

Jabez was relieved to hear Anderson's instructions to stay near the back of the battle. And to protect Goodman.

*

The start of the battle neared. Jabez was struck by the silence as Anderson's men dismounted, tightened their saddle belts, and remounted. The only sounds were from horses shuffling and snorting and leather saddles squeaking as the men set themselves.

It was a soft, Indian-summer afternoon, with a cloudless blue sky. Jabez looked at the large meadow of prairie grass that rose slightly to a hillock where the Union force gathered. The meadow showed its seasonal colors, and Jabez watched the tall bluestems, rust colored now, wave slightly in a soft breeze. In the woods along the creek behind and the sloughs on right and left, the red maples blazed their autumn blood-crimson. The sycamores with their yellow and tan leaves spread along the creek, and trees that had not turned yet showed flashes of green. This was his favorite time of the year. What a contrast to the carnage coming in the next minutes. He dreaded it.

Jabez's stomach tightened as he watched the Union militiamen stand in formation with their rifles, waiting for the rebels. *Will they cut us down like wheat before we even get close?* He thought of his life ahead, with Cait. The prospect of losing that future for a cause he really didn't believe in left him once again feeling trapped and angry . . . and this time afraid. *I'm not afraid of death; I just don't want it now, here.*

He saw some of his comrades closing their eyes and mumbling prayers, and he knew they were trying to smother their fears too. Arch and Jesse showed no signs of anxiety. They were laughing and joking and full of energy, as though they couldn't wait for the battle. He figured they believed they were invincible, indestructible.

Jabez looked to find Frank among the riders. He caught Frank's eye and gave him their open-palm sign to show he would have Frank's back. Frank flashed the sign in return.

Anderson, dressed in black and riding his black Arabian horse, moved along the line of his men, repeating, "Mow them down but don't stop break through the line and keep straight on to the horses and scatter them. Keep straight on to the horses."

Jesse was beside Arch. "Race you to be the first man to the Yankee line."

"C'mon, I'll whip you."

Anderson lifted his black hat high. His men moved forward about fifty yards. Then Pool's men emerged from the wooded creek behind Anderson's line. When the riders got about three hundred yards from the standing Federals, they cantered their horses and leaned forward, beneath the horses' heads, to lower their profiles—a Comanche tactic—then broke into a full gallop. When the guerrillas galloped into range, the Union muskets fired. The slope of the hillock was not great, but it was enough to cause the shots aimed down at the riders to go high, missing all but a handful of the charging rebels.

Then, from the flanks, burst the hidden riders, startling and distracting the Federals, who panicked while scrambling to reload their rifles. All the guerrilla bands raced to the top of the hill in a fury. The noise of over a thousand hooves and the high-pitched battle cries of the guerrillas mixed into a terrifying din. The September sun shone in a cloudless sky, but a gunpowder cloud formed over the crest of the hill.

Some of the men assigned to hold the Federal horses spooked and mounted and rode for their lives toward Sturgeon. Arch was the first to the Federal line. Jesse was close behind, and he shot Major Johnston in the head, killing him instantly. Then, along with brother Frank, Arch and others he broke through the line to scatter the horses and chase the escaping Federals. Only eleven fleeing men made it to safety.

Some of the Federals on the battlefield attempted to use their bayonets and were shot by guerrilla revolvers. "Surrender, surrender," yelled the guerrillas. The survivors threw down their now-useless rifles, and the riders herded them into a circle. Some guerrillas dismounted and began to collect bayonets and the swords of officers, and some unsheathed their own Bowie knives. The fate of the Union militiamen was sealed.

Jabez could only watch as one of the bushwhackers called Cousin cut the throat of a badly wounded soldier and held the dead man by the hair. "I'm gonna give you bluebellies a demonstration in scalping. Just take a sharp blade and start here at the top of the forehead, and cut to the bone of the skull, then carve around the scalp, over the first ear, then around the back of the neck, then over the other ear, and back to the beginning. Hold the scalp by the hair, bend the head over your knee like this, and pull off the scalp like you were skinning a rabbit. If the man is bald, use your teeth to pull. Easy."

One of the living soldiers was on his knees, praying, "Please, Father have mercy on me."

Cousin said, "Shut up, boy. I'm giving a lesson," but the soldier prayed louder. Cousin pointed his revolver at the praying figure, but this did not stop the beseeching. Cousin shot the man, finished his demonstration of the scalping technique, and carried the scalp to his saddlebag. The front of Cousin's stolen Union coat was red with blood.

Shortly, all of the Federals on the battlefield were slaughtered by blades or bullets. The bloodletting intoxicated the guerrillas. They walked from body to body, crushing skulls or putting more bullets in heads, sometimes pinning the dead to the ground with Union bayonets. The killers carved off seventeen scalps, a number of ears, and one nose. A few men decapitated bodies and tossed the heads about like pumpkins. They laughed as they exchanged severed heads with different headless bodies. One guerrilla castrated a body and stuffed the organs in the mouth of the corpse.

Some guerrillas had so much blood on their clothes they needed the uniforms of the dead. They searched the corpses for those of equal size and exchanged their bloody coats and pants for those of the fallen soldiers.

Anderson said he wanted to know the total of the number killed. Dave Pool hopped from corpse to corpse as if dancing, waving his arms and counting with each hop. On the final hop, he yelled, "Got one hundred seven dead bluecoats on the battlefield!"

# BLOOD

Jabez and Frank were tending to a wounded guerrilla. During the charge, a man riding to Frank's immediate right had been killed instantly. Frank said there was only one more guerrilla killed in the charge. "Hundred and seven to two. Not a bad score."

As the bushwhackers prepared to leave the battlefield, Jabez pointed to a severed head stuck on a bayonet and said in a whisper, "Frank, why this?"

"It was a fair fight, and they would have done the same to us, but we whipped 'em good. This is as big a victory as Lawrence and Baxter Springs. The Good Lord was watching over us, I reckon."

"No, I mean all this butchering."

"Well, once these boys get juiced up for a fight, it's hard to bring them back down."

Jabez felt a wave of disgust. *Nobody stopped them. Why didn't I speak up while they were doin' it?* But he couldn't say those words to Frank. All he could say was, "I know you and I didn't join in this butchery, but we're a part of this outfit. We've all got it on our hands."

Frank shrugged. "Remember Macbeth —'They canst not say we did it.'"

# 36

## SGT. GOODMAN

Jabez watched the prisoner Ted Goodman scan the mutilated bodies of his fellow soldiers. Jabez thought, *Poor fellow. What he has seen today.*

Goodman bent forward and vomited. Jabez walked close to him to whisper, "Try not to show weakness, soldier. And don't say anything unless you're asked. Don't provoke these men. They're drunk on blood, and they'll be looking for a chance to take your scalp."

Goodman appeared taken aback by the words. "Appreciate the advice. What's your name?"

"Just call me Jabez. Where you from?"

"From Iowa. Live in Hawleyville, just over the Missouri line. Where you from?"

"Liberty. Clay County, here in Missouri." Jabez looked around. Say, we can talk later, but for now we should not be seen as getting familiar."

Goodman reached as if to stop Jabez from leaving. "This is the worst thing I've ever seen. I saw lot of men killed in Chattanooga and Georgia, but the murders today in the town and the mutilations on this hill are things beyond a nightmare. I'm a religious man, and I prayed God to save me, but when I saw what happened today, I questioned why God would allow it. How could this be God's will? How could he allow this to happen?

Jabez tried to pull away. "I feel for you, soldier. I don't have a hard heart, but you can't talk like that and survive if they hear you. You need to be quiet. I have to go now."

# SGT. GOODMAN

The assignment to guard Goodman prevented Jabez from finding ways to forget about his role in burning the depot and smoking the soldier out to meet his fate. It seemed that every time Jabez looked at Goodman, the scene of the soldier crawling out from under the depot platform flashed in his mind, and feelings of guilt and shame washed over him. Jabez took an opportunity to leave Goodman with the other two guards for a short time and concentrate on tending to minor wounds on men and horses. But this respite couldn't erase his feelings about what he had done at the depot nor about what his fellow bushwhackers had done in the town and on this battle-field.

*

In the Indian-summer afternoon, the guerrillas returned to their camp. Whiskey drinking resumed, and several of the men came up to Goodman, cursing and threatening him. More than once  the guards had to push away a gun barrel aimed  at Goodman.

Jabez offered to spell the other two guards for a while. When they took a break, Jabez asked Goodman how he was feeling, and Goodman said, "No change." Jabez nodded and tried to think of what to say.

He held up some clothes. "I brought you a shirt and pants one of the boys took at the store in Centralia. "The fella said they don't fit him, and anyway he has some new Union soldier clothes now. I'm tired of lookin' at your underwear. Wear these. You'll need something for the cold tonight."

"Appreciated. How about shoes?"

"Nope, no shoes is insurance. If you get loose, we'll catch you easier if you're barefoot."

The other guards returned, and Jabez took his leave and strolled through the camp. He spotted Arch and Jesse. Arch was talking to a group of guerrillas. Jabez could see Arch was high with excitement.

"I got to the Yankee line first," said Arch, his eyes wide and his arms spread out, hands open, looking like a preacher hitting his stride in a sermon. "And I killed the most. Fourteen, including four of the cowards who spooked and rode away."

Jesse shoved Arch out of his way and said, "Yeh, but I shot dead their leader, the Major. Shot him in the head with one bullet."

Arch wheeled around and asked, "How many of the Federals did we kill on the run?" Jesse estimated the number killed off the battlefield was about fifteen. Arch whooped, "Total of over a hunnert twenty kills here. Plus twenty-two from the train. We got some fine vengeance today!"

Three men were cleaning and brushing the scalps. Jesse said, "I was so busy chasing the cowards running from the battlefield that I didn't have time to take any scalps. Give me one."

A man tossed a finished scalp to Jesse. "Here's your prize for killin' the Yankee leader."

Anderson ordered the men to return to camp, rest, and then rise during the night and depart. "There will be Federals swarming all over this territory," he said.

The guerrillas curled up, heads against their saddles and tried to grab a few hours of sleep.

*

On the night of a day that had seen the massacre in Centralia and the destruction of Johnston's Union troops, hundreds of Confederate guerrillas and their Union prisoner broke camp and began their trek toward the Missouri River.

Preacher, Thrailkill, Gordon, and their men split from Anderson and Todd and headed in a separate column to the river. Goodman, Jabez, the other guards, Jesse, Frank, and Arch stayed with Anderson and Todd.

Arch made a slip knot in a short rope and threw the

loop over Goodman's head, with the tail of the rope dangling over his horse's haunch. "If he don't do right, pull on that rope," Arch told the guards.

After about an hour of travel, a blue rocket lifted in front of the troops. Then another. Anderson called forward his signal man, who sent a red rocket, then a white one. From the guerrillas' right came the supernatural-sounding hoot of a well-imitated owl call, and then the emergence of some of Todd's men who had chased down one of the Feds during the battle. The riders spoke with Anderson and Todd at the head of the column, and the group passed toward the rear. Frank shouted to them, inquiring who they were and where they were going.

They replied, "We got a prisoner, one of Johnston's men. We had to chase him a long way, and only settled him after putting six bullets in his body."

"Ain't he dead yet?"

"Naw. The devil can't kill him. We was impressed as how tough he is, so we thought we'd try to keep him alive."

"Do you think he is some kind of lucky charm?" Arch asked. "Well think again. He'll slow us down. Take him down to the farm below and shoot him. Bill Anderson don't take prisoners."

Jabez felt his stomach tighten.

One of the riders said, "What about this fellow you have, the one with no shoes and a noose around his neck? He's a prisoner."

"Yeh, but Anderson says he's reserved," said Arch.

The column wound down to the farm, where they found creek water for the horses and men and stacks of hay and oats for the horses. The riders continued until noon the next morning when they stopped for a bivouac in a woods. By this point, Goodman's presence was no longer a source of agitation with the men.

Jabez and Goodman sat apart from the main body, gulping creek water.

"What kind of work do you do?"

"I'm a blacksmith," said Goodman.

"Well, I'll be damned! that's my line of work too. Also a farrier, but I suppose most blacksmiths know that trade too."

"Yep, I know a bit about caring for hooves."

"How long you been smithin'?"

"Long time. I ain't a spring chicken. I'm thirty-five. Been a smith since I was younger'n you. I like it. It's physical, and it keeps me in touch with the people, and horses too. At some point everybody needs to come see the smith and the farrier."

"Me too. I like it. Bushwhackers go through horses like nothing you ever saw. They need me. So, they put up with my quirks—like I ain't so fond of killin'. But don't get ideas about that quirk, because if you try to escape now I *will* shoot you."

"Did you say, 'now?' What do you mean?"

Jabez gave no response.

The two men sat without talking for a while. Goodman said, "What Confederate outfit are you all in?

"We're not regular cavalry. Anderson doesn't want to be bound by all the rules and orders. We're not even partisan rangers. We're guerrillas, one hundred percent independent. Jeff Davis doesn't pay us a dime."

"I heard one of your fellows say your captain doesn't take prisoners. Why are you all keeping me?"

"Prisoner swap, for one of our men. I'd say that is unlikely though, unlikely the Federals will even talk about a swap, after what we just did." Jabez instantly wished he hadn't said that to Goodman.

In the night, the guerrillas were on the move again, but the horses were tired, and Anderson called a stop at midnight to give them rest. The men fed their horses from a cornfield and a pasture. There was little food for the men, and Goodman got nothing. He told Jabez he hadn't eaten since St. Louis, and he was weak. Secretly, Jabez shared his portion with Goodman.

At first light the next morning, Jabez roused Goodman and took him where the horses were feeding and told him Anderson had commanded him to curry Anderson's mount. Goodman, a big man with powerful arms, told Jabez, "I'm gonna give him such a rubbing and scratching he'll remember it as long as he's a horse."

About an hour later, Anderson passed by Jabez and Goodman. "Well, Sergeant Good Man, you gave my horse a fine curry. How do you get along?"

Goodman replied, "Very well, sir."

"Well, Sergeant Good Man, you should know that you are the first man that was caught in federal blue whose life I ever spared!" Jabez's heart jumped at the word "spared." *Maybe Anderson will let him live*, Jabez thought.

The march continued for another ten miles and then stopped for another feeding. Some men went to a farmhouse, seeking food, but came rushing back, shouting "Yankees are coming!  Yankees are coming! They're hunting us."

Anderson took charge and moved the guerrillas through the brush to a road, where on signal the men formed into a neat column of twos and broke into a trot. Shortly afterward, a cannon boomed and shells began to fly near. The column turned and crashed into the brush. Coming to a hill overlooking a small valley, Jabez saw a huge number of Federal cavalry troops.

# 37

## GOODMAN'S FATE

Jabez yelled to Anderson that he had spotted Union soldiers. Anderson screamed, "Fours, fours!" The men scattered in groups of four—each rider knew his assigned group. Anderson kept three men with him, and they rode over to join Goodman, Jabez, and the other two guards. Anderson said, "Ride for your lives. Prisoner, that means you too." With Anderson leading, the group—including Goodman—rode at full gallop.

In nearby woods, the Federals fired shots at the scattering bushwhackers. Jabez wondered what would happen to Goodman if his group got into a gunfight with the Union troops—*Would Anderson command me to shoot the prisoner?*

After a couple hours of riding without ever reining in, the group had evaded the Union riders, and they came to a grove. Over the next hour, a stream of guerrillas rode in. Jabez could see that this had been a camp Todd had used before. Discarded Union uniforms were strewn all around. Here and there were shelters made of limbs and branches—regular shebangs—where they had stashed grub and whiskey.

The men tore into the whiskey supply with a vengeance, and by the time night fell, they were full-on drunk, racing around the camp like they had rabies. Anderson was drinking heavily, and at one point, Jabez saw him on his black steed riding through the camp, shooting his revolver in the air. The other men began to fire their guns too.

Jabez could see Goodman was anxious. The prisoner told Jabez he was scared that a drunk might shoot him. Jabez and the other two guards formed a protective ring around the captive. All three were teetotalers, and their abstinence kept them alert for danger.

It had been a long and hard day in the saddle, and after a while, the whiskey finally knocked out the drinkers. Jabez thought, *It's like a wizard has cast a spell on them, making them fall in their tracks.* The exhausted and very drunk men slept on the ground in whatever position they had passed out in.

After the drunks were asleep, Jabez and the other guards split up guard time, so that only one had to stay awake while the other two slept. During his watch, Jabez could see that Goodman was not about to sleep—he seemed to still be scared, reacting to every movement and sound in the camp and the woods.

Next morning, one of the men was bawling, crying for help on his hand, wounded in the battle. The hand was red open, looking very raw and crawling with maggots. Jabez was called over. His medical experience was derived from his amateur work on horses and from performing emergency field bandaging on bushwhackers injured in battle, but he was all they had. He examined the hand and said it looked like he would have to amputate, but then Goodman said he had seen oil of turpentine work on a wound such as this type. One of the men found some turpentine in the camp, and Goodman applied it. The turpentine brought the wounded man some relief. After that, it seemed to Jabez that a lot of the men began to take a liking to Goodman. Anderson gave Goodman his old coat, after the leader had replaced it with one taken in Centralia. Jabez began to feel better about Goodman's chances to survive.

A group of twenty-four—including Anderson, Arch, Frank, Jesse, Goodman, Jabez, and the other guards, left the camp, moving toward an undisclosed destination.

Jabez found a bird's feather and stuck it in the band of his hat. He was feeling a bit more jaunty, and in turn he tried to raise Goodman's spirits. They had a short conversation about their families—both from Kentucky originally—and about the blacksmith trade. When no one else was around, Jabez asked the prisoner, "Did your outfit ever do any scalping?"

Goodman shook his head. "No it's forbidden in the Union Army. Rules of war."

Jabez said, "Also not permitted in the regular Confederate Army. We're not regular army, but I don't know if that's a legitimate excuse." Jabez could tell that the carving the guerrillas did to the Union troops after the battle was weighing heavily on Goodman. As it was weighing on Jabez.

The guerrillas spent the night in the neighborhood, and next morning they moved at a lazy pace, looking for the best conditions to cross the river, going roughly in a circle. That night, they camped close to the river town of Rocheport. The town was on fire, burned by the Federal cavalry in revenge for Centralia. The fires and a full moon gave enough light for Jabez to see that the troops were departing.

It was October 1, and Jabez knew that a full moon on this date meant there would be two full moons during the month, a blue moon. He recalled the old myth of a full moon causing lunacy. He thought, *To be moonstruck twice in a month will cause more lunacy, and we can stand no more.*

Next morning, they followed trails in timbered brakes and hollows until they came to a shanty in the woods.

There they found a cadaverous specimen of guerrilla. The man was the keeper of what Anderson called a "remuda." Jabez had never heard that word before, and he asked someone the meaning. The man replied, "It's a Spanish word that ranch hands in Texas called a supply of extra horses."

Everyone was to get a fresh horse. Anderson and Todd got first choice, but Anderson said he wanted to keep his magnificent black horse. Goodman's horse was not swapped for a new mount, which made Jabez worried that the prisoner's end may be near.

After a night in the woods near the remuda, they moved to another camp, at a place called Maxwell's Mill. This camp was like a palace in comparison to past camps. It possessed an everlasting spring of very high-quality water and a still to produce whiskey with these waters. Once again, the men indulged their custom of drinking to the point of extreme excess, with Jabez and the other two guards being the teetotaling exceptions.

In the midst of the drunken madness, one of the guerrillas pulled Jabez and the other two guards aside and whispered, "You boys won't have to mess with this prisoner much longer. If Anderson doesn't make a prisoner swap before we cross the Missouri—and it don't look like he is gonna—he'll have Sgt. Good Man shot."

Jabez tried not to appear upset at this statement, but he wanted clarity. He said, "I'm not surprised. Where did you learn this?" The man pointed at one of his own ears and walked away. Jabez decided not to pursue the question.

The next morning, Frank asked Jabez to look after a man who was having seizures that would last for several minutes. The seizures would stiffen his whole body, he would tighten his arms and stretch out his feet as far as they would go, and you could see extreme tension in his neck and jaws—they were tight as banjo strings. Frank said the man, whose name was Richard Kinney, was riding beside him in the battle when Kinney was gunshot. It was only a minor wound, no infection, Frank said.

Jabez said it was a serious situation. Said it was probably lockjaw. Said lockjaw is not an infection but comes from a poison the ball could have been carrying, especially if the bullet was old and rusty. The poison causes the seizures and stiffening.

Frank said, "Why do you think it's lockjaw? You're a blacksmith, not a doctor."

Jabez said, "I've seen this before, and I heard a doctor tell what causes it and what happens. I don't know what to do if it is lockjaw. If it is lockjaw, the man soon will not be able to open his mouth, and the seizures will get stronger and longer, and the man will just wear out and die."

Frank moaned. He said the man was one of his best friends in the war. He said, "In the battle, the men on both sides of me were hit in the charge, Frank Shepherd, who is dead, and now Richard, who may be soon. Why am I spared and they are taken? My father was a preacher who used to quote this piece of Scripture at funerals, 'Two men are in a field. One shall be taken and the other left.'" Frank took a long pause, almost like an actor on stage, and then he said "That's Scripture, and that's life."

The group remained at the camp for three nights, as the separate groups of "fours" came drifting in. The crowd swelled, and each night the men took to staging drinking contests and telling tall tales about their exploits in killing Yankees.

Jabez saw a group of citizens from the area come to camp on the second afternoon. There was much shaking of hands and congratulations, and Anderson exhibited Goodman as the 'sole survivor' of the Union force at Centralia. Jabez liked that the chief used the word 'survivor,' but he wasn't going to put much stock in it. Time was running out. No effort had been made yet to negotiate a swap.

Jabez believed that all the friendly things Anderson had said to Goodman were probably just Anderson's way of toying with his prey before killing it.

The group moved on to a place they called Harkers, through paths and roadless terrain, stopping at the home of a family that was obviously affluent. They all left Goodman and Jabez at the gate and went inside the mansion. Jabez jumped on the opportunity to have a brief conversation with the prisoner without anyone around. He said, "Your friends are at a town called Fayette." Before Jabez could give him any information about how to find Fayette or how far away it was, the other guards walked up, and Jabez repeated the word "Fayette" in a whisper and then shut up.

The group proceeded to Harkers, which was about a mile above Rocheport. All the guerrillas from different bands were massing there to cross the Missouri, along with new recruits wanting to join General Price. A violent storm prevented any attempt to cross the river that night. The weather cleared the next day, and at night they set out for the river crossing.

Anderson had collected thirteen skiffs to ferry the mass of men, and he dictated that either four or eight men would go in each boat, depending on its size. Horses would swim behind the boats, held by the men with ropes and halters or tied to the tail of another horse. Anderson's system meant that multiple trips would be required.

The men appeared confused about how to load and launch the thirteen boats for the first crossing. The many men and horses were crowding the edge of the river, trying to learn how to handle the boats and take horses along too. Some of the first horses entering the water pulled back toward the bank, striking the mass of men, boats, and horses behind them. Men and beasts stumbled wildly.

Jabez asked Anderson, "When should we take prisoner Goodman across? Want us to go first?"

Anderson looked annoyed, and replied, "Hell no, you and the other guards go last." So, the guards and the prisoner moved back to the rear of the chaos of humanity and horses and waited. Jabez looked at Goodman, who was watching the men carefully.

Jabez said to the other guards, "We ought to watch the loading and learn how to do it, because we're going to be last. The two guards moved toward the front, all the way to the edge of the river.

Jabez hung back for a moment. He looked at Goodman, straight in the eye, and nodded. The prisoner nodded back. Then Jabez said just two words, said them very clearly—"head north." Jabez turned and moved toward the commotion at the river and joined the other guards. When the three returned, Goodman was gone. He had slipped away into the darkness and the thick underbrush.

Jabez looked at the clear night sky and found the North Star. He hoped Goodman understood his message, and he hoped Goodman knew about how to use that star. Helping that man felt to Jabez like a great relief flooding his body. He wondered if what he had done would be penance for smoking out the soldier at the train station in Centralia.

# 38

## THE CHOICE

October 7, 1864, Boone and Cooper Counties, central Missouri
Bill Anderson exploded in a fury over Goodman's escape during the crossing of the Missouri. He screamed at the three guards, "How could you pitiful sonsabitches lose that goddamn Yankee? What in hell were you doing leavin' a prisoner alone? You've got shit for brains." Anderson pulled out his revolver and smacked one of the guards across his face. When the man fell to his knees, Anderson hit him again with the gun across the shoulder.

Anderson's mouth foamed saliva. He turned to Jabez and the other guard. "I should put your sorry asses in front of a firing squad right now.

Anderson caught himself before firing his revolver, spun, stuffed his gun into his belt, and walked away. Before Anderson could take any further action, Jabez said, "Captain, leave those men be. That escape is on me. I was the last man in the back, and then I came up to the river."

Anderson slowly turned but did not look at Jabez. "All three of you were on assignment and under orders to guard the prisoner. You all failed. We'll have a trial tomorrow."

*

Later, during the night, Jabez stuffed some hardtack and personal items in his rucksack and a revolver in his belt and wrote a note admitting responsibility for allowing the prisoner to escape. He wanted to be honest, and he wanted to save the other two guards from punishment. The note made clear that he intentionally allowed the escape. He placed the note where he knew it would be found, and around two o'clock in the morning he slipped out of Anderson's camp. He was careful in taking his horse, for fear someone would hear or see him leaving, and he led it through the woods, keeping an eye out for the pickets guarding the camp. When he had covered a sufficient distance on foot, he mounted the horse bareback and rode into the night.

He headed west toward Boonville to catch the ferry at its first crossing of the morning. He figured his note would be discovered when the men rose at an early hour to feed their horses, and so he estimated he had a head start of three to four hours on anyone who would chase him. Riding in the dark of night forced him to go more slowly than normal. Riding bareback had a similar effect. His backside and groin were feeling plenty sore. By the slow pace, he was losing time against potential trackers.

As he neared Boonville, Jabez stopped to rest and wait for first light. He knew he could be losing more time against any chasers, but he had to wait for the ferry to start up. Shortly after dawn, he spied a couple of horses saddled and hobbled at the edge of a field. He saw that the owners were far away, walking through high grass heavy with dew, toward a wood. They seemed so distanced from the war and the violence and killing. Just two farmers, everyday men, probably friends, walking in a field of prairie grass and autumn wildflowers. The scene was so peaceful, almost as if a dream. Then he snapped his attention to the matters at hand, stole the saddle from one of their horses and dashed. *Better a live thief than a dead deserter,* he said to himself.

He came to the ferry at Boonville and crossed back to the north side of the Missouri. Jabez lied and told the ferryman that he was going to the Union garrison in Fayette.

In fact, his secret destination was the O'Kelly farm outside Richmond.

At this point, Jabez was beginning to convince himself that Anderson would not send trackers after him, but simply take the entire unit to meet up with General Price. *They have more pressing business than to waste time in chasing me.* He didn't know if that was an intelligent thought or merely a hope. In case Anderson did send someone to chase him, and he crossed the Missouri with the Boonville ferry, the tracker would likely ask the operator about a soldier traveling alone. He figured the ferryman would describe a man of his size and features in Union uniform heading to the Federal garrison at Fayette, and Fayette was in a different direction from Cait's farm. Jabez wondered, *Is this good thinking? My mind is so crazy now. I hope I'm thinking straight.*

As Jabez departed the ferry, he asked the ferryman which road went to Fayette.

"Take the right fork to reach Fayette. Don't take the left fork, that will take you along the river."

Shortly after crossing the river, Jabez came to a fork. He took the road to the left and in a short distance found a secluded spot, slightly elevated, from which he could view the fork without being detected. There he settled and waited to see if any of Anderson's men were following him.

Jabez was beginning to nod off from lack of sleep when he saw three riders, dressed in Union blue and riding from the ferry landing on the north side of the river toward the fork in the road. He could tell that one of the riders was Arch, whose diminutive size and too-large uniform were the giveaways. *Which road they gonna take? Will they see me? Would they know I am headed to Cait's place and go there? Do I dare go to Cait's place and put her in danger? Do I go back to the south side of the river? Or surrender to the Federals?* His mind was flaming, and he leapt to his feet, then realized he had no idea why he had jumped up. *I'm panicking,* he thought.

He saw the riders take the fork toward Fayette. He sank to his knees as the anxiety drained from his body. Trying to collect his thoughts, he figured they would ride hard toward Fayette, and not finding him, they would believe he had arrived at the Federal garrison and surrendered. Then they would rejoin the guerrilla band. *Hope my mind's working right.*

For the next days, Jabez rode along back roads tracing the north side of the big river, traveling at night and sleeping and resting in the woods or in tobacco sheds in the daytime. To test whether Clement and the other two were following him, he set up a couple observation posts, and to his relief, he saw no trackers.

Jabez had not traveled much in this part of the state, so he lost his way a number of times. He had to rely on the celestial bodies and occasional glimpses of the river for general direction. He knew about foraging wild food in the woods, but it wasn't the season for berries and such. He stole from the last remains of summer gardens. He had little money with him but enough to allow him to make a few food purchases at general stores along the way.

His mind puzzled over whether to continue to Cait's place. He decided to press on, figuring he would hide in the loft in her barn in case Anderson or Arch came there looking for him. *Hopefully, they will forget about me and go straight to join Price.*

A few days later, Jabez reached his sanctuary outside Richmond.

# 39

## GLORY

October 10, 1864, Boonville, Cooper County, central Missouri
Confederate Major General Sterling Price was in Missouri, astride his horse Bucephalus, named after Alexander the Great's celebrated mount. The General was one of the most famous men in the short history of the state of Missouri. He had served with distinction in the Mexican War, and he had served as a U.S. Congressman and as a governor of Missouri. Initially, he had voted against secession, but later he embraced the Confederacy and was placed in charge of the newly created, pro-Confederate state guard.

Price had been nursing revenge since Union forces had driven him and his state guard troops out of Missouri in 1861 and defeated him in Arkansas shortly after. Now was time for Price's comeback—and vengeance. Proceeding from northeastern Arkansas on September 19, 1864, Price led an invading army with orders to attack St. Louis, then move west to the capital city of Jefferson City, where he would depose the pro-Union government, inaugurate the Confederate governor-in-exile, and officially proclaim Missouri as a Confederate state. Then, he would sweep west along the Missouri River to Kansas City and exit the state. The intent was to show Northern voters that the war would continue, prompting votes against Lincoln in the upcoming election. The plan met trouble early on, as Federal resistance turned Price away from St. Louis, then from Jefferson City.

Price's invasion was a ponderous plod, burdened by

the need to carry supplies and military paraphernalia, including five hundred wagons, eighteen pontoon boats for river crossings, numerous pieces of artillery, and a drove of five thousand head of cattle. Many of the soldiers were scraggly and unarmed—hardly soldiers—and many used the procession through the state as an opportunity for plunder, taking from Unionists and Secesh equally.

On October 10, after Price decided not to attack Jefferson City, he and his men streamed into Boonville, a port town on the south side of the Missouri River, west of the capital city. Boonville was in Little Dixie, land of the Secesh, and hundreds turned out to welcome the Confederate army. The town organized a celebration in honor of three of their heroes: General Price, Brigadier General Jo Shelby, and Thomas Reynolds, governor of the rump Confederate government-in-exile.

Part of Price's plan had been to pick up recruits along the way, but only a disappointing couple thousand had joined his army. Price hoped the local Secesh young men in the Boonville area would eagerly join. Down the main street rode eighty new recruits, the guerrillas led by Bill Anderson, dressed in their best bushwhacker garb, flamboyant with plumes and ribbons in their hats and multiple revolvers poking from their belts, and riding beautiful Arabian horses. Anderson was dressed all in black, his black shirt embroidered in a fanciful sky-blue pattern. The guerrillas made drama with their slow and showy parade, and they tipped their hats and smiled to the crowd like conquering heroes.

The crowd cheered and raised the cry, "Centralia!" The bushwhackers waved and grinned.

As the guerrillas approached Price and his men, one of Anderson's men pointed to a herd of captured Federal soldiers. "Yankees! Kill the sonsabitches!" The bushwhackers drew their revolvers and prepared to attack the captives.

General Price shouted, "Halt, do not touch these men, they are my prisoners."

The guerrillas backed off.

Reynolds took Price's arm and whispered, "My God, do you see those pelts on the bridles? People say they collect scalps, and it's true." Price groaned. When Anderson rode up to the platform where Reynolds and Price stood, Reynolds snapped an outburst. "Goddamn it, get rid of those scalps, they are a disgrace to the Confederacy."

Price joined in, "Captain, if you are going to fight with us, you must throw away those scalps. Scalping is against our military code."

Anderson dismounted, pulled off a scalp from his bridle and turned to his men. "Boys, the General says we have to toss these symbols of victory."

His men collected the scalps and stuffed them in an empty saddlebag.

"Throw them away!" yelled Reynolds.

"That's an order," said Price.

Anderson responded, "Yessir, we will," and then faced his men and grinned. He turned to Price. "But first, Sir, we have a special gift for you." Anderson presented a wooden box containing a brace of shining silver revolvers.

Price appeared momentarily undone. He shook Anderson's hand and walked to face the crowd, held the revolvers aloft and said, "If I had fifty thousand men like these bushwhackers, I could hold Missouri forever." The crowd roared. Anderson grinned again and winked one of his gray eyes at Arch Clement.

An hour later, Anderson met privately with Price. By this time, Price had recovered his disdain for the guerrilla chief and wanted to station him as far away from his troops as he could without offending him. "I need you and your men to go back across the Missouri and shut down completely the North Missouri Railroad."

# 40

## A ROBBERY

October 21, 1864, Glasgow, Howard County, central Missouri
Bill Anderson did not spend much time disrupting the
North Missouri Railroad. Following orders, most especially orders he didn't like, was not in his blood. As Price's
army moved west along the Missouri, the local Federal
troops along the river in central Missouri moved westward in the direction of Kansas City. The shift of the Federal military presence out of central Missouri and toward
Price's advancing army opened the door for Anderson to
engage there in his favorite activities—harassing and
killing Unionists, burning and looting. Easy pickings
now.

Anderson learned that his old chief, Quantrill, was
on the prowl too, with a reconstituted band of guerrillas.
The most important intelligence Anderson received about
Quantrill was the news that Quantrill and his guerrillas
had kidnapped a banker in Glasgow and had forced the
victim to take $21,000 from the bank's vault. Anderson en-
vied this huge haul, and he knew where he might be able
to replicate it.

One of the richest men in this part of Missouri also
lived in Glasgow, a man named Benjamin Lewis. There
was more to interest Anderson about Lewis—he was an
ardent Unionist and a friend of President Lincoln. Even
more, Lewis had manumitted all of his slaves, one hundred fifty in number, paying the transportation of those
who wanted to move to Kansas and employing at a fair

wage those who wanted to continue working for him as freed men and women.

Lewis had built an imposing mansion, Glen Eden, on the outskirts of Glasgow, overlooking the Missouri River. On the night of October 21, Anderson and his orderly, a man he called Weasel, strong-armed their way into that house and sat in the drawing room gulping from Lewis's Kentucky bourbon supply. Each had placed a revolver next to his glass. Lewis and his wife sat on the sofa, immobile, frozen in terror, as Anderson trimmed his fingernails slowly with a pocketknife and finished the last of the bourbon.

Anderson said, "Mr. Lewis, you have been accused of being a Unionist pain in the ass to the Southern cause. You've done more damage to the South than any ten men. The Secesh here hate you. Hate you! You've been accused of being a nigger lover—and worse, a nigger lover who freed his slaves. And you have been accused of being too rich. How do you plead?"

Lewis was trying to appear cool, but he sweated heavily. "I have Confederates in my family, some are even connected to General Price. The General arranged to protect me when one of his brigades came through Glasgow."

Anderson slammed the blade of his pocketknife shut and stomped his right foot on the floor. "Shut up. What about niggers?"

"I still have some here," pleaded Lewis.

"Are they slave or free?"

Lewis didn't answer.

"Never you mind. We'll get to that later. If they're not your slaves now, they can be mine. What about the accusation of riches? That's the first thing we need to talk about. We can help you deal with that accusation."

Lewis was trembling. "Look, gentlemen, I have some land bu, but little money. I, I, I'll give you what I have."

Anderson snapped open the pocketknife again and

pointed it at Lewis. "Bring it, if you're interested in living."

Lewis left the room and returned with around $1,000 in coin and bills. "This is all I have."

Anderson rose from the chair, took the money and yelled, "What? This is nothing." Anderson picked up his revolver and grabbed the front of Lewis's shirt, then bashed the man's head with the barrel of the gun. "Bring me ALL your money. Now!"

Lewis held his bleeding head. "This is all that's here. And the bank was robbed last week. They took our savings."

Anderson was snarling now. "Don't lie to me. I hate liars." Anderson hit Lewis again and knocked him to the floor.

Anderson and Weasel kicked and stomped his body. Lewis was barely conscious. Anderson held Lewis by his hair and with the other hand shoved the barrel of the revolver down his throat. Lewis gagged, and Anderson thrust the barrel back and forth, up and down the throat until Lewis was coughing blood. Anderson threw Lewis back down on the floor, beating him again with the gun, and he and Weasel fired their revolvers so close to the man's pants that the cloth was scorched and so close to his face that it suffered a powder burn. Lewis was thoroughly thrashed, unconscious, and his wife was screaming, believing he was dead.

Whiskey and hate had driven Anderson out of control. He turned to a black female servant, barely thirteen years old. "You think you're not a slave, that you've been freed by this son of a bitch, but once a slave always a slave. You're *my* slave now." He pushed her into a bedroom and raped her.

Anderson returned to Lewis, dragged him out of the house, and commanded Weasel to mount his horse and run it over Lewis' prone figure.

Sobbing, Lewis's wife cried, "There is no more money

here. I will borrow the money from our friends. Please don't kill him. If you let us be, I will get you the money. How much? How much?"

"If you can raise $5,000, this piece-of-crap husband of yours will live. Otherwise, I'm sending him straight to hell."

An hour later, the wife returned with the ransom.

Lewis was alive but still unconscious. Anderson said, "I would kill this sorry snake, but as a Southern gentleman, a man of honor, I'm true to my word. You can have him now."

# 41

## RETURN

In the late afternoon of October 15, Cait O'Kelly heard a steady rapping on her front door.

"Who is it?"

"The Jaybird is back," he said.

Cait laughed and pulled Jabez inside and wrapped her arms around him. "You crazy fool. I'm so glad you're back. But you look a mess. What happened to you?"

Jabez looked like a mendicant—rail thin, his face bearded and darkened from filth and weather, his hair long and greasy. He was exhausted from his days with the guerrillas in the brush and his days afterwards as a fugitive. He leaned back. "I can explain later, but right now I could stand something to eat. Could you spare a fella a meal?"

"You stink. First thing you got to do is take a bath." She laughed again. "Seems like that's always the first thing when you come here. You get on now and bathe, then I'll give you some of pa's clean clothes. Then you eat. Then you sleep in the hayloft."

"Sounds good. I'm beat. We can hold the talk 'til the morning."

After an early supper, Jabez and Cait walked toward the barn, then stopped and gazed at the sky. Jabez showed her the bright star, Venus, which was an evening star in this period. "Pa called it Ol' Phospherous. Said that's what his people called it because it was so bright. It's the first star to be seen in the evening for part of the year and the last star to be seen before dawn for the other part.”

They walked on. Neither spoke. Jabez pulled Cait close, his arm around her waist. She rested her face against his chest. “I’m so glad you’re back.”

“I’ll stay in the barn loft,” he said. “Some of Anderson’s men may be looking for me. I’ll tell you about it tomorrow.”

*

Jabez slept long and hard, and the next day he rose and walked the fields and woods of the farm in contemplation. The morning was cloudless; the leaves of the trees were at peak autumn color; chickens were making their noises in the coop; and Jabez felt like his world, which had been racing like a locomotive at full throttle, had come to a sudden and peaceful stop.

At breakfast, Amanda asked if Jabez wanted to speak privately with Cait.

Jabez responded, “I think you also should hear what I have to say. You’ve supported us bushwhackers, and I think you should know what I’ve seen. And what I’ve done.”

The three finished their breakfast and cleared the table. Jabez spoke slowly, his voice and his face displaying the anguish he felt. “These last two months have torn me up. I’m finished with bushwhacking and guerrilla war. All we do is kill and rob, and it don’t matter if the target is civilian. In fact, bushwhackers believe the best target is an innocent civilian, because killing innocents spreads the greatest terror.”

Cait rose and stood behind Jabez, smoothing his long hair. “Tell us what happened.”

Jabez reached above his head and took her hand and pulled her to a seat at the table. “We were working the north side of the Missouri, tearing up railroads and telegraph lines and generally raisin’ hell. Well that’s what we were ordered to do. Exept when Anderson and Clement go to work, it gets awful, it goes from cutting up telegraph lines to cutting throats and scalps. We stopped work on the lines and went on a bloody tour of Howard, Randolph, and Boone counties. I won't go into details, just know that it was awful bloody."

Cait interrupted, "I've told Amanda about the scalpings and murder of innocents that have troubled you."

"Well, glad you did. So, Amanda, you know this guerrilla life has been a long nightmare for me. There is no honor, no glory to it. It serves no honorable purpose, just terror and revenge."

Cait said, "Sorry I interrupted you. Tell us what happened."

Jabez took a deep breath and filled them in on what had transpired. His voice quavered. "Those Union soldiers on the train were just heading home. They were unarmed. It's not like they were fighting us in a battle. Nothing would be accomplished by killing them. But Anderson and Clement lined them up and our men shot them down in cold blood, slaughtered 'em like pigs at a hog killing.

"One soldier broke and ran and ducked under the depot's platform. Anderson ordered me to build a fire and smoke him out. . . ." Jabez' voice broke. After a pause he gathered himself and told the women the details of what happened in Centralia. "I feel awful about what I did."

Jabez averted Cait's anxious face and paused.

Cait rose again and put a hand on his shoulder. "I know it was so hard for you to be the one to burn him out. But you had been ordered by your commander."

Jabez nodded, but didn't speak. He looked at his folded hands on the table. "That battle against the Federals outside the town was a mighty victory. But here's the bad part—our men killed those who tried to surrender, Arch killed a number by cutting their throats. It gets worse— after the battle was done, some of our men went around the battlefield and scalped a lot of the Yankees, cut off the heads of a bunch of the dead bluecoats, and switched their bodies or propped the heads on their chests. It was, it was, it was . . ." he stammered, searching for the words, "not human. Hell, even animals don't do that kind of cruelty to their prey." Jabez stopped and couldn't go on.

Cait looked away. "Oh no, that's awful."

Amanda said she might get sick. "I can't believe I helped men who would do that kind of thing."

Jabez didn't take his eyes off his folded hands. "In Centralia we took a soldier as a prisoner.  His name is—or was, I don't know if he's still alive—Ted. Anderson ordered me to be one of his guards. I talked on and off with that fella Ted, and I could see that he was a good man. He was just like me, a simple man from a small town, and he too was a blacksmith and farrier. How about that? I said to myself, What if the shoe was on the other foot? What if the Yankees had captured me and I was a hostage? Anderson never takes prisoners. I believed Anderson was for sure going to shoot Ted, unless he could swap him out for one of our men, and the chance of a swap was next to zero. After what we did in Centralia, the Federals would surely not make any deal with Anderson. Anyway, Anderson didn't even try to set up a swap. My heart was softening for this prisoner. I couldn't help it."

Cait put her arm around his sagged shoulders.

Amanda said, "We have heard about the victory in Centralia, but Secesh around here think Anderson is a hero for that victory. But now I see. To witness such—I can't even think of the word for it—must have been like the worst nightmare. It's unbearable to hear of it."

Jabez continued. He didn't look up. He was afraid that what he was going to say next could end forever his relationship with Cait. "When we were crossing the river to meet up with General Price, everybody's attention was on the details of getting the boats and horses to the other side. I asked the other guards to go up to the bank to watch and learn how to handle the boats and our horses. I stayed with the prisoner Ted for a while, and then I went up to the river too. It was a chance for him to slip away, and to tell the truth, I let him disappear. I pointed the way to where Union soldiers were stationed. Maybe his escape helped ease my mind about the soldier I burned out of the depot. I can only hope.

"When Anderson learned Ted had escaped, he went crazy, cursing us guards for losing the prisoner, and he beat one of the other boys with his pistol. He was about to shoot them, but somethin' came over him, and he checked his temper and said he was going to try all of us the next day.

"I was so sick of Anderson. I could have killed him on the spot. I had to face up to the truth, and I didn't want those guard fellows to be shot for losing the prisoner. So that night I wrote a note saying it was my fault because I let the man run. Intentional. I put the note where it would be found. With that I slipped away in the dark of night while everyone was sleeping. Anderson sent three men after me. One of them was Arch. But I made it here, thank God.

"I don't know if Anderson's trackers are still coming after me. I believe—maybe I should say I hope—Anderson and his men have gone on to join Price's army. Catching me is nothing in comparison to the work Anderson wants to do with Price, but to play it safe I have to assume they are still looking for me. I have to assume I'm a wanted man, wanted by the Federals for being a bushwhacker and wanted by Anderson for what I did. I'm double wanted."

Cait took his hand and looked into his anxious eyes. "Make that triple wanted—also wanted by me."

# RETURN

Jabez looked up and smiled. "Well, the most important thing is that they don't come after you for giving me shelter. So, I probably should leave in a short while, then come back after they either join Price or go down to Texas for the winter.

# 42

## BAD NEWS

October 24–25, 1864, O'Kelly farm outside Richmond, Ray County, western Missouri

After Cait and Amanda got Jabez in shape to spend time in the woods, he left the farm and set up a campsite about a mile away, returning nightly for brief visits. He repeated the pattern for about a week.

When Jabez came to the farmhouse in the dusk of the 25th of October, he saw Cait hugging Amanda as they stood on the front porch. Amanda was crying, sobbing loudly.

Jabez walked to the porch. "What is it?" he whispered.

Amanda was distraught and couldn't speak. She twisted her bonnet in her hands and wiped her eyes with the hat.

Cait said, "Amanda was in town to get news. She said Anderson invaded the house of her uncle and aunt in Glasgow four days ago and brutally robbed them."

"Her Unionist relatives?"

"Yes. Anderson and another man did it. They got a lot of money. But it wasn't just a robbery. The worst part is they beat her Uncle Ben almost to his death. He's in terrible shape, may not live."

Cait clutched Jabez's arm. "Then—this man is so horrible—Anderson got angry about Ben freeing his slaves, and after Anderson finished beating Ben within an inch of his life, he raped little Mattie, one of the freed slaves who stayed on as a servant. That poor girl!"

Now Cait was crying too, and Jabez wrapped his arms around the two women, and they pressed their faces against his shoulders.

"Anderson is the devil himself, pure evil," Cait said.

Amanda lifted her fists. Her eyes were screwed shut, her face reflecting deep pain. "Yessss! Pure evil!"

Later, after Amanda composed, Jabez said, "He may still be in this general area. Glasgow ain't that far away. We may get a visit from him and his men."

Cait went to a closet and removed a gun. "I have Pa's shotgun, and I know how to use it. Let him come."

Amanda said, "I have one too. Wipe him from the face of this earth."

*

The next day, one of the Secesh women from Richmond came to the house to speak with Cait and Amanda.  "I have war news," the woman said. "General Price's men lost a major battle near Kansas City, and they're fleeing, on their way out of the state, heading south through Kansas and Indian Territory. People say the Confederate Army west of the Mississippi is pretty much finished now. She said a number of guerrillas were killed in the battles around Independence and Kansas City, including George Todd."

"What about other bushwhackers?" Cait asked.

"Some who joined Price were killed. But Anderson's guerrillas had not joined Price and were not in the battle. His gang split up. All the boys from Clay County moved up there. Our network says that Anderson and the other guerrillas with his band have moved here to Ray County, and they're staying at a new camp near where the Fishing River joins the Missouri. Soon they will go to Texas for the winter."

*

That evening, when Jabez came to the house, Cait and Amanda told him of the war news and Anderson's whereabouts.

Jabez said, "So Frank and Jesse and my friends from Clay County split off and went up to their home territory? That's good. Without the Clay County boys, his camp has about sixty or seventy guerrillas. Still, that's more than enough to wipe us out here at the farm. They ain't far away. I wonder why they made camp there?"

Cait's eyes were on Jabez. "Do you think they'll be coming for you?"

Jabez didn't respond.

"Lord help us," said Amanda. "What can we do?"

# 43

## REAPING THE WHIRLWIND

*"Let all your fighting material be placed on a war footing to chase and kill . . . Anderson, to follow him until he is dead . . . ."*
Orders of Union Brigadier General Clifton B. Fisk

October 26, 1864, Richmond, Ray County, western Missouri
Lieutenant Colonel Samuel Cox, called Cob by his friends, the commander of three hundred troops of the Thirty-third and Fifty-first Missouri Militias, was in his field office tent and feeling especially good this evening. Union troops, Missouri militia forces, and a Kansas Jayhawker brigade had defeated Confederate General Price on October 23 at the outskirts of Kansas City, routing Price's army and chasing them to Kansas and on toward Texas. The pro-Union newspapers were calling the victory the Gettysburg of the West. Cox believed that it ended for good the potential of a Confederate takeover of Missouri. The job now would be to quell the remaining guerrillas. Cob Cox was a designated guerrilla-hunter, and he was pleased that many guerrillas had joined Price's army and were now leaving the state with Price. He was especially happy about news that the bushwhacker leader George Todd was killed by a sniper on October 21 while he was scouting for Price.

A lieutenant named McGriffin McGuffin Mitchell, known as McMac, raised Cox's spirits even higher by advising him that an unidentified woman had come to the camp asking to meet Cox and pass along some important information about guerrillas. But McMac was wary and said, "Watch out. I'm pretty sure she is Secesh. Can't trust them tricksters."

Cox said, "Stay and listen after you bring her in."

The woman wore a big coat and bonnet that hid her features. She entered Cox's tent and sat away from his lamp and spoke softly. Indeed, she did have important information, but she wanted the meeting and the revelation to be confidential.

Cox gave her the assurances.

She said, "Bill Anderson and some of his guerrilla band have come back to Ray County after they left Clay County. They will likely leave for Texas soon."

Cox's pulse quickened. This was the opening he had waited for. "How many are here?"

The woman looked around to assure that Cox and Mc-Mac were the only ones within earshot. "Not sure. I think about seventy."

Cox smiled. He could handle that number. "Where are they camped?"

Again, the woman looked around before answering. She spoke in a low voice. "They're on the east side of Fishing River, a bit before it enters the Missouri." She pulled a paper from her clothes and pushed it on to Cox' desk. "Here's a map I sketched. It's kinda rough."

Cox and McMac looked at the paper. McMac said, "I know that area well." He showed Cox several key features on the map.

Cox was beaming. He looked at the woman. "Do you know how long they're here?"

"No."

"Do you know their plans?"

"Not really. But I've heard that just about every day,

they ride out after breakfast, looking for opportunities. I hear they're looking for plunder."

"Yes, like what they did in Glasgow."

She appeared as though she would speak, but she paused and just put her hands in her lap.

Cox said, "Anything else you can tell me?"

She leaned toward Cox, her voice even lower now. "One other thing. I know Anderson is the one you want. He always rides at the front of his men, on a black horse. He'll be dressed all in black."

She leaned back and put her hands in her lap again and paused. "That's really all I have. Promise me again that you will keep this meeting confidential."

"Count on it. Anyway, I don't even know your name, or why you came here."

She rose to leave, "That's not important."

Cox rose. "Lady, thank you. You have provided a very useful service to this nation."

After the woman left, Cox turned to his aide and said, "What do you think? Is this a trap?"

McMac said, "Hard to tell, but yes I always assume a trap."

"Maybe. We have enough troops to foil a trap. And if we set our own trap, maybe we can beat them at their own ambush game. The most important question is this—was she accurate about Anderson being over near the Fishing? We'll find out tomorrow."


October 27, 1864, Ray County, western Missouri
Early morning, Cob Cox left his tent and spoke to McMac Mitchell. "It's about time for Mr. Anderson to have his breakfast whiskey. We'll let him have it. He'll probably take another, and then we'll have a big surprise for him."

McMac assembled two hundred Union militia men for the operation.

Cox explained his battle plan. "We'll stop about a half-mile from the camp area and send out a few scouts to confirm that the guerrillas are truly there, and how many. If all looks good, we'll send fifty men, with revolvers, in on a decoy run. They'll run into Anderson's pickets who will fire shots and rouse the guerrillas, and then our decoys will turn and head back up the road toward where our main force will be waiting with rifles. The guerrillas will chase them. Our main force will dismount and hide in the fringe of trees along the road. Every fourth man will hold four horses back in the woods. Those along the road will fire when the guerrillas are within a hundred yards. Those on the right side of the road will aim for the horses first and those on the left aim at the guerrillas. Our main target is Anderson. He'll be at the front, wearing black bushwhacker clothes and riding a black stallion."

The fake attack on the guerrilla camp worked. The decoy party poked the hornet's nest and turned and raced toward the ambush site, followed by the pursuing guerrillas. Within two minutes after the fifty decoys passed the line of hidden Federal troops, the guerrillas galloped near that line, and the Federal rifles opened fire.

Horses fell, some men were shot too. The guerrillas pulled up, realizing they were in an ambush, and milled about in confusion. Men who lost their horses were frantically trying to be pulled on to the horses of their companions. Bill Anderson, at the front of the rebel squad, sped on and blasted through the trap, but as he passed the line of ambushers a Minié ball caught Anderson in the head.

Bloody Bill Anderson was dead.

Cox's troops carried Anderson's body back to Richmond, propped him up in a chair, folded his right hand around one of his pistols, and invited the locals to gaze. A man with a camera took photographs that would proclaim to America the end of Bloody Bill's reign of terror.

# REAPING THE WHIRLWIND

The soldiers buried the scalps they took from Anderson's bridle. At first no one knew what to make of the silk cord they found on his saddle with fifty-three knots, until a woman wearing a bonnet commented that he was reputed to make a knot for each man he killed.

# EPILOGUE: A RECKONING

Jabez Cooper: *After the Yankees killed Bill Anderson, things quickly went to hell for the Southern cause in Missouri. George Todd was killed. Price was whipped in a decisive battle at Westport in late October, and his army was run out of the state. Quantrill pronounced bushwhacking as dead in Missouri, and he and Frank led a group to Kentucky, where Quantrill was killed and Frank surrendered and was paroled. The rest of the bunch went to Texas for the winter, and even after General Lee's surrender at Appomattox—which crazy Arch pronounced a Yankee ruse— they came back to Missouri and fought on. Finally, most all guerrillas accepted the end of the war, surrendered, and took the oath of allegiance to the Union. But Arch refused. In the chaos after the war, Arch and (I'm told) Jesse and Frank and other former guerrillas, robbed a bank in Liberty, and the governor put out a reward for Arch. Still, Arch pressed on, and he tried to take over Lexington, but a posse organized by the governor shot Arch dead. It seemed almost all the top chiefs in the bushwhacker gangs that I had served with were killed by the end of this needless and cruel war.*

*Ignorance or pride or both allowed the South to get into this for-sure losing war without any idea of what life would be like if we lost. We never imagined that we would lose. Southerners are better fighters, and God was on our side, that's what we told ourselves. Hundreds of thousands of our countrymen died, and many more than that number suffered. The South is in ruins that will take a century to repair. This war has cursed the entire nation.*

*I believe the worst of it was in western Missouri. Sure, we didn't have big battles like in Virginia, nor a torching like Georgia got. But those were states where the people were of one mind and purpose, fighting an enemy from the outside. Here, in the towns and counties of western Missou-*

# EPILOGUE

*ri our people were divided between Secesh and Unionist, neighbor against neighbor, family against family, repeated across our land countless times. This became a personal war, face to face, and when the hate flamed like a bonfire, it was impossible to stop the killing. Every time there was a killing, revenge raised its ugly head. As the war went along, the fruit of revenge got more and more poisonous.*

*We bushwhackers did some awful things. I will feel the effects forever. The Federal soldiers and the Union militia and the Jayhawkers did some awful things too. Revenge seemed to spin in every direction.*

*I know I have seen the darkest part of the human heart, and I have seen the Devil himself in the human form of Bill Anderson and Arch Clement. I still have nightmares about the bloody scenes in Lawrence where Arch burned the men in the store and where Anderson made the man get down and lick his boots and then shot him in the back while his wife begged for his life. In those dreams I see farmers in their fields and travelers on the road who are killed for no reason. I can still hear Little Arch squealing his high-pitched laughter as he cut a man's throat or ripped off a scalp. I tell you the world is a better place now that Anderson and Clement have gone to Hell.*

*I'm haunted by those ghosts, those scenes. The worst ghosts are the murdered innocents. I can say that I never took the life of a civilian, and I never took a scalp or an ear. But I have to live with the truth that I was part of an outfit that took many, and I don't know if I can ever forgive myself for riding with men who did those deeds.*

*Even killing enemy soldiers is worrisome to me. For God's sake, they are our countrymen. I can't shake the memory of Centralia, when we killed those unarmed Feds who were going to their homes on furlough. I didn't fire a gun at those boys, but I burned the depot to smoke out the soldier hiding under it. I chose to obey the order to do so, although it didn't seem like a choice at the time. In my nightmares, I see that man crawling under the depot, see him choking and coughing as he crawls out and then is shot. I see the twenty-one other unarmed soldiers on that train murdered in cold blood. I see Union soldiers at the battles on the field outside Centralia and at the fort at Baxter Springs raising their hands in surrender, only to be shot in their faces. I see the scalping too. So much scalping.*

*Another thing is how I feel now about slavery. My father was an evangelist for that institution, even though he never owned a single person nor wanted to. I never could really understand why it was so important to him. It was a cause that he followed with all his heart, and eventually that heart gave out. In a certain way, he died for slavery. But why? And look at me—I went to war for slavery. Why? It was imprinted on me, I suppose, by Pa saying slavery was the law of nature and the Bible and the Constitution and state law and so forth. All our friends were proslavery. But now I feel ashamed about fighting a war to keep colored folks in bondage. On top of my shame and guilt is the knowledge that both my father and I gave so much for a cause that was rotten. That's hard to admit, hard to live with.*

*I would like to say I had to join the bushwhackers, that it was a matter of fate I couldn't avoid, not a choice. That it was in the Cooper blood. But I have come to know that fighting for the Confederacy was a choice and remaining in the guerrilla gangs while their work got crazier was a choice too. When I came to understand how wrong it all was, I was frozen. I could do nothing. Cait reminded me that doing nothing is in fact a choice—a choice to not choose. Well, I finally made some choices. So did she, so did Amanda.*

*I think a lot about letting the prisoner Goodman escape. It was my choice. Was that mutiny? Or was it the right thing? I know this—if pa were alive, he would disown me. But I believe Goodman would have been shot or lynched by Anderson if there was no prisoner swap— and there was no real chance of swapping—so I believe I saved an innocent life. Maybe that makes up for the soldier I smoked out from under the Centralia depot. It's good I owned up to letting Goodman escape. It would have been awful if those other guards had been punished, or shot, for my action. So, maybe I saved their lives too.*

*Deserting was another choice, a choice not to continue under the command of a crazed killer. Never in a thousand years would I have thought of myself as a deserter, but I chose to turn against Anderson, and I believe I did the right thing.*

*I know my fellow raiders would say my choices were not right. We were all bonded together, so turning against Anderson was turning against them too. Frank and I were good friends, and we had made the blood oath. I hated to leave him.*

*My choices made me a different man. It's like I've started life over, a fresh start. Am I fourteen years old again, with life stretching before me in all its possibilities? Or am I older and wiser? I know this—I'm damn lucky I've got a good woman named Cait who helps me as I try to chase away my nightmares.*

*We make our choices. Or we think we do.*